ALLNIGHTER

ALL NIGHTER

FICTION THAT BURNS AT BOTH ENDS

cardigan press

Published 2006 by Cardigan Press
www.renewal.org.au/cardigan
Copyright © remains with the respective authors
Cover and text design: Design by Committee
Typeset by Steve Grimwade
Printed by McPhersons Print Group

ISBN 0-9581304-3-4

Thanks to all
and onward with the cavalry.

How to Use This Book

Many books are read in bed as a sort of hors d'oevre before sleep – a quick five minutes gets you yawning and you cast it aside until the next night's nibble. This book is different. These stories will have you reaching for 'just one more'. A quick snack turns into a midnight feast and soon you're gobbling up the small hours. This book won't let you go 'til the sun comes up.

At *8pm*, everything looks lullaby-sweet. The stories are charming, you recognise the situations and you're pyjama-comfy. At *11pm* the night is blackening and the stories are sinking deeper into unsettling, brink-of-midnight territory. At *2am* the stars have wheeled, your head is reeling and your ninth coffee is cooling on the nightstand: the stories have passed though the looking glass and reality is looking shaky. By *5am* you discover the fragile clarity that strikes the over-stimulated just before dawn. The blue hour is rising in the windows, the birds are singing especially for you and the stories are wringing the last hallucinatory drops out of your limp, sated brain.

You've just had an *Allnighter*.

Contents

8 PM BEDTIME STORIES

Leather-Clad Promise *Jane Ormond* 3

On the Bit *Paula Hunt* 10

Lucky *Julia Inglis* 14

Atmospheric Pressure *Ellie Campbell* 23

Mac Attack *Sally Breem* 31

Runt *Catherine Hamilton* 39

Bad Deal *Kate Reeves* 43

Wandong Wingding *Melissa Bruce* 47

Buddhas *Brooke Dunnel* 56

Child's Play *Caroline Petit* 63

11 PM BRINK OF MIDNIGHT

Sometimes Being Beautiful,
Being Sleepy Beautiful *Sean M Whelan* 73

Ralph's Bay *Scott McDermott* 77

Tuning *Lucy Lawson* 84

The Postcard of Dorian Gray *David Cohen* ..92

The Pudden Olympics *Euan Mitchell* 103

The Jazz *Paul Dawson* 111

Byron's School of Method Reading
Carolyn Court 123

The Little-Big Soldiers *Mira Cuturilo* *126*

Upside Down in Parallel *Melanie Joosten* ...*132*

Lights *Claire Thomas* *142*

A Raga Called Milk and Honey
Pete Nicholson *153*

Downsizing *Adele Smith* *163*

Electric Cherub *Andrew Morgan* *173*

His Painted Self *Rose Mulready* *180*

Orange *Ann Bolch* *185*

A Goitre-Shaped Protuberance *Ryan Paine* .*188*

Life After Death *Daniel Wynne* *192*

Low Flying Planes *Adele Smith* *194*

Hemingway's Elephants *John Holton* *200*

Floating Above the Village *Lee Kofman* *203*

365 *Carolyn Court* *214*

The Line *Phil Guy* *218*

Brackets (the story of) *Andrew McDonald* ...*225*

So Many Things to Think About
Marika Webb-Pullman *228*

A Frangipani Friendship *Leigh Coyle* *235*

5 AM HALLUCINATORY BIRD SONG

George Robertson Was *Helen Addison Smith* .245

Blood Drunk *Adam Browne* 254

The Honey Machine *Rose Mulready* 258

Fith *Mischa Merz* 261

Since She Hasn't Gone *Nathan Curnow* 268

Molluscan Princess *Rachel Leary* 270

On My Goat *Jamie Buchannan* 278

Cicada *Leanne Hall* 282

Counting Buttons *Meg Vertigan* 286

Leather-Clad Promise
JANE ORMOND

Jimmy was the only one who didn't have to wear the dorky paper hat and Mr Walter had given up trying. Jimmy would let his rock-star waterfall of foxy brown hair swing down past his collar, arrange it to form a tousled backdrop for his skyscraper cheekbones and girder-grey eyes. He would hum, low and tigerish, look up from under the flame grill as he basted the ribs, and lock eyes with Arlene on burgers or some girl who would forget herself as she tried to order a milkshake. He would give a half-smile drenched in testosterone and let the flushes ensue.

Del kept stacking sesame buns into the warmer, his 'Walter's BBQ Rib Shack' hat sliding down over his small, oily forehead, the cartoon piglet winking over his third eye.

Del felt the familiar sting of Jimmy flicking him on the shoulder on his way to the back door for a smoke. Del instantaneously stopped what he was doing and aimed himself like an automatic missile in Jimmy's direction. This was the highlight of Del's day, these ten minutes when Del could nod and agree mindlessly as he watched Jimmy smoke in the hazy sunlight. Jimmy, with his mirrored shades, leather boots and musky aura, blessed by the gods of charisma, a vision being drunk like an elixir by Del; Del and his embarrassment of pimples, his thin, pale arms and mousy colours, the constant smell of spicy, watered down ketchup and dirty palm oil clinging to him like a reminder of his ordinariness; a smoggy veil without a wisp of exotica.

That night, as they had done every Tuesday night for the past three months, Del and Arlene hung up their greasy aprons, ate left-over hamburgers too deformed to be sold, smoothed and spritzed themselves into shape in the staff bathrooms, then headed to their regular table at Heaven Lea's to watch Jimmy shimmy and throb on the tiny stage. Backed by a glassy eyed, rangy blond guitarist and a lazy drummer whose beer gut was the only thing stopping his chin slumping on the skins, Jimmy would slither and sing in masculine trembles; songs that sounded like B-grade, tin-can Led Zeppelin, or Deep Purple set in jelly. But no-one cared; certainly not the rabble drenching themselves in pitchers of cut-price beer, and least of all Del or Arlene.

When their set was finished, the three men would splinter without a word; the drummer to the free nachos at the end of the bar, the guitarist to the nearest pack of girls on the town, and Jimmy to the spare seat and adulation always reserved exclusively for him at Del and Arlene's table. He flipped the chair around and straddled it.

'You were great again tonight, Jimmy,' gushed Arlene. 'I love that song about the diamond thief who falls in love with the rich woman. That's always my favourite. I love that one.'

'I think the crowd really liked you tonight,' said Del.

Jimmy swigged from Del's beer.

'Yeah, well, I guess they liked me as much as a bunch of retarded shitheads from this dump of a town can. They got no idea what they're hearing. They don't know how good they're getting it.'

Jimmy finished Del's beer and said he had to make a phone call.

While Arlene was fixing her lipstick in her compact mirror, Del stashed his beer glass in his pocket.

It was mid-afternoon and a sci-fi sun tried to burn through the thick smog clouds as Del squinted into the depths of the onion buckets as he hosed them out at the trough in the backyard of Walter's. He aimed the jet hard into the corners, a fine spray splashing back up into his face. He felt a shadow to his left. It was Jimmy, leaning his back against the trough, smoking and squinting and steaming in his leather pants, taking in the bleak backyard of Walter's, with its piles of bulging black garbage bags, its stacked empty boxes and catering-size bottles of 1000 Island dressing pushed up, tornado style, against the cyclone fencing. Del kept working, chin down to hide his blush. Jimmy smelt sweaty but waffle-sweet. Syrupy.

'Thinking of splitting, Del.'

'Huh?'

'Thinking of splitting. I've gotta get my show on the road. I'm dying here, y'know?'

Del felt like he was choking on a tennis ball.

'No-one wants to stay here.'

Jimmy flicked his cigarette.

'Umm, gee, would that have anything to do with this place being a dump, Del? Seriously, why do you stay here?'

Del thought 'because of you', but said 'because I've got work to do.'

'So get Arlene to refill the ketchup bottles.'

Del meticulously dried the bucket, his head bowed low, his chin snuggling his small shoulder. Jimmy lit another cigarette, nodding as he scanned the sky.

'Yep, definitely time to go.'

He watched Del, all crumpled and jittery, wiping up. Jimmy noticed the reddening of Del's nose, the glisten across his eyes. He nudged Del with his hip.

'So why don't you come with me? I'm probably going to need an assistant to, you know, take calls, hook up interviews, deal with hotels, that kind of thing.'

Del swept the tea towel across the base of the bucket.

'Really?'

'Umm, yeah, sure, why not?'

That sweltering afternoon as he hosed the onion buckets for the last time, and as he saw the dropped jaw of jealousy on Arlene's goodbye face, Del envisaged his future of a life on the road with Jimmy. A future of deflected spotlights, swelling stardom, increasingly lavish hotel rooms and eventual Colonel Parker-esque tell-all biographies; a future of deep-down love and an upstate getaway.

Del told Mr Walter he was sorry but he had to resign. He was taking a job in the music industry.

Del and Jimmy were crammed into the men's bathroom at the International House of Pancakes just outside of Tallahassee. Del was trawling through Jimmy's rebelliously aging mane of long, wiry hair.

'This is so not what I signed up for, Jimmy.'

'Ah shut up and keep pluckin'.'

Del was latching with sharp tweezers onto any strand of hair that dared to shine silver, yanking it out as gently as possible while Jimmy stared at himself in the mirror, drawing his lips back to practise his smile and examine the porcelain veneers he'd got done a couple of months back by his brother-in-law in exchange for faking a mild break and enter.

'Vain fucker,' thought Del as he stumbled upon a posse of greys loitering at Jimmy's temple. 'Look at him, practically hypnotising himself.'

So much for the high life; eating bulk-buy soup in a cask, never to stagger into a theatre foyer of gleaming promise, but more often a dissolute shack with a mechanical bull or a shrimp buffet with a begrudging Polynesian theme. That leather-clad parcel of promise had turned out to be nothing more than a box of beatings; unrequited love and always getting the lumpy bed and the kid-sized blanket.

'Ow! Easy! That hurt! Fuckin' idiot.'

'Sorry Jimmy.'

Showtime. Jimmy was crooning in the corner to his backing tape as a Mormon Youth Group chattered with their mouths full. Del slouched to the soft serve machine, and waited behind a man in a grey business suit worn to a shine on the seat. The man turned slightly towards Del as he expertly wound the ice cream inside the bowl, and said 'some people don't know when to give up, huh?' as he cocked an eyebrow towards Jimmy.

'Excuse me?'

'I said, some people don't know when to give up, do they? Look at this guy. Did he used to be big? I don't know. But I'm looking at him and all I can think is 'buddy, go home. Get out of here. You're depressing people.'

Del sniffed in agreement and moved with the man as he pushed the nozzle of Blue Heaven topping down over his ice cream, letting it flood the creamy peaks and ripple down the slopes.

'It's like that joke about the guy who works for the circus. You know this one? This guy, he works for the circus, shovelling up all the elephant crap, and every day he complains about how bad it is shovelling elephant crap. Then one day someone says to him, well, why don't you quit? And he says what? And give up show business?'

Del gave the man a half smile and picked up a bowl.

The in-house stereo system kicks in before Jimmy's finished his last chorus, but he doesn't notice. Del drags himself to the bathroom to wait for Jimmy with a wad of paper towel. Jimmy always jogs off-stage, shaking imaginary beads of sweat from his face and distractedly grabbing a towel (or whatever Del can improvise) on his way into the 'dressing room'. Jimmy runs past Del, snatching the napkins and disappearing into the men's room. Del wanders in behind him to see an all too familiar sight of Jimmy, shirt off, hands on the edge of the basin, leaning into his reflection over the sink, still shaking the fake sweat from his brow. Del sits on the toilet in the stall behind him.

'Think I spotted a couple of record execs out there tonight, Del.'

'What, at the IHOP?'

'Yeah. The two suits in the corner. Kept looking over. I think one of them was taking notes. I'd better get out there, press the flesh. Maybe they want to negotiate.'

'Oh yeah, you do that. I'm sure they're ready right there with their cheque books, ready to sign you up for a mill.'

'Jesus, what's with you, bitch?'

'What's with me,' says Del, getting up from his seat to face Jimmy, 'is that I'm sick of shovelling your elephant crap.'

'Ah shut up, you and your stupid fucking metaphors. I seen you reading books in the van. You think you're so fucking smart, don't you? So fucking wise, oh master, well you're not. You're nothing.'

'Better to be nothing than a tweezer for a has-been who never was.'

Jimmy stares at Del.

'I can't believe you'd throw all this away, Del.'

'All what? All this? All these stinking bathrooms? All these crummy pancake joints? All your goddamn disgusting grey hairs? I've had enough. It's never gonna happen, Jimmy – admit it. It is never. Going. To. Hap-pen.'

Jimmy turns back to the mirror, runs his hands through his hair and doles Del a serve of 'you're dead to me now.'

'For someone who's had enough, you sure are hanging around, Del. Fuck off. Now. I don't know what the hell you wanted from me anyway…'

Del pulls the tweezers out of his pocket and throws them in the basin.

'I guess I wanted a TV embrace. Not a Hollywood ending, just a TV embrace.'

'A what?'

'Nothing.'

As Del leaves, into the clatter of crockery and chart hits, he can hear Jimmy yelling 'Did you swallow a book or something?' and the unmistakeable sound of metal being chased around porcelain.

On the Bit
PAULA HUNT

'You can live without it indefinitely, if you really try,' says Toad McGuire. He hasn't picked a winner since 1978. He's sorta famous for it.

Toad's been fishing around in the pocket of his beige dress slacks for a repulsively long time. At last he finds what he wants. Next to him Rover gazes at the TV screen, watching the horses making their way out to the starting barriers. As he always says, Toad's a gentleman; he turns his head before hacking a bucket-load into his crusty hanky.

Toad has a pretty impressive mop of hair, black; he does the dye job himself. Rover can tell cause there's always a patch he's missed, and sometimes, when the place is steaming, his hair leaks a little. Toad folds the hanky and puts it back into his pocket. He catches a glimpse of a betting slip in Rover's small fist.

'You got a little something on one of these nags?' asks Toad.

'A gorilla,' says Rover. The enormity of it hangs in the Winnie Blue-fuelled air for a bit, before he adds, 'Big Daddy Cool. A bit of Braille came my way.' Rover slides the slip into his fleece-lined pocket.

Toad plays it down, drains half his pot in a single gulp. Rover, he's one of those kids that never had it his way. Too big to be a camel driver, too small to play footy. Not bright enough for school, but smart enough to know it. Ends up hanging around Flemington in his trackie daks, running errands and chasing futile promises. Not the sort of fella who'd get a grand without putting up something valuable as collateral.

'Ya wanna watch the race from the stand?' Toad asks the kid.

'Nuh.' Rover's happy enough to stay put. He's only just knocked the head off his beer and he doesn't like skolling, seems a waste. Makes not an iota of difference to the horse where he watches it from, he knows that.

On the telly the horses are being manoeuvred into the stalls. They're beautiful – flanks brushed shiny, manes clipped neat, fighting the jockeys every step of the way. Toad pays attention, makes a note of Big Daddy Cool's silks. He worries Rover's nag's drawn too wide. He worries about the dead track. He worries the jockey ain't gonna ride flat out, and that the trainer's just giving a roughie a bit of a run. He worries about how the kid is going to pay back what he owes in the more than likely event that his horse isn't first past the post.

When the starter's gun goes off the kid isn't even watching. He's at the bar, ordering a couple more pots from the bird with the short skirt. Rover's glass is still near full but it's his shout and Toad's is empty. Toad wouldn't have minded if the kid waited till the end of the race.

Dead certs and sure things, Toad worked that fairytale out years ago, after a few busted noses and a stint in the pound. For a short time he'd been a contender, always won enough to play another day. But he didn't have the temperament for professional punting, too easily hooked. Not just horses either. He'd also punted, without success, on featherweight boxers with lopsided grins, tails in two-up and girls with green eyes. In the end he was betting with rubber bands and there wasn't a bookie that'd take his wagers – they couldn't afford the standover men. So he'd kicked it – the desire. These days he took pleasure from hanging around the bird cage, saying g'day to his mates in the gutter, and making them laugh with his few bob each-way and his unerring knack for picking no-hopers.

But right now he's got a knot in his guts like he hasn't had since before 1978. Back when he couldn't exist, if not for the promise of another winner. He's got that knot in his gut and he hasn't even got a penny riding on it.

Rover brings back the fresh pots and turns his attention to the race.

'*And Glorious Girl holds the lead, followed closely by Big Daddy Cool and Breezy Blue. Hamilton brings out the whip and Big Daddy Cool tears off; he's going faster than last weeks pay…*'

Toad's eyesight ain't what it used to be but he can eyeball a set of navy and white silks heading up the field.

'*Glorious Girl won't give up, she's making up ground on the outside…*'

The head of his beer slops over the side of the glass; Toad puts it down and concentrates on the last few furlongs.

'*Glorious Girl and Big Daddy Cool, neck and neck…*'

Rover stares at Toad's hands. The pinkie on the left is missing the top joint. Toad gave him a story about a bad dog he couldn't pay off and some nasty debt collectors, but the other blokes reckon the old man lost it on a bandsaw chopping two-by-fours. Rover isn't sure he minds either way.

Six races later Rover heads off. Saturday night, roast at mum's. Peaches and junket for afters. It's been a good day but he won't get too worked up about it; there'll be bad days too. He misses

Toad in the half light, pecking through the rubbish for uncollected tickets. Lubricated by a gallon of cheap champagne, the dolled-up birds and toffy ponces sometimes toss the winners and keep the rubbish.

Toad had survived a decade without a whiff, but one collect, enjoyed vicariously, and he's stuffing his pockets with betting slips stained with beer slops and tomato sauce; hoping he'll make it to the dishlickers in time for the second race. The Toad's an emu again.

Lucky
JULIA INGLIS

The People's Palace was a tall, skinny building on Pitt Street, run by the Salvos. A 'budget hostel for country travellers' they called it and it was on a grand street leading right to the heart of the city. But inside the Palace doors, the smell was like all the boarding houses my Da had dragged us through in Newcastle. It smelt like every other in-between, waiting place. A wee woman called Mavis came from the kitchen to show me around. She had a tiny moustache and wiry frame with the smell of boiled cabbage hanging over her.

'This room is for modest young ladies,' Mavis said and I heard the message in it.

There were three women in the room but none of them looked to greet me. Caught up in themselves, they were tired and silent. I felt them waiting, their faces thin and worrying. I thought of those anxious, unsleeping eyes with me in the same room every night. All of us trying to breathe the same air, like birds trapped in a crate.

Outside The People's Palace sat a woman with grey hair piled high in the front with a knitting needle rammed through it. She sat on the steps smoking and staring out at something across the street. 'Aren't ya stayin'?'

'Nah,' I told her. 'Too cramped up with people.'

'That's nothing, wait till you eat the food. Worst in Sydney.'

I sniffed and smelt bad luck and boiled cabbage and something else I couldn't put my finger on.

'Religion,' she said, 'takes the bloody fun out of everything, doesn't it? Even cooking. Bet they can't dance, neither.'

Straight across the road stood The Wine Palace, a bright yellow shop covered in posters advertising all kinds of alcohol. The little bottles danced in front of our eyes.

'Some joke, eh?' she said licking her lips. 'Like living between heaven and hell.'

'Which one do you reckon came first?' I asked and we both cracked up.

I walked up Pitt Street with a sound thumping in my ears. It was a big heart beating, loud and slow. Past the glittering shops and fancy theatres I went, past the tall, shadowy buildings and dark little lanes. At the end of Pitt Street, the tall buildings fell away and the sun hit full. The sound was all around, rolling back and forth and over me. I opened my eyes and there it was waiting – Sydney Harbour.

The water had dragged me back to it again. Green and vicious, the whole thing was alive and moving. That water was hungry for land, it lapped sharp at the shore and bashed at the ferries in Circular Quay. Over us all, the two half-finished arms of the Harbour Bridge sat broken and reaching out for one another. I felt a grand sadness for it all.

The pubs and hotels lined the water, their thirsty doors open wide for punters. Some of them had rooms to rent and I tried careful to choose one from them all. On top of the Paragon Hotel, I saw a monstrous white horse, standing twenty feet and rearing up wild. Sydney Bitter Ale the sign said and I agreed this city was no easy drink. I couldn't tell if that Tooths Ale horse was spooked or in fight, so I didn't stay there under it. I chose a shark instead.

The Port Jackson Hotel sat on George Street in the hub of The Rocks. It was a rough and ugly little pub but it had a woman sitting freely in the open front bar. One woman cutting her own track in a pub full of men. The window of the front bar kept an open eye on all that water and I took it on that. The woman wore her golden hair loose and it frizzed out behind her like an orange halo in the dark pub. From the knees of a sailor she smiled at me while I lied to the barman. I bumped my age up three years and told him I was nineteen and he still shook his head – no. The golden-haired woman stood up and the rest of the bar arced up for fun. Finally the barman gave in and handed me a key.

My little room sat high at the top of The Port Jackson Hotel, three flights up. It had a sink, a bed and a window looking out. I felt a queer calm in staying at a pub named for a shark. I let myself fall into the bed and the sheets were cold, quiet. It was soft in the belly of the shark.

It was growing dark outside the Port Jackson hotel when I opened my bag to take the jars out one by one. My Da put his drink into anything, the old bugger didn't care what had lived in it before. Plum jam, pickles, or jellied eels – empty jars were just more bottles for homebrew. I stood them all out like shiny soldiers on the window ledge. Outside, the city lit up with flashing words outside shops and the harbour flicked on-off-on with ferry lights. I picked a jar with my eyes shut trying to make a game of it, only I was deadly serious. I was teaching myself to drink.

Da told me that when things got desperate some men turned to metho and after drinking his homebrew I didn't think there'd be much of a leap. The stuff was rotten. I started with the smallest jars first and took deep breaths between swallowing mouthfuls. The more I drank, the wilder the sea grew outside. I pulled the little picture frame from my pocket and looked at my baby's curl trapped behind the glass. I remembered sneaking the scissors and cutting his hair quick before they took him away from me. Through the window I could see the lights from boats on the water and other sailors riding it out inside them.

I couldn't tell if it was morning or afternoon but it was another day and with the waking came the guilt and misery. To stop crying I went for the last jar. The last jar was the biggest and it sat on the window sill like a dare. It was a pickle jar and the rotten things had cured the brew. Vomit followed the first mouthful. The sink was beside the window and in between vomiting, I rested on the cold glass and goaded myself into taking another swig. I sat back on the bed clutching the jar like some precious object in my lap and looked at myself in the mirror. It was a sad picture I made in it. The shame came up with a dark howl that knocked me down. The last jar hit the floor and lay leaking out on the stained brown carpet, turning the little flowers dark. I grabbed hold of the sink and squatted beside it. I heard myself howling like a dog tied up too long and forgotten.

The knocking started soft at first and then the door shook with the beating.

'It's Launa, lovey-dove,' said the woman from the bar and she stood shimmering in front of me. Launa hurt my eyes in a dress sewn bright with gold sequins. She'd brushed her hair out full and the silky pelt fell around her arms. 'We haven't seen your little bum for days. What're you running here, your own drinking competition?'

'Yeah, me against me.'

'Who's winning, then?' asked Launa and gave the window a shove. A cool wind blew in rifling through everything. 'Here's the Southerly, that'll take some of the stink.' She came over and sat with me on the bed. 'Where are you from?'

'The Hawkesbury. The river.'

'Ah, a little river rat.' Launa picked up the picture frame and I saw her eyes flash, reeling the story in. She looked at the lock of hair inside it for a long time. 'Must be a beautiful baby,' she said. 'Let's put it somewhere nice.' And she stood him up on the weak bedside table.

When I got back from the bathroom, my room was empty with the bed made and the sink clear. There was a note, an invitation to meet Launa outside at 11 o'clock and I took it slow getting ready.

There was a mighty crowd down at Circular Quay but I found Launa by the red of her hair. 'Give us a kiss for New Year's,' she said and I kissed her two times. She grabbed my hand and dragged me to the front of the ferry line where all her boys were waiting. 'Sheila, you look a smasher,' she said to me with no joke at all. 'Cha-cha-cha.'

The bells rang for midnight and I rode Sydney Harbour in a boat with a screaming, cheering crowd. The ferries blasted calls back to each other, I gave kisses to anyone who asked and saw fireworks turn the whole city purple and green. An enormous cracker exploded over the Harbour Bridge, and the Paragon horse sparkled white-gold. For the first time in my life I smelt good luck next to me. The bells rang in the New Year and in the middle of Sydney Harbour, the ferry turned around and we all sailed into 1930.

Launa stayed at the Port Jackson Hotel so she could see when her ship came in. She knew them all by name – the Queen Mary, The Oriana, The Arcadia. Of an afternoon, we'd sit down at

Circular Quay and name our country. Most of the ships were bound for England, but for Launa, they didn't count. It was Paris or nothing.

'I'm not going to London, like every-bloody-one else,' she said watching the ships and waiting.

I finally got it out of Launa that she was only nineteen. 'Feeling fifty,' she said rolling a ring on her wedding finger round and round. 'That's me,' she said smiling. 'The fox.'

The fox ring was a tatty bit of silver with a button stuck in the middle. On the button was the head of fox painted so it looked like it was staring right at you. In the pawnshop, they told her it came from a foxhunter's coat and she reckoned wearing your enemy's ring was the best protection. Launa wore that ring like it was the grandest jewel and decorated her scruffy dresses with sequins and beads sewn by hand in rough lines along the edges. She had fellas calling to her night and day and she reckoned this was why the Port Jackson was getting ready to turf her out.

'I'm not on the game,' Launa was forever telling Stewie in the bar and she was right. I saw her giving it away for nothing to any bloke she fancied.

When Launa got the hump with waiting for her ship, she took up with a French sailor and disappeared for days. On the third morning, a liner turned up in the Harbour heading for Marseilles and there was Launa tap-tapping at my door, looking as pleased as if she'd worked her own magic spell. 'Close enough to Paris,' she said.

Launa the Fox had a going-away party that started in the back bar of the Port Jackson, moved through the Whaler's Arms and ended up in a skinny terrace in Millers Point. Archie's Bar was a dark little room dug out from under Arch Fergal's rooming house in Argyle Place. You couldn't see it from the street. We entered from a laneway behind and mixed in quick with the sailors and wharfies and everyone else on the hunt for sly grog. At the door sat an old man called August with a jack russell pup sleeping in a baby carriage. 'Don't give him any more drink,' August said and tapped the dog on the head. 'S'pose you've come to Sydney to gawk at that bloody bridge?' August tucked the blanket in around the sleeping dog. 'Look at her,' he pointed out a posh-talking woman with a glittering arm full of bracelets and treasure. 'Don't you give that one any money.'

Arch was a human cricket ball, red all over and perfectly round. He played the trumpet when he wasn't serving sly grog and when he got hot, he took off his shirt to everyone's applause. His shiny round belly was covered in inky drawings – Lady Godiva naked on a horse, the Welsh flag with its dragon prancing and an angry duck just above his belly-button pointing to itself, saying 'who me?'

On top of the makeshift bar, Launa did a speedy dance. She waved her arms back and forth showing her shaved armpits and making the bangles crash on her arms. The higher she kicked, the more leg she gave and the more the boys below egged her on. Arch stood on a chair behind Launa playing his trumpet in piercing blasts. The cheering grew with the galloping horn and the fox danced faster as we all chased her on and on and on. At the end of the song, a man yelled 'CHARGE' and the police kicked in the door.

The rats scattered as we ran up the lane and I said to Launa, 'I don't want to go back yet. The night's too grand to sleep on.'

We climbed the windy road up to the Observatory to check that Launa's ship hadn't left without her. On the floor of the rotunda, Launa laid out her stolen goodies – a battered watch with a gold face, mother of pearl cufflinks and a sailor's wallet. She smiled, chuffed and proud. I put my hand inside my bra and felt for the cold, sharp stones. When I pulled out the bracelet, the posh woman's treasure, Launa fairly choked in disbelief.

'You're a dark horse, aren't ya? God, give me a look at that.' She spun the bracelet and watched the stones catch the light.

Inside the Observatory rotunda, Launa showed me the dance steps slower this time and hummed with it. When the steps clicked in my head we did the Foxtrot back and forth and sang loud on our own round stage.

'You can move, Sheila,' Launa said holding the stitch in her side from all that alcohol rattling around inside her. We sat in the cool grass right out on the edge of the hill with the Observatory watching over us and I tried to take in the whole harbour. I could see down to Balmain, Peacock Point and Lavender Bay. I smelt the city mixed in with the sea.

'You've come a bit late for the party, Sheila. Sydney's already losing its sparkle. It's such a small city, really…like Melbourne. It always gets too small.'

But I saw a magic city, awake and breathing in the middle of the night and it was glittering. 'Sydney is still sparkling, Launa. It just sparkles darkly.'

We walked barefoot down Argyle Street sniffing the pure, clean air from the Chinese laundry and as we passed under the dark arch of the Cut, two bats swooped low and musky over us. Launa started running down the hill with her arms outstretched.

'Look at the foxes,' Launa called back stretching her wings and inviting me to fly down Argyle Street with her. 'Flying foxes…'

For the first time I saw what a night could be. What it could be used for and the fun to be found in it. I knew it was this same pull that had drawn my Da out every night – the shiny, dark night.

Launa's boat sailed away the next day and I went up to her empty room. On the bed was a black dress with a silvery crescent moon beaded onto it. When I pulled it over my head, I smelt a clean, animal smell – Launa. '*Keep sparkling*,' the note said, '*Love, Launa.*' I twirled in front of the mirror until I noticed something shiny in the middle of the bed. The little horseshoe pendant was pure silver and the word Lucky was carved into it.

I set the bottles up one by one on the ledge and they were different from my Da's, they had fancy names and labels written in a curly hand. The bleaching came first and it was potent. The longer I left it on my head, the more my scalp itched and bubbled. After the bleaching, I rubbed in the sticky dye straight from the box. Scarlet Kiss, it promised and like the bleach, it was cold on my scalp at first and then burnt like hell.

To wash it all, I had to lie with my head flat against the bottom of the basin and hold my breath while the tap ran cold. The water was freezing and I felt myself waking from a heavy place. I opened my eyes and watched the dye slowly leave me, leaking out like blood. When I was finally done, my hair was red. Or brindle. Bright red sat in patches with browns and blondes and black. Good enough or bad enough, I was a redhead. I put the moonlit dress on, shook my hair back and stared at her, the new girl in the mirror. I went down to the bar.

'Look out, here's the bushfire blonde,' a sailor called out and patted his knee.

I wore the horseshoe on a velvet ribbon, it was cold at my throat and gave me a power as I crossed the bar. Behind the sailor's bloated face, the eye of the Port Jackson Hotel looked unblinking at the broken arms of the Sydney Harbour Bridge while high on top of the Paragon Hotel, my horse burned orange and reared for the fight.

Atmospheric Pressure
ELLIE CAMPBELL

He displayed all the symptoms of a man contemplating suicide: a tendency to stare at children and small animals – puppies, kittens, whatever – and ponder the gift of youth long lost. He had developed a predilection for frequenting empty pubs – workers pubs – just before the 12pm lunch crowd, specifically to remind himself of his awe-inspiring loneliness, his thought-crippling maladjustment.

More telling than this, however, were calls he made to his daughter, Amelia, just to listen to her voicemail.

John, 65, wrinkled, recently widowed. Grey-haired and liver-spotted, sitting in his Honda Civic, wedged towards the back of Sydney's Kingsford Smith Airport carpark. John, former airline manager, Cathay Pacific, now retired, sitting in the driver's seat – alone – with two bottles of his late wife Joanie's Temazepan.

No-one bothered to look in at John, but he was looking out; out at a backpacker, a young man with long limbs and a slouching gait, sloping towards the terminal. John breathed deep; the things that boy was yet to learn. Businessmen passed, though not as many as John had expected. He envisaged files of businessmen passing as he drifted out of the world, all of them dashing beside the little Civic and tipping their hats as he said his goodbyes. But it was midday. They were meeting, working. Why hadn't he thought of that?

A car pulled up beside him, a little bubble car – a Japanese-looking number. The carpark was full, John noticed, as he completed a final survey.

John gripped the Temazepan bottle in his hand. Joanie hadn't touched the pills. The doctor prescribed them when they discovered she only had a month or two.

'You might get a few sleepless nights,' the doctor said. 'Take the tablets and you'll sleep like a log.' But Joanie wasn't convinced. 'Silly bastard,' she said to John on their way to the chemist. 'As if I'm going to sleep it off. This life with a month left? God. I won't be shutting my eyes till my last breath's done and I can tell you that much for free.'

But they bought the tablets regardless. They were not from a generation known for willful acts of rebellion against doctor's orders. Doctors were simply unpopular gods.

The carpark was full but still no-one had noticed him. Invisible already, John thought. Oh, sure, there was a lifetime of memories here. A lifetime of early mornings, work, beers at work, beers after work, years of Joanie and Amelia. The smell of aeroplane fuel never left you, not after 30 years. And three months. And two days.

His daughter Amelia called him to task during his wan, self-sorry moments. If she were here she'd pretend to play the violin, but she was back in Singapore with James. John picked up his mobile and dialled her number. Voicemail.

He spoke quickly. 'Amelia? Amelia, love, it's Dad.' He paused. What to say? How to say it? 'Amy, I just wanted to say.' He paused again. 'Remember when your mum used to make your school lunch? You know, your nice pink lunchbox, that plastic one? Well remember how it used to be packed full? Ham sandwich. Always a ham sandwich. And you had your nice box of sultanas and your muesli bar too?' He was conscious of time passing, the potential voicemail cut-out. 'Well what if you opened it now and it was empty? That's how I feel. I feel like I'm all out of sultanas. No ham sandwich.' He hung up. Bugger it, he thought. He dialled her number again then hung up. What else was he going to say?

A car behind him beeped. He swung around in his chair so that his head pushed between the window and headrest.

'You going?' The driver yelled.

John shook his head and waved. 'No, sorry.'

He stared at the roof. There was a funny smell. Mildew? Water had seeped in somewhere.

Another car beeped him. He swung around waving no. The driver, young, swarthy, sped off, braking suddenly as he turned the corner. Why all the aggression? John wondered, his thoughts turning quickly back to sultanas.

The sleeping pills looked like tiny pearls. Joanie hated pearls. She told him, 'Buy me a set and you will die a painful death, John Barcom.' He bought her opals instead, asking every hapless shop assistant he encountered, 'They don't look a bit like pearls to you, do they?' Joanie was adamant about the pearls and about her name: Joanie. Hated it, too. 'Makes me feel like a pearl wearer.'

But everyone called her Joanie, to differentiate between John and Joanie. 'Peas in a pod,' their friends all said, until the end, when Joanie went first, which wasn't ever part of the plan. The man always went first and so John didn't speak for a little while, not at the funeral, not at the wake.

Another car beeped at him.

'Jesus.' He turned. Quick, agile now.

The driver was middle-aged, her hair wild with humidity. She made John think: menopause. Hotted-up mid-lifers, Amelia called them. John smiled at his cynical daughter's sentiment. He was allowed to now, being well past mid-life. Next to the mid-lifer sat the woman's mother, he assumed, her hair wilder still, with blue rinse and roller-induced Roman curls. The mid-lifer pointed to the top of the wheelchair in the backseat and smiled, ingratiating. He hated that smile. Really. He honest-to-God hated it yet knew he wasn't meant to think that. Uncharitable, definitely uncharitable.

Once, he might have censored knee-jerk irritation. He might even have rushed at the prospect of chivalry.

She beeped again as he turned away.

He took the open bottle in his left hand and shuffled the pills onto his tongue. He shut his mouth.

The car beeped.

He swallowed. Aagh. No. The pills were sour. His cheeks were full, puffy like the Japanese car still parked to his right.

Beeep.

The mid-lifer and her mother grinned and waved at him. He nodded and smiled back. What was so special about this spot? Was this spot designated? No.

The mid-lifer kept smiling. She pointed again at the wheelchair and then at the little ramp and path next to John's car.

'Oh,' he nodded.

The driver inched forward, her face that of a hunter's.

The tablets were loosening. Melting. Were they melting?

'Christ.'

He turned his key in the ignition. There were tablets wedged between his front teeth and the backside of his bottom lip. He pushed the car into reverse and stopped, spitting the tablets out.

Find another parking spot, he thought. Am I drowsy? he wondered. He feared passing out at the wheel of a moving car. You just can't, he thought. Irresponsible. Lives At Risk. He tried to spit the remaining pills back into the bottle but couldn't find the energy. Some stuck to his chin and dropped onto his Lacoste t-shirt – his favourite t-shirt, picked up in Singapore after a week of duty travel. 'They might have told you it wasn't a fake,' Joanie told him. 'But that shirt smells like nylon on a stinky summer's day.'

As the car pulled into John's spot, the elderly mother gave John a smiling thumb's up. The mid-lifer parked her car then burst from the door like some crazed gameshow contestant. She raced across to him. Her legs were long in their tight shorts, her high heels spangled and her sunglasses large and fly-like for a face that, John realized, wasn't unpretty.

She ran to his open window then stopped, dropping her hands to her thighs. 'Oh,' she said. 'I'm sorry. It's not you after all.'

'What?'

'It's not you. Sorry, I thought you were Geoff.'

'I'm John.'

'Right.'

'You look like my wife,' he said.

'Really?'

'You have longer legs and more freckles.'

She didn't say anything.

'That was inappropriate and I apologise,' he said. 'Are you going to Fiji?'

'Yes. Now how did you know that?'

'I work here. I can tell.'

'Really?'

'I'm the terminal manager for Cathay Pacific. Just heading home, actually. Gave myself an early mark.'

The mid-lifer was stepping away. He couldn't stop staring at her legs and simply wanted to stretch his arm out the window and hold her wrist and say, don't go! And then, once he had her... He censored the thought. The thought surprised him. He'd forgotten thoughts like these. Did this signal recovery? Was this his comeback? Was it therefore nothing short of foolish to be skolling a jar full of pills and dreaming of the kind of sleep that might reunite him with his wife on some fluffy heaven cloud where the food was abundant, the foot-rubs frequent and the music jazz? His thoughts about this mid-lifer were tangled: Joanie would always be there with him, like the soundtrack to his life, commenting. How could he possibly explain this to the mid-lifer? That should they, you know, hook up, there would be three of them there. An actual threesome. And what if the mid-lifer had her own Joanie – a Geoff? Who was Geoff?

'Who is Geoff?' John asked.

'An old friend.'

Bingo. A foursome. Faced with that possibility, he shrank in the driver's seat.

'My mother's boiling in the car. Better rescue her,' the mid-lifer said, tottering away.

He stared across to his usurped parking spot. Damn it, he thought, I can see the overpass and the planes on the tarmac from there. And the old office window. I need another spot. In the shade.

John continued down the lane. An old Holden with an 'I own a GUN and I VOTE!' bumper sticker cut across him. Why was everyone rally-car racing around this quiet old carpark? It was like Rome with roo-shooters. Another car found his bumper and sat on him as he inched forward. There was no turning around. He drove up to the tollbooth.

He wound down the window, feeling in his pockets, emptying the ashtray, the glove box, searching under the seat.

The tollbooth attendant stared at him. 'Are you alright?'

'Yes.'

'Your chin,' the attendant pointed.

John pawed at his chin and smeared the pills off.

'Your ticket please.'

'I think I lost it.'

'That's the maximum fee.'

'I didn't get it out of the machine on my way through, you see.'

The attendant looked up from his phone. 'Right. So that's $90.'

John looked down at the mini-pearls on his Lacoste and on his lap. 'I don't have any money.'

He snatched a pair of gloves he had brought off the passenger seat and threw them on the floor. What if the attendant saw them? They were pink and new and he had planned to leave them in the car so that when he was found, his finder could wear them to avoid touching the skin of a dead person. As he rummaged through his laundry that morning after his black tea and cheese toastie, those gloves had seemed like the finest, most logical idea in the world. Now they looked kinky.

'Credit card?'

'No cash, no credit card.' John shrugged. He plucked pills from his crotch. 'I didn't think I'd be coming out, see.'

'Well I don't know what planet you're thinking I just flew in from but I'll have your licence thanks.'

John shook his head. 'I threw it away.' He undid his watch. 'Here,' John said, handing him his 30-years-of-service Rolex. 'It's real.'

'This isn't Bolivia, mate,' the attendant said. 'How am I supposed to add this to the tally?' He sipped his Coke. 'Permanent parking's out on the freeway. First on the left. Is that what you're after? I've got your licence plate. We'll send you the bill.'

'I work here,' John said.

'No you don't.'

'I do. This is where I work.'

'Recently?'

John's mobile rang. It rang twice then stopped. No message. Number withheld. What if it was Joanie? he thought. Calling from the dead? Maybe in the afterlife you could call the living but you couldn't leave a message? It got him thinking about ET, the movie: Joanie, phone home!

'I love my wife and she's not here,' John said. 'My lunchbox is empty.'

The attendant nodded. He flipped the Rolex into the air and pocketed it.

John shifted into gear and drove out onto the freeway. As he accelerated the bottle of Temazepan slipped off the dashboard and onto the floor. On John's left, a flashing neon sign: PERMANENT PARKING.

He passed the neon sign and sped back towards the attendant. Damn that brat, he thought. He's not getting my Rolex.

Mac Attack
SALLY BREEM

Back in the very early nineties McDonald's is still number one. Before Nando's and Subway and juice bars, and sushi trains, and fancy delis and ubiquitous alfresco dining. Before cardboard salads and Supersize Me and pistachio gelati, Macca's is still the big thing. The big 'M', the Golden Arch glowing on every built up horizon; the only thing open in Queensland apart from 7-Elevens and NightOwls and service stations on long quiet roads in the suburban night. One of the only places where a young kid can hang out, pick up or pick a fight.

I'm thirteen when I start work at McDonald's Aspley. You have to be fourteen to work legally in Queensland but with my parent's signature on a yellow form everything can be arranged. McDonald's Aspley is huge, part of the old school manifestation of Ronald McDonald Architecture; not express size or arranged boutique, it's mega-eighties and mega-American. The drive-through does not wind around the car park inconspicuously; it's definitely hard on the clutch. You inch up to the Taj Mahal of cheese on a massive concrete ramp. Like something out of *Star Wars*, the cars bank up, headlights rearing, awaiting assignment or expedition to space or another land. People cue endlessly, on the ramp or twelve-deep on the registers in the dining room; an unquestionable popularity; and owing to the status of the gastronomical monopolist there's a certain amount of cred that comes with working there. Every working class kid in my generation is lining up for the big gigs – Hypermarkets, Westfield Shopping Centres, Pizza Huts, KFC or Sizzlers (though Sizzlers, it is widely known, is only for spastics). If you work at Macca's you're part of a scene; a code developed out of both its public and covert reputations. Macca's, every kid knows, is no walk in the park. In the mini-nations of suburban megaplexes, Macca's is the warmonger. I know I'm up against the unquestionable standing and rhetoric of the great suburban coloniser, the international giant of late capitalism, and I'm determined not to get beat. I'd do anything to salvage my spirit and subsist. I get a uniform, a badge, a half-successful brainwash and the ability to develop my own cloak-and-dagger survival strategies. Surviving with stripes. Failure is not an option.

Lots of cool kids work at Macca's in the eighties and early nineties. And there are many more who aren't cool because Macca's requires much young flesh to fill its coffers. There are hundreds of us. Kids working the vats and the grills and the double-decker drive-throughs like we're sending up coal from mines. Macca's likes us young; it means it takes us nearly three hours to make ten bucks. The going rate for your average thirteen-year-old in the late eighties is $3.75 an hour. The volume of what we move, cook and pack is incredible. Every few days the massive semi-trailers come, subtly branded, opening their back doors and unloading a torrent of perishables and merchandising. The sugar buns arrive in great yellow plastic tray towers and stack up everywhere in the rush. There are thousands of boxes of pre-cut meat patties and French fries in plastic bags and countless varieties of lids, cups, wrappers and accompanying implements. Buckets of pickles and packed-down pre-shredded lettuce, and great cylinders of sauces which are loaded into guns and shot over toasted buns at high speed. The stock is all downstairs in colossal bays and freezers and no matter how well prepared we think we are, kids are constantly running up and down the stairs to collect, coming back with so many boxes and trays stacked in their hands they no longer have bodies just fingers and legs. There are always hundreds of buzzers going off. The last thing you want to be is a gumby. The last thing you want to hear is 'bus load'.

The only people on staff older than sixteen are the managers and sometimes the day ladies who fill in when us slaves go to school. The day ladies are cool – plucky middle-aged women who find themselves, mid-term, wiping down plastic tables for some reason or another. They never seem able to move fast enough. It's as if the tiny spaces, work stations and production units of the Macca's assembly line have been built to factor in the agility and fearlessness of youth.

The managers are another business. They wear blue uniforms just like cops. Steely and infallible. They aren't packing guns but something a whole lot worse – McDonald's boot camp procedures; all laws, expectations and punishments non-negotiable. We all know that McDonald's managers have been to McDonald's managers' schools: they are no longer human.

The worst and the most feared of managers at McDonald's Aspley is Wendy; tall and thin as a steel pole with a manner and constitution just as hard. Her uniform, hair, and shoes are always perfect. Wendy is never late and she never makes a mistake. Wendy is a machine. The skin on her face is smooth and taut with the thin-drawn-on eyebrows and impenetrability of an old-school movie star. Indeed, there is something very Joan Crawford about her; something nasty and impeccable. Wendy doesn't like anybody but if you're good at your job she gives you shifts. Playing ball with her is always tenuous. You have to be nice; you have to perform even though all you ever want to do is tell her to fuck off.

Wendy is Store Manager – often on shift. When I'm arriving (usually flustered and late), rushing through those great glass doors, my heart sinks when I see her. The vibe's edgy; inevitably she's gonna strip shreds off somebody; it might as well be me. Wendy expects 180%. The type of manager who asks me to mop the entire three-storey dining room twenty minutes before the end of my shift; who makes me wait in the dingy crew room downstairs for over an hour before the call is sent down for me to start; who rags me out in front of customers for some minor trespass or other. Wendy reduces less capable crew members to tears and bears down on them with her unfailing capability until gradually they are reduced to mush. It's painful even to watch. Kids shake and choke and stumble on their words. Whatever fuck-up they've made gets worse as their cheeks burn and their tears slide unceremoniously into brown paper bags or hot vats. A strange kind of silence descends over the rest of us. We work harder to cover for them like we're giving penance to the fallen or as a mark of respect but in the end there's nothing we can do. We know what's coming. This is their last shift. If Wendy's really pissed she'll fire them on the spot.

Nothing's harder or more humiliating than walking out of a McDonald's, heart in your stomach, bag in your hand, trying not to look back. Some kids are confident enough to rage against her, yelling out something funny as they leave. Most go quietly. Wendy will ring their parents three days later to ask for their uniform back. The only time Wendy smiles is at customers and even then the movement on her face seems mechanical like the button to her mouth is stuck and has to be held down hard to make it work. You can't fault her service but something about it leaves me cold. She's drawn too tight and she's too officious. No wonder the more adventurous of us want to be Rockstars. By the time we're seventeen we know working for the man sucks.

Wendy only tries to fire me once. She calls me into the party room downstairs, the same room she does the rosters in; the same room where (on her good days) she displays enough acquiescence to let me sit with her. There's a hint of something between us but really I'm just trying to get good shifts for my mates. By this time I'm a bit of a Macca's favourite; a success story; having mastered the transitions of Macca's stations from the pre-pubescent suffering of Dressing to Chicken and Fish, to Fries, to Front Counter, to Children's Party Hostess and Queen Bee Drive Through. It's amazing how important you can feel wearing a Macca's head set. When your voice is the one the boys can hear on grill when the cars come in relentless. Speakers pump the sound into the kitchen so the crew can be prepared for the unexpected call of twenty-five Big Macs, which has the power to throw the whole delicate system of sending those burgers down the shoot way out of whack. The boys keep half an ear out while doing five million other things at once cos that's just the way it is at Macca's – not more staff to take the load – just more multi-tasking. I learn pretty fast how to have three conversations at once – to the speaker, to the car next to me, to the chicks on the floor. How to punch in orders while taking the money for another one; run two registers; left hand punching, right hand taking. Brain and body split right down the middle but almost not even thinking about it. That's the thing about being hot crew. You learn how to act like you're not even doing it. Getting flustered is not cool. Only when you get home do the synapses start unravelling. When you've had five showers and just can't get that smell of white fat off your skin and the phone rings and you say, 'Welcome to McDonald's Drive Through, Can I Take Your Order Please?' That's when you know this imitation machine shit is just no good for you.

Sometimes when I'm up in the solitary confinement of the Drive Through 1st Window I miss the rush and heat of the floor; my common days – getting down and dirty with the rest of the crew. I stare out the plate-glass windows through the pixilated forms of Grimace and Hamburgler to the blue sky rising over the Hypermarket, thinking that being here's like reaching any kind of pinnacle: you look around and there's just no one there with you.

I like it out back – where all the guys are – cutting my teeth on the vats; pining for a chance to be out on front counter with the other girls who aren't all greased, thinking it'd be better, but Wendy keeps me on Chicken and Fish cos I'm a legend at it. I can make thirty Filet o' Fish, sixteen apple pies, answer calls for packs of nuggets, and still have time to help pack for the Fry guy and cut tomatoes in the mega-slicer for the geek who's losing it on Dressing because really, I'm not like those slick counter chicks with their perfect hair and big asses in their tight Macca's pants out the front who act all superior and yell at us when there's not enough hot stock. I'm one of the guys. By the time the managers do eventually let me loose on the floor, I've got enough gumption to remember where I've come from. I can cut it both sides.

But now it's all over. Wendy's giving me the sack. Leading me into the party room which looks sinister unlit; plastic, plastic and warped Ronald heads. What is it, I wonder, that I'm supposed to have done? I've done enough bad shit before and got away with it. I've filled those brown paper bags with free burgers for the cute friends of the cool crew. I've put two thousand sachets of salt in a bag when some asshole screamed into the speaker for extra. I've told my Dad to piss off when he pulled up to the speaker in drive through – everyone thought that was a cack – especially when he leaned in and asked rather sheepishly, 'Is that you, Sal?' I've passed out one early morning under the front counter and no one found me till the store was open; stolen a 1kg bag of caramel sundae sauce when fetching stock, changed the timers on the food from, 'should throw out at big hand 6' to 'ok to sit here and harden until big hand hits ten'. And like everyone else, I've also eaten and drunk anything I could; nuggets under the Bain Marie, orange juice in the walk-in fridge; apple pies in drive through; and handfuls of French fries inhaled en-route to the wash-up bay. But it's not for any of this that Wendy gets me. Wendy gets me for giving a staff member a Summer Size Chocolate Shake when he only paid 50% off for a standard. That's approximately 50 mls extra of sugared milk and he looked like he needed a decent feed anyway but McDonald's is not in the business of forgiving empathetic lapses in judgment.

I look at her and wonder. How can she do this? How can she after four years fire me for 50 mls of shake? Four years: nearly my whole high school life. I wonder too why she's brought me down here into our room, why she didn't just fire me on the day. It's been three days since the alleged crime and Wendy's been stewing on it. Like Terminator, like her programming's all fucked up, like she wants to be human but the procedure, always the procedure. We're in here and the lights are dim as if she doesn't want anyone to see and I realise that I'm just not gonna let her do it. I need this job. How else am I supposed to get into town on all those nights I tell my Dad I'm closing and the boys pick me up from round the back, Macca's uniform and clothes suitable for a dark nightclub in the Valley in my bag. Macca's is where I meet the guys in the bands for godsake, the ones who have the cars, and the cool hair, who pick me up and drop me off, who watch me take my legs out of trackpants and into black stockings in the backs seats of their cars, Macca's is my ticket – for sometimes what amounts to less than fifty bucks a week – out of Albany Creek. There's just no way Wendy is ever going to understand this.

I try a different tack. I incite her Macca's patriotism, I tell her this place is just like another family, that maybe someday I might be able to wear blue, just like her, that I'm very sorry, it was a mistake, and I'll never do it again, that I'll work harder and never even spill a bit of shake let alone black market it, that she can't do this because I've worked hard for her, that I've given my all to this place. I'm getting heated. She really can't do this. I look around the room for inspiration. My last line: And anyway I'm the best damn party hostess you ever had.

Then Wendy's crying. I can't believe it.

And it's not big crying with hints of sound and movement; it's more like her eyes are leaking. And they're softer but her face is just the same. I know I've won. Won my freedom, won my key to the city from the big suburban coloniser. From Wendy. I don't even really hear what she says next, some quietly-spoken spiel about chances and departures from courses of action and exceptions because *I've* had a victory, *I've* kicked a goal. I look up at her and catch just the last sentence. We will never mention this again. Of course. Of course. I say. Never. And I know Wendy means the crying more than anything else. When we leave the room I almost salute her.

Runt
CATHERINE HAMILTON

We all crammed into the powder-blue Ford Fairlane: me, she, the stuff I'd left at my mum's house for years after I'd moved out, Sasha's stuff that she'd accumulated since she moved out, her guitar (not that she could actually play it), her cat, and seven two-week-old kittens that still needed a good deal of looking after. It was a twelve-hour drive.

I felt sorry for the kittens, all crammed together along with their mum, in a sweaty, towel-lined cardboard box, stuck in the metal car-box, travelling at a hundred kilometres an hour, but we decided fuck it, we'd go, we'd just have to take them with us. If I'd waited a couple more weeks to visit her, it'd just be all our stuff and the one cat, still claustrophobic but less so. But I called myself an animal-lover, and I couldn't stand the thought of them being drowned just so she could move interstate. I was making a fool of myself.

Twelve-hour drive turns into fifteen. Drive for two hours, stop, stretch the legs, take nursing mother outside attached to a lead, give her some pet-milk mixed with water, walk her around the truck-stop, see if she'll do a poo, but she never does. Who wants to poo with the whole world watching? Who can poo with a leash around their neck and tits dripping milk? It's embarrassing, humiliating. Makes the poo back right up. I, of course, am the only one performing the cat-leash-walk-poo-ritual. She doesn't care. She sits there, twanging her guitar in a bad rendition of the Indigo Girls. Playing with the kittens and gurgling over them with baby-talk.

'Woo are sooo cwute! Wittle puss-puss, wittle kitty.' It's so degrading. Then she smokes a cigarette and resumes her twanging.

'Melbourne's going to be sooo cool, isn't it babe?' She calls me babe like I'm hers and I don't know why I like her so much. She's all wrong.

We arrive at 2am and my housemates are still up. They've even left us half a bottle of vodka, but eyeing the empties next to the sink, I don't think they could fit any more in anyway, not unless they wanted their stomachs pumped later.

'Hey! You're home! You have to try this drink I made up, it's awesome. Lime juice, tonic, two shots of vodka and a teaspoon of caster sugar. But here's the thing…you don't mix the sugar in too much, so when you reach the bottom of the glass, there's this syrupy vodka stuff. It's great! Alcohol and sugar rush! Oh look! Kittens!' Susie stumbles over to the box of kittens and coos over them like a clucky hen.

'They're soooo cute! Can I touch them?'

I tell her to be careful, that they've just had a really long drive and that they're all a bit fragile right now.

'I know, I know. I'm not stupid. Oh, this one doesn't look too good though.'

I look over into the box. I thought there were seven kittens, but there's eight, only the eighth one is just lying in the corner, skinny and panting with its eyes shut. A small white ball of fluff on a white towel, lying next to some yellow vomit. It looks like its neck is broken.

'Don't worry Grets, there's still seven good ones. You always get one runt in a litter.'

Susie was from the country. She speaks like she knows about these things, survival-of-the-fittest crap. Her mum worked in a supermarket. There's no farming blood in that family.

She leans over and whispers into my ear so loudly that the whole room can hear what she's saying.

'Is that Sasha? She's cute! You did alright there Grets. I reckon she might pop your cherry tonight.'

Thanks a bunch Susie. Wanna tell the whole world about the intactness of my cherry next time? Sasha just grins at me.

'So, who wants one of these vodka things?'

'I reckon I'll just go look after these little fellas.' This is her out. She can come with me, to my room, we can fawn over the cats and, whatever. We can whatever. Drink vodka for all I care. But she just shrugs.

'Ok, I'll see you later then.'

'Right then.' I pointedly pour a massive vodka, with a very small dash of lime, and balance the drink in one hand and the cardboard box of wriggling kittens in the other and herd them up to my room. Mother cat races behind me. She's not leaving her little ones, she's the walking kitchen: breakfast, lunch and dinner. As soon as I put the cardboard box down, she's picking them up, one by one, and making a bed for them all in a pile of jackets I have in the corner of my room. She makes seven trips and leaves the smallest one alone as if to say, 'she's yours if you want her, I got enough on my plate.'

I set up a clean towel on my bed and switch on the electric blanket, making a warm nest around the runt. Its head lolls around as I carry it and I can see its little chest heaving. It's going to be a long night.

Every hour I dropper some pet milk into its tiny mouth and stroke it so very gently. I don't know if I'm helping it or if I'm drowning the poor thing. I just want it to live. I wish it to live, but I don't think it will. It's like it was doomed right from the beginning, the other kittens pushing it out of the way until it just hid in the corner. At least it's quiet up here, comparatively anyway. The sounds from downstairs get progressively more and more raucous, and it's only when the sky has turned that pale washed-out green of pre-dawn that the giggles and the stumbles climb the stairs. There is no knock on my door, only the creak of another bedroom door opening, closing, laughter, thumps.

The little white kitten-runt shudders its last breath and wets itself.

Bad Deal
KATE REEVES

This photo's of my first fiancé Alex Hadzis. His dad was a professional gambler and the most gorgeous-looking man, much better looking than his son. Not that I ever let on to Alex that I thought so. He was far too sensitive; like all Greek boys, incredibly sensitive about his looks.

Alex had immaculate hands like his dad, and dressed like his dad in the most beautiful suits. Even in the middle of the day, even when driving the taxi, he got about in Italian suits and shoes. He was different to a lot of Greek boys, he loved getting all dressed up and looking good. He hated it when I dressed down. If I didn't look a million dollars when we went out with his family or his Greek friends, he wouldn't talk to me.

See the Silver Top taxi he's standing next to. This was taken the day he drove the taxi for the last time. That's why he's looking so cocky, that's why he let me take the photo. He would never have let me take it if he'd still been driving.

He drove taxis to supplement his card playing. He'd become a professional just like his dad even before he left school. He was very good, very sharp. Clever at knowing in advance what moves the other players would make, reading their minds. Well, this is what he told me, and I believe him because he made a bomb playing cards. Still, he would invariably lose to me when he came home after a big game.

Oh, he let you win, I bet you're thinking.

Which is true, of course. If we'd been playing for money, he would never have let me win because he's so tight. But we weren't playing for money. We were playing for anything of his that I wanted. I won his apartment, his dad, his dad's house, his mother (fabulous cook his mum), his future children with his wife thrown in, his land on Rhodes, his Howard Arkleys, his sports car, his deerskin boots, and his genitals. Not that he handed any of this stuff over, of course.

The way it would happen was this. Alex would get me to do a little painting of whatever I won, and then he'd write on the back 'this house (or whatever) is yours' and sign it and say it was mine. I once asked my cousin Helen how it'd stand up in court, just out of interest, and she said all I had to do was to buy a mini-disc recorder and tape the card-game and then get him to write my name instead of 'yours' – like 'this house (or whatever) is Carla's'. She said that would fix it because the paintings were so lifelike.

Behind the Silver Top taxi, is the apartment he bought when he made his first big killing with the cards, and a bit further up, out of view, is the art gallery where I met him at an opening not long after. There were people all over the place that night, swilling beer, carrying on. I'd gone out the back to have a smoke with Mark the gallery owner. Alex was out there with him looking at paintings. He had the exact same look of concentration on his face as when he played cards.

'That's what I call real painting,' he was saying. 'Real painting, not junk painting.'

When Mark told him they were mine, all six of them, sitting pretty and jewel-like on the little ledge in the back room of the gallery, he bought them straight away – much to Mark's and my amazement. He pulled out a big wad of notes folded with a rubber band and shucked off the band with his fingers so it made a loud twang. Then he just started peeling off these notes at Mark, one after the other, giving them each a tiny snap in the corner with his thumb.

This upstairs window over here was his study, and that's where he kept the card-game paintings when he won them back. Very occasionally, there was a whole wall of them up there, but usually only one or two and the rest I kept in the gallery with Mark. I could always tell when Alex was going to try and retrieve his property. It was after he'd lost, big-time, with the cards although he never let on, never looked miserable or angry. Still with the bottle of Maker's Mark, still with the 'Come on, Carla, let's you and me have a little game.' But I could tell because he was more thoughtful than usual, and these times he would always win the paintings back.

When it ended, when he broke off the engagement after he got the girl of his parents' dreams pregnant, the card-game paintings were in his study. Not because he'd won them all back, but because he hadn't wanted to keep playing when we got engaged and it had seemed kind of stupid to keep them stored in the gallery. He never said anything but I knew he thought they were his. He liked them. You know how things happen like that.

I took the paintings the day I returned the key to the apartment. I carried them down to Mark who sold them that afternoon to a collector who'd already made at least one offer for the lot.

But I only sold the best ones. The ones that had the potential to leave Alex property-less, soulless; a lonely and unloved man.

There was the painting of his lucky deck of cards, the cards he used when playing the really big games; the painting of his apartment from across the road on a summer's day; the painting of his imaginary Greek bride and the two beautiful children who looked like him – one boy and one girl; the painting of his mother holding up a steaming plate of stuffed zucchini flowers; the painting of his gleaming yellow Boxer with number plate STUD5; and the best of the lot, the painting of his erect penis, painted with all the skill and subtlety and lasciviousness I could muster – the one that had the collector comparing it excitedly with the vagina paintings of the famous French realist, Gustave Courbet.

And that is how Alex Hadzis lost his job, his home, his wife and kids, his mother, his sports car and his genitals all in the same day.

Wandong Wingding
MELISSA BRUCE

Today's the day. I woke this morning with the ready feeling Jess is here, she stayed the night. I thought it all through before she woke up. 'Today's the day.' She knows exactly what I mean. I bring her in on my plan – she's not participating or anything, just agreeing, accompanying, supporting. She hasn't done It yet either so she listens – like all ears.

I've chosen the most experienced boy in the school. He's also the best looking. He's not going out with anyone at the moment so the timing is just right. I'm feeling ready for the initiation – quite matter-o-fact really. It's time. I'm not the legal carnal age yet but just about. I tell her I chose *him* because I'll get a good example of the experience, I mean it won't go wrong (he's the expert) and it won't get complicated either. There's no contemplating him as a boyfriend. He's like the school's Romantic Lead; maybe even the whole district's. No – this will be a clean and clear exercise and by this evening I'll be a very different woman, well, I'll have graduated to being a Woman full stop. I've been looking forward to knowing how this feels – for years.

Jess isn't giving me any bullshit about romance and morality and stuff. You can always trust Jess to get it. That's what you really need in a friend, I reckon. She was born on the other side of the railway line (in every sense) but she always gets what I mean, gets who I am; 'The posh bitch up from the big smoke'.

I'm not nervous, just a bit more awake than usual. Kind of alert, and pretty, pretty alive. My objective is not to impress or possess, but I do still wash my hair and wear interesting underpants.

Jess is like my bridesmaid – if it was a wedding – but not all giggly and stupid – she's just calm and knowing and beside me. As though I was going to sit a special exam or make a political speech. She knows I'll be alright, but the preparation requires focus, accompaniment and respect.

We know he'll be there – everyone will be. This is The Wandong Wingding –there's no-one who doesn't come. This is the *second*-largest truck and country music festival in the southern hemisphere – but that's not why we're here – any of us. None of us particularly like truckin' country music. It's just the excitement of the event.

We arrive mid-morning. Perfect day. Hot. It's at the football oval where there's a huge wooden stage in front of the creek. The field's surrounded by millions of parked cars, trucks, tents and caravans. Stevie's friend, Jimmy, has bought a caravan for us all which his parents usually keep in the backyard. Apparently he does this every year.

By lunchtime there's a whole pile of the tribe, (I'd like to say 'our tribe' but I'm still trying to wedge my cityself in) gathered on the dusty ground in front of the outdoor stage. Akubra hats, cowboy hats, t-shirts, jeans, thongs and girls in sandals and skirts –everyone's hippy-happy, well off their face to be honest – except Jess and I, we're not because we've got a job to do.

There's hot dogs, meat pies, beer, Winfield, Marlboros and marijuana. I'm wearing a Cinderella dress which I borrowed from my not-so-ugly Step. It's totally divine, a lot of fabric in the cut, it twirls and floats when you walk, a dark colour, sleeveless, cool. And I like a pretty dress with boots – kind of soft and hard all together.

I grace my way through the crowd, so Romantic Lead can see what a godforsaken angel I am and have no doubts at all when it comes to the time. If you were stoned, you'd probably think I was walking an inch off the ground.

Occasionally Jess and I wink – like a slow-motion, clock-ticking countdown. I can't say I'm expecting anything amazing for the actual event (although there is a curiosity) – no, it's more that I'm ready, eager, needing to experience the amazement (after all these years and imaginations) of how it feels to *not* be a virgin.

I can tell Stevie Pallin's caught a whiff of my transcendent charms. You've got to be careful not to light the wrong fire. When you're putting out a strong scent, it's hard to focus it only in one direction, without the Unwanteds seeing the sign. Stevie's been looking for a sign. He's a nice guy and cool enough with his panel van which everyone gets to use if they shout him a beer. He's like the dad of our group – the reliable one – a little misplaced – looks like he should be running safaris in Africa – a gentle soul, strawberry-blond beard, longish hair, tall, strong, big heart. But a liaison with Stevie would come at a high price. He's not the sort of guy you could just experiment on. And besides, Lisa wants him. Badly. Wish he'd stop looking at me. Why do people want what they can't have?

The boys want another smoke. Jess and I wink again. They have to head off for the caravan hide-out because the festival's teaming with police. Already today, the Hells Angels got into a fight and somebody was knifed. We pass their Harleys, all lined up, gleaming in the heatwaves of the one o'clock sun. A flock of kids are magnetised towards the bikes but afraid to go too close.

When we get to Jimmy's caravan, four people are piling out. One of them is Tina – she's so off her pretty little face (prettiest in the whole school) that she's talking like she sucked in a helium balloon. 'Hi Luce,' she says in a breathy squeak. She floats down the step all delirious and divine and says, 'What's to eat?' It's hard to imagine her eating at all – ever. She's at least a whole size under everyone's goal weight. Plus she's just about got a cleavage, already. There's nothing fair about the human race.

On our way up the caravan steps, Romantic Lead checks her out and she winks, or maybe her eyelid just falls over. They often end up together at parties but they're never really an item. She doesn't seem too concerned (about anything much) as I follow him in. Good. She smiles one of her pearly sweets and walks a foot off the ground into the distance (in tight-fitting jeans). I was attempting that ethereal float with the use of a dress and *without* the dope. Cheat.

Inside the van we're all piled up on the bed and bench and seat while they pass around the joint. I'm cool about dismissing every offer, every round. To be honest it's nothing moral at all, I just have a phobia about being sick. (I think I must've just about choked and died as a kid.) Lucky in a way, because I have an addictive nature.

I do feel a little bit smoked-out but you can't get stoned without directly smoking the joint, so Jimmy says. Everyone gets word-fully boring around us. Jessica has a couple of puffs but nothing mind-altering. It's like I'm watching everyone disappear.

You'd think the countdown would speed up time as it got closer to the event, but everything has spiralled into a slo-mo zone and my experiment is taking a century to mirage itself into actual formation. Jess does an even more slow-motion wink.

I sit beside Romantic Lead and notice that his identical twin brother's face is actually kind of wider, like maybe he got squished a bit on the way out. I've chosen the one who came out first. They're both cute. Twin-two is funny but I prefer the sex appeal of the silent smouldering, wise elder who (like me) braved it first into the world. There's still time to change my mind (they're all pretty available) but no, I stick with my plan.

Everyone's all relaxed and limbs are touching limbs – more by chance than by purpose – except for me – I'm sending messages all along my left leg which parallels his right hip to tell his whole body about my calling.

The slurred conversations continue. Johnny talks over the lot – a kind of monologue of his inner mind like a toilet roll unwinding in a Kleenex ad. You keep waiting for the end of the roll but there isn't one. The voices form a hovering cloud above our heads, which lets me and RL kind of get in touch under the smoky, non-verbal, communications blanket. He's getting the call.

Then (move of moves) RL puts his arm around me during Jimmy's particularly bad rendition of an unfunny joke (so unfunny we all crack up). It must be a boy-sign because when the joint is done they straight away all pile out of the van except of course me and RL. I catch the tail end of some half-hearted barrackings and a glimpse of one of Jess's droopy winks but I'm too busy, too focused, to respond. Before they close the caravan door I can hear that song from the main outdoor stage, 'Desperado', you know, the one about the fences.

RL maintains his trademark reticence in verbal communication, which leaves a lot of room for the job at hand; however, after some zip-reaching gymnastics amidst the tangled old blanket, when we're finally all smudged up with the saliva-juice of excitement – he does find it in himself to speak. He says, 'You got a condom?' Told you he was a man of words.

Well I'm not the sort to jump off a cliff without a rope, so I'm like 'Yeah' and I reach for my money bag. He shows no surprise at all about me being so well prepared. Must think I do this all the time. So, like a pro, I hand him the necessary device.

I can't look. I've never seen a condom go on – except in the pictures and on a couple of bananas and it seems to me it's something that's not going to inspire me to continue – so as I hear the tearing plastic I look up, out the window, at the sky. Some kind of Currawongy type bird goes by – ah the beauty of country life.

He seems more blasé about this than me which is perfect really because it would've been tricky if he got all special while I was on my experiment. It's almost as though he knows the requirements of his employment and is quite ok with doing me the favour.

He certainly knows what he's doing. Definitely a good choice. I don't have to initiate anything –– just be willing. I can't say it's like great or awful or anything really, it's just happening. Well, it's sort of not quite happening at first. This is when he says the second thing so far. 'You a virgin?'

I don't know *why* but I answer the *truth*, really casual. (Maybe I *am* stoned.) 'Yeah' I say before his next effort but frankly I should've said 'Nuh' because almost before I get the word 'Yeah' fully finished I'm actually not one anymore.

Well it sort of hurt a bit but not really, hardly at all but now, *after* the de-virginisation moment, well frankly now I don't feel anything at all. I mean like nothing. Just his weight. I'm thinking ok – we've done it, right, good, experiment over, but he keeps on going. I really just want time out now, to be alone, to experience the true depths of how it feels to be Not-A-Virgin. As the rhythm increases, the whole caravan starts creaking and shifting. I guess that's what they mean by the 'earth moving' and bullshit like that but when I hear laughing and joking, I realise it's the guys outside, stupidly rocking the van.

It gets all out of sync – the van is not in a rhythm with us and I'm feeling dizzy and have to check the sky again like you do in a boat's cabin so you don't get sea-sick. Things kind of start to speed up – like in the movies, with the breathing and stuff but we've also got the guys outside chanting and rocking the shipwrecked van. Then he lets out a sound, not too loud or too long, like a farm animal or something and then the van just stops. I can hear the guys laughing off into the crowd. RL is like dead for a moment.

He rolls off without looking at me. I guess he's kind of checking when he asks me his third (and profoundly considered) question, 'Did you want that?' Funny thing is – I did, I planned it of course, so even though it's beginning to be a recurring theme I say it again, 'Yeah'. (I'm sure I've said all three 'Yeahs' exactly the same – with a kind of casual certainty.) 'Yeah', I say it again, just to wrap for the last time.

We get dressed – it's all a bit sticky really, getting out of bed. It's all very casual, but sort of sticky. Like neither of us feel anxious or anything, just a bit stunned, detached – kind of, *what the hell just happened over there sort of feeling*.

When he opens the van door it's totally bright outside and they're playing that golden oldie Joplin song about Me and Bobby McGee. A sad song, but a nice song, really. I'm waiting for the feeling of revelation as I come down the caravan steps. I guess I think it will fall upon me like a sunbeam or something. Nothing yet. No-one I know is around until I see Jess. She's sitting on someone's Holden station wagon, smoking a cigarette, staring longingly at the dream career of the singer up on the stage.

I'm sure she notices us walking past but she stays there on the car without a wink. RL and I head for the pile of guys at front of the stage without talking. Nothing bad or anything. Just nothing. I mean he's not horrible, not rude; he's just not making a big deal of this if you know what I mean. No-one says anything – like nothing happened at all. It's as though we just bought a Coke at the school canteen. I spose this is good.

Jess finally arrives with a drink and sits beside me facing the stage. I think I must stink. The band starts singing some other Joplin song about a ball and a chain. The guys have decided to head off to Tina's house for the rest of the afternoon – her mum and dad are away. We don't want to go to Tina's. She's nice and all but somehow she kind of makes you feel like shit. Besides, I've got some revelations to feel.

They all walk off as a big bunch, leaving us on a dusty patch of grass-less earth. Before Jess even gets to ask the first question I turn back to see RL in the distance, putting his whole arm around Tina. Right then I feel a wave of, I don't know, sickness, but it must be just the heat. So what. I got exactly what I planned. I'm ok.

'How was it?' she says quietly. We're both staring at the band. I shrug my shoulders. I want to be quiet and think about things a minute. I'm still waiting to feel the Difference – the feeling of Womanly Difference – the Wave of Wisdom – the Weight of Significance – the Graduation Thing…

'You alright?'

'Yeah…'

'You did it didn't you?'

'Yep.'

'Was it alright?'

I shrug my shoulders again. We're quiet for a minute, just staring at the stage.

'You sure you're alright?'

'Yeah' I say.

The song is ending. I'm still waiting for the Feeling but it hasn't arrived. I'm beginning to wonder about the Feeling altogether, I mean this idea I had about how I would undergo some kind of memorable change… Jess is worriedly waiting for some feedback, I can tell. Still staring at the stage, I finally say out loud what I've been saying over and over and over in my head:

'I don't feel any different.'

As the crowd applauds, we savour one of those anticlimactic, life-disappointment moments, which we understand together without having to say another word.

Buddhas
BROOKE DUNNEL

He packs slowly, calmly. It's so different from the earlier rages that she's fascinated. She sits in the vinyl armchair, fingering the industrial tape that holds the armrests together, and stares. He wanders through the house, placing things in boxes, plucking the Buddhas from the shelf above the fireplace and wrapping them in old newspapers. She doesn't protest. They bought the figurines together at a succession of markets, but, to be fair, he was obsessed first.

She threw one into the fireplace once; she'd been confused. It didn't smash or burn, which was the intended result, but lay in the grate, forlorn. The wall would have been a better target; the smash would have said something. Or she should have thrown something flammable into the fireplace, for the sparks, though it hadn't been lit at the time. As it was he'd said nothing, just retrieved the Buddha, dusted it and reset it on the shelf. Then he went out.

She speaks, her voice crackly with apprehension: 'What am I supposed to put on the shelf now?'

He looks up from his box, surprised. 'What did you have there before?'

She has to think. It's been so long. 'Nothing,' she says, equally surprised. She wasn't aware she'd been that boring before.

He shrugs, returns to his precious Buddhas. 'There you go.'

They can speak civilly now that it's all decided. Before it was all shouting, or questions with no answers. It enraged her that he saw no need to acknowledge her once they lived together. Once she said, 'Every question I ask isn't rhetorical, you know. I don't talk just to hear myself speak.'

He'd retaliated, of course: said she asked stupid questions half the time, and why should he answer if she can find out for herself in the next ten seconds? 'You ask me if I've bought any milk. Check the goddamn fridge and you'll see whether I bought any milk. Don't ask me.'

'So I should go to the effort of checking, but you shouldn't go to the effort of responding?'

'Hey, I went to the *effort* of buying the goddamn milk!'

'How do I know that unless I ask you?'

'Check the goddamn fridge!'

He wraps the last Buddha and rests it with the others.

'Pass the tape.'

He keeps his back to her, stretching his fingers out behind him: he expects her to just hand it over, to do his bidding. Shithead. She'd like to throw the tape at his head, or reach out and snap a finger or two, but that would be counter-productive, and anyway, she can't reach.

Her friends told her not to hang around while he packed. They told her to get drunk and leave him to it, they'd get her out on the town, pump her full of vodka, find her a man. A new man, a better man. She declined, told them she wanted to make sure he didn't touch any of her stuff. She didn't want to make sure of any such thing, he's not a thief, and anyway, he thinks most of her stuff is lame. What she wanted was to watch the slow disappearance of him, to feel his essence seep from her house. She's not stupid, she knows it will hurt, but it's better than coming home drunk and being shocked by the emptiness.

He takes the tape (no 'thank you'), seals the box, scrawls 'BUDDAS' on the side. His poor spelling always gave her the shits.

'Right,' he says. 'Kitchen?'

'We smashed all the plates.'

'Kettle's mine.'

She sighs and waves her hand at the door. 'Be my guest.'

Listening to him potter, she realises that's what he is. A guest. This is her house; her ashy fireplace, her dusty carpet, her ancient recliners. Those are her cockroach carcasses under the fridge. That's her TV with the fuzzy lines at the bottom of the screen that puts everyone's torso two centimetres to the right of their chest. He used to hide the remote and watch her tear the room apart trying to find the damn thing, then pluck it from a pot-plant and switch to the footy the second her back was turned. Well, not any more. She can watch whatever she likes now, on *her* TV, eating *her* popcorn. She bought the popcorn maker.

He reappears, sipping a Coke.

'Fridge light's busted again.' He yawns easily.

'That's mine,' she states, staring at the aluminium can sweating in his palm.

'What?'

'I bought those last week. They're mine.'

He rolls his eyes. 'For God's sake.'

She scowls. She's not immature, he's immature. 'So, what? Packing a bunch of Buddhas is a really exhausting job? You need a drink that bad?'

'What, sitting around watching me pack is a really exhausting job?'

'I'm not drinking Coke!'

'Want one?'

She explodes. 'Don't offer them to *me*! They're mine!'

'Damn and fuck,' he shouts, retreating into the kitchen. She hears the wet buzz of bubbly liquid gushing down the sink. 'There!' he calls, ferocious. 'Sorry for drinking your goddamn Coke!'

'You're forgiven,' she says sarcastically, but he is, really. Suddenly it's just a can of Coke.

He re-emerges, holding the kettle. His kettle. She'll have to remember to buy another; she'll die without her morning coffee. 'Why've you got to be such a bitch about this?'

She wonders about this as he crosses into the bedroom. Why's she got to be such a bitch about this? Because it's easy. Because it stops her from crying. Because what does he expect?

She unsticks herself from the armchair and follows him into the bedroom, curious to see what he'll take. He paid for the new pillows, but surely he won't be *that* anal?

He's facedown on the bed, his back rising and falling. He might be crying; he does it silently, a real man. She stops in the doorway. Now what? She could say, 'Don't cry', but the man says that to the woman, doesn't he? She fingers the doorframe and says, accidentally, 'Christ.'

He's startled, he sits up; evidently he expected her to stay in the lounge, bitching, being a bitch. He didn't expect to be caught. 'Oh,' he says hopelessly, wiping his eyes. He *was* crying.

He was crying the first time she saw him, too. She wasn't supposed to tell anyone that, he said they'd think he was a loser, so she didn't tell, and it was a nice little thing for the two of them to have, that memory. It was at uni, in the library. She was working there, re-shelving books. It was late, and there was a guy hunched over in the reference section, face in hands. She didn't know he was crying, because he was so quiet about it; she thought he'd gone to sleep. She touched his shoulder to wake him up and he shrieked like a little girl, then cried in her arms.

Of course she took him out for coffee after that, it was the nice thing to do. He was an American on exchange, he had four assignments due he hadn't started, his mother was badly sick and he hadn't made any friends yet. She liked his accent, liked his shaggy hair and too-big nose, liked the fact he could cry in a library. She took him back to her house, did one of his essays and slept with him.

The beginning had been bad, she realised later, but the rest was worse. The tension, right away, like they already hated one another; the shit with his visa; his mother dying; the shit with his father, that red-necked ex-General bastard; more shit with his visa, like it would never end; the Buddha in the fireplace; the plates; and now, the can of Coke. It had all been really truly awful, she thinks now, sitting beside him on the bed. Even the good bits had been shitty because there had been badness right before them and there would be badness right after. She says, to fill his snuffling silence, 'What is it? What's wrong?'

'Nothing,' he says, staring at his hands, fingers twisted in his lap. She's told him knotting his fingers together will give him arthritis but he never listens. He amends, 'Everything.'

And so they sit, side by side on the bed, facing the mirror. The mirror always freaked him out, but she can't live without it. It fills the whole wall, and she rolls over to look at herself the second she wakes up. It's humbling to see yourself seconds from sleep, crud clogging your eyes, hair everywhere. Not that she thinks she's such a babe when cleaned up, but it's a different perspective, isn't it? She likes to think that she can really face herself, she really *knows* herself.

He thought it was demented. 'Who wants to look at themselves the second they wake up in the morning? Everyone looks crap.'

She tried to tell him that was the point. 'If you can see yourself at your ugliest and accept it, it'll make you a better person.'

He refused to understand. He would shake his head in that dismissive way she hated. 'I accept I'm ugly at seven in the morning. I don't need to see it.'

It was like talking at bricks. It was like talking at rubber, because her words bounced back and smacked her in the face.

There they are in the mirror – him lanky, shoulders hunched, eyes pink. He smells meaty, like fresh mince. He smells raw. She's wearing her ugliest tracksuit, hair unbrushed, no makeup, deliberately. She didn't want him to try to sleep with her. She'd be well and truly stuck then, messed up all over again, and it always takes so long to untangle herself.

He says, 'This sucks.'

They watch one another in the mirror warily, like animals. Time expands, stretches like a rubber band. Soon it will snap. Someone could get hurt.

He pushes himself up off the bed, doesn't look at her. 'I'd better finish packing.'

'Right,' she says. '…Right.'

He goes back into the lounge. She stays on the bed, looking at herself in the mirror. She watches herself breathe. *This* is facing herself, *this* is knowing herself: not seconds from sleep, but seconds from disaster. She shuts her eyes and covers her ears. She hears her blood rushing and begins to calm down. She is still alive.

Then there's a presence: he's back, pushing something into her palms. 'Here, you should have these,' he's saying. She opens her eyes.

Two Buddhas, one in each palm. Fat and benign, they smile up at her. They are still warm.

Child's Play
CAROLINE PETIT

The bastard knew, he knew. Hilary couldn't stop shaking. Her husband Bernard had eyed her as if to say: Hold on Hil, just hold on. But she couldn't hold on, she didn't want to hold on. The pumped-up pompous ass, her father, then had the temerity to look her eye in the eye and blandly say, 'I don't know what you're talking about, Hilary.'

Shocked, she rushed out through the other diners, who tried to conceal their eavesdropping interest in her progress. Her father's stern voice rang out: 'Hilary, come back.'

Outside in the busy street, she was swept along with the crush of late office worker boozers and Friday night shoppers. She washed up at the entrance to Myer amongst the flute-playing Peruvians and a has-been tap dancer. Feeling sick and light-headed, she headed to the Ladies' Lounge. She stood on the crowded escalators, ignoring her anxious face reflected in its hard mirrored walls.

Harassed women laden with shopping bags rushed past the connecting hall that joined the rows of sagging leatherette armchairs to the toilets and washbasins. She flopped into one of the vacant chairs. Dazed, she tried to make sense of what had happened.

When she was little, Hilary had believed her mother spent hours regaling her father with little stories about her successes. As in: 'Hilary likes to draw. She can read single words now.' This was pure childish fantasy, she had come to realise. Her father didn't know these things about her then, or now. He left for work early and came back late. Often she was in bed. On those rare occasions he was home, he sat in the chair and consumed the newspaper. He was an educated man. Children did not interest him.

If she played too loud with her sister Eve, he'd called out to her mother, 'Can't you keep that racket down, Ruth?' Her mother would appear from the kitchen and gently suggest they play in their rooms. Daddy was busy.

Later, when they were older, Eve and she were allowed to eat dinner with their father. It was a formal affair. Her mother spent hours cooking. The food had to be exactly the right temperature, piping hot. He worked hard. He expected a hot meal when he came home. Was that too much to expect? It wasn't, her mother acknowledged, red-faced after cooking on even the hottest days. There was always a main dish, two vegetables, a salad and a dessert. Sometimes, there was also homemade soup, or, as a concession to summer, pâté.

You had to have interesting conversation at the dinner table. Hilary made up stories based on books she had read. Eve was very good at imitating the voices of her teachers, that naturally superior tone when teachers corrected you. She'd say: 'That didn't happen.' Then Hilary would say: 'Well, it could have.' And her father would ignore the entire conversation, not commenting at all, and speak only to her mother.

Other times, her father would deliver pronouncements on the food. The sprouts lacked flavour, or the lamb was too tough. He'd rant and rave. Hilary and Eve would continue to chew as their mother ran sobbing from the table.

When she was grown up and married, Hilary and Bernard always went over to her parents' house for dinner, every fourth Friday. After her mother died, the ritual had been moved to restaurants, for which Hilary was eternally grateful.

Tonight's dinner had started out well. Her father behaved himself around other people, was charming and polite – a genial host. She was sure Bernard thought she was neurotic the way she railed against her father. 'Invite him over. He can have a home cooked meal for a change,' kind, magnanimous Bernard would say. Hilary would shake her head – case closed. She had vowed never to cook for her father.

Her father spent his days discovering new restaurants. He lingered over his food. Waitresses liked him. Even in retirement, her father insisted on paying the bill when Hilary and Bernard met him for a meal. He tipped big. This surprised Hilary. When she was growing up, he'd been a penny-pinching miser, didn't believe in pocket money. He would ask via her mother, 'Ruth, haven't you fed these children today?' If Eve and she whined and wheedled, he'd say: 'You'd only spend it on lollies. Rot your teeth. Another thing I have to pay for.' Recently, Hilary had noticed how her father's teeth had yellowed and his face had a lupine quality.

How did her father appear to an outsider? An old man eating alone, savouring his food, drinking too much wine and she, the heartless daughter. Eve, Goody Two Shoes Eve, was well out of it. She had moved to New York, her superior teacher voice had become her own. Her answer was: 'Don't go see him, if he makes you upset. I'll pay for a full-time housekeeper.' Hilary admired Eve's ruthlessness and her pay packet.

The acrid smell of the toilets roused Hilary's first memory of the euphemistic Myer's Ladies' Lounge. She must have been four or five. Her grandmother, her father's mother, had dragged her there, her mottled hand tight around her own thin arm. She had passed through the arm-chaired room, bitter from the toilets and overlaid with Yardley Lavender Water. She'd made a face.

Her grandmother had said, 'Watch it. It will stay that way.'

Alarmed, she had run into the toilets and stared at her face so long she had wet her pants a little. She didn't tell her gran.

Her grandmother's scent came in a blue bottle with a glass stopper. She had coveted that blue bottle. But her grandmother said, 'Little girls sweat too much. It's a waste.' Hilary knew it was true. She turned puce in the heat.

Hilary remembered the rows of old women who had sat in the black leather chairs with wooden armrests, legs apart, shopping bags by their sides. Nowadays, Hilary supposed those permed ladies would be found at the pokies, or dead.

A fat woman sank with a sigh into a chair across from her. The woman took off her shoes. Hilary couldn't drag her eyes away from the bunion-riddled feet. God, they must hurt, her feet crushed into cheap red high-heeled shoes. Why do women do that? Her grandmother's feet were awful: long-toed, yellowing, toenails curling. She had thought of them as baboon feet.

It was meant to be a treat to go shopping with her grandmother. Her mother never accompanied them. She never had the time. She ran the house. There was always something to do. Her mother said to her father, 'She likes Hilary. Your mother much prefers the company of children.' This was a lie, but Hilary was too good-mannered to argue.

A well-dressed woman in a harsh voice complained about how even designer clothes were manufactured in China. 'Shoddy work,' she declared to her sleek-haired companion who was busy marking down the price tag on an Italian wool suit. 'None the wiser, eh?' she said looking up at Hilary. Hilary nodded absently.

She didn't think Eve had been there the day her mother had spoken to her in hushed tones. 'Your father wants to discuss something with you, Hil.'

For a moment Hilary thought she must have failed a subject. But it wasn't report card time. Anyway she sailed through school, despite the fact that her teachers complained she hid novels inside her textbooks. 'What are you reading, now Hilary? You need to participate more in class.' Hilary hadn't bothered to answer. Someone sniggered. Right then, she had been reading *Rebecca*. She had cast Eve as the conniving, evil Rebecca and her maths teacher, Mr Torrens, as the dreaded Mrs Danvers. There were no quadratic equations in books. She didn't tell Mr Torrens that.

There were no novels in her father's study. It was a dark place. Her mother kept the curtains closed. It was full of dry tomes on law and journals with small print. In all the journals, there was a letters page. The letters began: 'Dear Sir'. Hilary had never gotten further then the first sentence: 'It has come to my attention...' She made it a point to stay out of his study, his den, his lair.

Hilary kept her books in a jumble. Schoolbooks with their spines broken littered the floor, making her bedroom impassable. She liked it that way. She kept her stash of adult novels piled between the wall and her bed, away from her mother's prying eyes. Already, at age thirteen, Hilary had decided she could read anything she wanted. It also meant that Eve never found her writing notebooks she lashed to the bottom frame of her bed. Oh, she was a clever girl.

Now, her father sat at his desk, his eyeglasses on. Her mother smiled at her father.

'Go on, Ben,' said her mother.

Her father said, 'I've written a children's story. I want you to read it.'

Unable to comprehend the words coming from his mouth and the typed pages he held in his hand, Hilary stared. She had never looked at his hands so hard. She noted his fingers were long and slender, his wrists delicate. He put the papers neatly into her outstretched hand. Their hands never touched.

She had taken the typescript to her room. She thought her father's secretary, Miss Bremmer, must have typed it. Hilary wondered what her father had told Miss Bremmer. Probably, he hadn't told anything, simply given it to her. And she transformed his inky scrawl into clear typed words. It was what he paid her for.

That's what she had heard her father say when her mother lamented she couldn't reach him the day Hilary had broken her arm on the playground. Her father said, 'I was in a meeting. It's what I pay Miss Bremmer for, to screen my calls. I knew you could handle it. She needed to go to hospital. You took her to hospital. Case closed.'

In her room Hilary had wished she had quadratic equations to do. She stared at the words a long time. Thankfully, the story did not begin: Dear Sir, It has come to my attention... Its central character was a boy. Right away, she had taken an instant dislike to him. He was stuck-up. He talked too much. The boy's sister was left at home to do the sewing or help their mother. It was unclear. The boy himself went off to fight Indians, American Indians. Her father, so far as she knew, had never ventured further than Portland. Summer after boring summer, they rented a windswept beach cottage that, despite her mother's relentless sweeping, was always gritty with sand. During their time there, her father often found excuses to return to the city.

For days, Hilary had worried what she should tell her father. She couldn't eat her dinner. It was hard to swallow, sitting on the edge of her chair waiting for his sardonic imperious look. Eve called it his hanging judge look. Her mother cooked more elaborate meals.

When Hilary had sought advice from Eve, she had laughed. 'It's crap,' she said. 'Tell him you loved it. He'll give you pocket money. You can buy more stupid books. He doesn't really care what you think.'

On the Sunday when her father visited his mother, Hilary had slipped into his study, laid the manuscript on his desk. She pressed a heavy book on top of it to iron out the creases. He never sought her out, never stood at the entrance of her bedroom anxious to hear what she thought, never mentioned it, ever.

Three months ago now, Hilary had posted him an advance copy of her first novel without inscription. He hadn't come to the launch of her book. 'Too many people,' he said on the phone after responding to her publisher's formal invitation. 'Yes, fine,' she said, 'I quite understand.' Bernard said she wasn't to take it to heart. He would have hated the cheap wine. The reviews were good. They appeared in the papers her father read. Still nothing.

Two monthly Friday night dinners had passed. This was the third. Stubborn, she had refused to mention it and warned Bernard not to discuss it either.

Tonight, her father talked of a recent court case he'd been following about a man who murdered his wife and gotten away with it, declaring he was provoked into it. Her father applauded the cleverness of the murderer's counsel. Insulted and enraged, Hilary argued with him. He fixed her with a triumphant calculating look and said, 'Living with women is never easy. Look at your mother and me and you girls. I –'

Hilary stood up and stared him. In a calm voice that surprised her, she said, 'What possessed you to write that crappy kid's American Indian story?'

'I don't know what you are talking about, Hilary. It's something you made up just like that lying, revolting novel you wrote.'

'I hate you. I've always hated you, you unfeeling bastard.' In the gasp of silence, she watched her father's face turn red, apoplectic.

Bernard placed his calming hand on her father's shoulder. She had turned on her heel and fled.

Hilary felt a welling of tears; they cascaded down her face. Her sobs echoed above the clatter of the women in the toilets. An old woman with a kind face touched Hilary's arm. 'Are you all right, dear?'

Hilary hiccuped through her tears, attempted to look in control.

'He's not worth it, dear,' said the woman.

Hilary nodded.

Sometimes Being Beautiful, Being Sleepy Beautiful
SEAN M WHELAN

Doyle wakes up from yet another dream about watching himself dream.

In these dreams he sits on the end of his bed watching himself sleeping.

And he wants to wake himself up and say, *what are you dreaming about Doyle? Mine are only ever about watching you and I need to dream about something else.*

This makes him so tired and anxious that by the time he wakes up, he needs to go to sleep again.

Doyle needs new dreams.

It's late afternoon, the sun is dying all over Melbourne, the nightly news is about to begin.

Doyle listens and imagines he can hear the street lights turning on one by one down his street. Every second one calls out his name and every other one calls out hers.

Doyle has taken to sleeping during the day to try and crack his habit of dreaming about himself dreaming.

He thinks if he sleeps during the day he might dream about the sort of things people do during daylight hours. He thinks it might be nice working in an office. He thinks up possible office dream scenarios, like placing a stack of clean white paper into a photocopier. He thinks about the weight and the smell of the paper.

He told Darlene about this and she told him it was the worst dream she'd ever heard of. She said 'can't you think of something more dramatic?' So he suggested an office dream about accidentally jabbing himself with a paperclip.

'Oh Doyle,' she said. 'You've got so much to learn about dreams.'

Darlene lives on the same block as Doyle. They are both in between jobs, haircuts and lovers. Doyle's heart conducts nuclear tests inside his ribcage every time Darlene smiles at him. Darlene likes the way he imitates the sound of a nuclear explosion every time she leaves the room, but it's difficult to love a man with such boring dreams.

Darlene has taken to sleeping during the day too, to try and help Doyle with his dreams. Sometimes she sits on the end of his bed watching Doyle. Sometimes she lies next to him and whispers fantastic topics into his ear to stimulate his dreams. She tells tales about the elephant-headed Indian God Ganesh riding a skateboard through Northcote plaza scattering blessings to random shoppers in the form of sandalwood-scented Barbie dolls. Sometimes she feels Doyle's dreamself sitting next to her resting his head on her shoulder and laughing softly.

But when he wakes up it's always with the same dead look in his eyes.

They get up between five and six every evening and they climb Northcote hill to watch the sun go down.

They spend the rest of the night talking and driving around the city. Sometimes they park in front of a twenty-four-hour supermarket and they watch the store like a big screen television and they discuss the types of food they'd buy if they had a job.

Around 3am sometimes they go back to Darlene's place and sometimes her beautiful friends are still up, sometimes being beautiful, being sleepy beautiful.

They lie around on the floor and they take turns throwing words up into the air just to see where they land. Doyle tries to join in, but he discovers that his words keep falling in the wrong places.

One of his words fell into her aquarium once and was eaten by her prize angel fish.

Nobody noticed and Doyle decided not to say anything.

He thought it seemed ominous, and must mean something.

He finds this happens all the time.

His words falling in the wrong places.

He thinks to himself that one day he'll come back to her house and retrieve them. All those wrongly chosen words that fell down the back of her couch.

She doesn't need them anymore.

What would she want them for?

It's 5am. Fours hours till bed time. Darlene suggests that they drive onto the West Gate Bridge and pretend to break down and from there they could watch the city wake up. So they park in the emergency lane on the highest point of the bridge on the city-side and turn their hazard lights on.

'Why don't you ever dream about me Doyle?' says Darlene.

'I do, but I do it when I'm awake. Like right now.' he says.

'But if I wasn't here,' she says, 'then you would have to dream about me when you're asleep.'

He nods and says 'yes, I guess you're right.'

And then they take turns counting the lights on each floor in the Rialto building until Doyle falls asleep to the tick-tocking of the car's hazard lights.

Doyle wakes up to the sound of somebody tapping on the glass of the car.

It's a cop saying 'what are you doing? You can't park here.'

It's daylight, the passenger door is open, Darlene is gone.

Doyle is grinning, he just had a dream. A *different* dream. He tells the cop all about it.

He says he dreamt that he bought a giant inflatable jumping castle. Then he had it filled with helium and he moved all his possessions into it. He bought hundreds of metres of rope and he moored his giant inflatable jumping castle to the flagpole of the Fitzroy Town Hall. Then he allowed it to float high into the air above Melbourne.

From up there he could see the entire city, and when he looked down he found he was right above Darlene's house.

And in the dream he watched her walk from her door to the cab carrying two large suitcases.

Ralph's Bay
SCOTT MCDERMOTT

The boy sets the acid of a soft drink to work on the chip oil that coats his teeth, tongue and gums. His feet are buried in the sand, hidden from the sun. Periodically he licks salt from his lips. He is fourteen years old.

School goes back in a fortnight. The beach is flecked with teens and younger children whose mothers watch over them from behind cigarettes and romance novels. Nobody is from far away. It is a good beach but there are many and the tourists and day-trippers are lured elsewhere. No serious thought has ever been given to developing caravan parks or campsites or motels.

The boy squints against the brightness of the day. Against the background of Frederick Henry Bay, children play in the shallow water, lobbing a tennis ball and lumps of wet sand at each other. They and others will be driven from the beach when the sea breeze arrives, abandoning it to sailboarders and kite-flyers.

The last of the soft drink is warm and flat but he shakes each sugary drop from the can. He looks at the sand around him for footprints that may not have been there a moment ago. He has become unsure of the world he inhabits. He reasons that if something like this could happen to him, it could happen to others.

Forty metres to his right is the boat ramp and, behind it, the failed canal. Intended to link Frederick Henry Bay with Ralph's Bay across the narrow neck of land separating them, it was prone from the first to silt up and was ultimately allowed to close at the Frederick Henry end. The boy thinks of it as a toppled test-tube spilling the shallow expanse of Ralph's Bay. He enjoys the idea that the community squeezed between the two bays has sprung from a laboratory accident. He thinks that would explain a lot.

He waits for the sea breeze. Three girls his age pass between him and the water. He recognises them from school. He was in several of their classes last year and it is likely he will be again this year. If they see him, there is nothing in their behaviour to indicate it. This is the way it has always been.

The girls each wear much the same thing: bikini top with a floral print sarong. The differing colours and prints are the only concessions to some notion of individuality. Beneath the uniform their bodies are elastic; stretched upward and outward at puberty's direction. Everything about them in that moment convinces him utterly that he is in love with each of them. He cannot even resent them for their failure to notice him. It is merely sad.

When he was younger he believed there was a God that made a home in the sky for good people to live in when they died. Now he is not sure. He has learned this is called *agnostic*. He still asks God for things. It can't hurt to ask. For a long time he asked God to make him invisible. Better to be ignored when invisible, he reasoned, than in plain sight.

Sand flicks around his ankles, warning of the sea breeze to follow. He looks across the water to distant Sloping Island. His father has told him that sharks cruise the deep water between the island and the rocky outcrop known as the Iron Pot; drawn, his old man says, by memories of the whale flesh to be had more than a century ago as the beasts were pulled ashore to be boiled down to soap and candles. He has never spotted so much as a fin but knows there is more to fear in the world than he has seen. He has always been afraid to stray too deep into the water that is now turning grey and whose lifting waves will soon spill white caps.

He checks that the young woman is still there. Along the beach she has been sunning herself since mid-morning. She wears one-piece bathers whose green calls an Asian jungle to life in his mind. She turns at intervals, reads a book and swims occasionally. She is a university student and has the run of a house in Aragoon Street while her parents are at work. Best that you don't ask how he knows.

If God exists, does He grant wishes? The boy doesn't know. This didn't deter him from contemplating the acts of heroism that might be facilitated by the power of invisibility; hostages saved from their captors; evil organisations infiltrated and thwarted. If he is sure of anything it is that the world can always use another hero.

God said ok. Or, if there is no God to bestow such gifts, perhaps he simply willed it himself. Perhaps the strength of his desire called to action some previously dormant gene or formed some new connection within the circuitry of his nervous system. Certainty of the true cause will elude him his whole life. Whatever the explanation, invisibility has been his to call upon for the previous eight days. It is time to be a hero.

Thus far he has neither liberated hostages nor infiltrated evil organisations. His exploits span only the liberation of a copy of *Penthouse* from his uncle's newsagency and the infiltration of the women's change room at the Clarence Municipal Swimming Pool. Some hero.

A toppled umbrella declares the arrival of the sea breeze. Sand whips high enough to sting unprotected eyes and mothers call their children from the water. The young woman marks the page in her book and gets up. Back to the wind, she shakes the sand from her towel. The boy that had been eating chips and downing a can of drink on the sand can no longer be seen.

His heart gallops as he follows her along the path that takes them from the beach. It is a short walk to her house. He is careful to time his steps with hers.

A driveway leads to the backyard. She hangs her towel from a clothesline. From under a pot plant she retrieves a key and lets herself in by the back door. The house is quiet. She places the key, her book and sunglasses next to a fruitbowl on the kitchen table.

He follows her upstairs. The carpet is soft under his bare feet. A number of the upstairs windows are open and their curtains dance in the breeze.

The showerhead is hung over a cast-iron bath. When she runs the water the sound is just noise, like radio static played into a cauldron.

In front of the mirror she slips the straps from her shoulders and peels her bathers to her waist. She examines the tan lines that the sun has left, adjusting her stance to capture the light from a small window. The boy stands in the doorway, invisible and trembling silently.

She pushes the bathers down over her hips and steps from them. Each cheek of her backside carries an indentation where elastic has pressed into the soft flesh. She bends from the waist, breasts swaying beneath her, retrieves the bathers from the floor and carries them into the bath, where she stands under the showerhead. She moves cautiously, slipping slightly on the enamel floor of the tub. Under the streaming water she rinses her green bundle and wrings it out, hangs it from a tap.

Until this summer he had not seen a woman stripped bare. Now it is a thirst he cannot quench despite the obvious objection of his conscience. The burden of guilt he carries is substantial but not so heavy as to hinder him as he acts on his compulsion. His gaze crawls every inch of her. Does he enjoy it? He is too nervous for that. He drinks her in, willing himself to commit every piece of her to memory. Ultimately, it is a type of torture to which he has subjected himself – to place himself in this room and be unable to touch her.

The young woman angles her face up toward the showerhead and pulls her hair back to form a narrow rope that clings to her neck. He is awed by the way the water navigates the contours of her body. To be a bead of water and make that journey, then he could die happy.

The breeze has picked up. A gust through an open window slams a bedroom door. The girl starts at the sound and slips. She reaches for something that isn't there, her head crashing into the bath's edge. He sees it all in time that has been slowed down and feels the blood draw back from the surface of his skin. Were he not invisible he would be shocked at the speed with which colour leaves him. His bowels are a hot soup. The girl sinks into the bath, crumpled. Water rains onto her upturned face.

First he needs to breathe. He takes deep, rapid breaths, muttering Jesus' name. He urges himself to calm down. He closes his eyes, slows his breathing, opens them. He walks to the bath, reaches for a tap and stops. He takes a flannel from a towel-rail and throws it over his hand. Now he turns the taps off. Unblinking eyes look up at him. He reaches an arm beneath the girl and another across her, careful to avoid any part of her that might be considered a liberty that is not his to take. He pulls her against the wall of the tub, rolling her onto her side. A trickle of water spills from her mouth.

He dials 000 from the hallway telephone. The emergency operator asks in her practised tone which service he requires. A hoarse whisper is all that he can form of the word 'ambulance'. For a moment he considers that this may be an effect of his invisibility – can't be seen, can't be heard. He grows terrified at the prospect of having to reveal himself to speak. He clears his throat and tries again. The word comes and it occurs to him that he has hardly spoken all day. He explains that a girl has slipped in the shower. His neighbour, he says, hoping that the lie will explain his presence. He gives the address, hangs up before he can be asked his name and is halfway down the stairs when he stops. Two stairs at a time he goes back up, pulls a towel from a rail and drapes it over the girl, covering her nakedness. Then he leaves.

He stands across the road, invisible still. He asks God to grant him another wish. Let her be alright. He asks that there be a God to grant wishes. He is sure that nobody has ever wanted anything so much. Elastic minutes stretch to their limit as he waits for the ambulance. When they come, the ambos are inside a long time. She is on a stretcher when they emerge, her neck in a brace. His heart hammers. Then she smiles and says something to the ambo nearest her head. He is a young man, handsome, with tanned skin and dark hair. He laughs and says something in reply. Relief wells in the boy like struck oil.

The ambulance leaves. He watches it down the street until it turns onto the main road. He is glad that there are no flashing lights, no siren.

The grass of an overgrown nature strip tickles his ankles and the air is moist with spray carried from the beach. He turns his face to the sky and takes in the kites that sail high above, their pilots hidden beyond the dune at the end of the street. A paper bag caught on the wind presses against him. Trapped against his invisible form it appears as if it has simply stopped and is unsure what to do next.

Tuning
LUCY LAWSON

When he was first learning guitar, Andrew's favourite part of his body was his fingertips. After only a few weeks of pushing up against the buzzing metal strings, they had hardened into oval calluses that he loved at once. The calluses were physical manifestations of work. He would rub them against the softer parts of his hands when he needed reassurance. Running his fingertips along his skin or someone else's, he appreciated the lack of feeling, the barrier between touch and sensation.

*

A friend got Andrew a job in a box factory. They hired him but nobody assigned him any work so he created his own job: he walked around the factory floor with a clipboard, which from time to time he would tick ostentatiously. He said things like 'good job guys,' and sometimes he would write on the clipboard, things like 'I am in a box factory. I am writing on a clipboard.'

No one said anything to the management. After three months they finally noticed and fired him. Andrew resolved to get a band together.

He put an ad up for a female vocalist but the girl he wanted never answered it; the girls who answered ads all had sitcom haircuts and carefully applied lip liner and had taken singing lessons. He wanted someone who he could stand behind in photographs, someone memorable. He pictured a beautiful, charismatic shaman figure who could perform songs about death without anyone laughing.

Andrew had noticed Kira many times and stared like other people did. He'd never really met her, yet her face had become precisely familiar to him. If he saw her in the crowd, whatever the event, he felt reassured that for that night at least he was in the right place, life was not being lived more intensely elsewhere.

Then one day Megan invited him to see a movie. He had known Megan for years and always emphatically kept things on a casual friendship basis; she was mopey and vulnerable and made wet sucking sounds when she ate. After the movie Andrew went to her house for the first time. Walking up the front path, he saw Kira lying on a couch on the front porch absorbed in a newspaper. She had been living with Megan for nearly a year. All that time Megan had known her, been privy to all sorts of things about her, and he hadn't any idea. Megan had mentioned her housemate Kira and Andrew had barely listened.

*

Andrew bowed his head to let his fringe protect him from the lights. He filled the cavernous pub with a squealing distorted sample of gospel that killed every conversation in the room – he wanted the breath to catch in their throats before they saw her.

Kira slipped from behind the bar (she knew the barman, of course she did) and ran onto the stage. He maintained the simple melody, but most of his attention was on her. She sang his lyrics, slightly flat and off the beat, about shipwrecks and dying horses. She wore ballet shoes and stood with feet splayed, holding the microphone with two hands like a child with an ice cream cone, and she nodded her tangle of black hair up and down as she sang. It worked. Andrew could tell.

At first, Kira disappointed him offstage, she was more ordinary than she looked: she had a cafe job, she was into environmental politics, she talked with a friend up the back about where she bought her skirt. Andrew wanted the girl onstage who sang about living in the mountains with her brothers, and being left an orphan when the plague swept through. She stayed alive in the snow by slashing open the belly of her favourite horse and crawling into its innards to keep herself warm. It was there, feeling the heart of her equine friend slowly cease to beat, that she had gained her soulful radiance.

Offstage, Kira made fun of Andrew's lyrics and got bored during rehearsals. While he obsessed over chord progressions, she would sit in the sun beneath a window with her legs up on an amp and do the cryptic crossword. It seemed an incongruous habit for her. She would frown slightly and read clues out to him. He never had any suggestions, and she would take the clues apart: 'about' often means 're', 'silver' will be its chemical symbol, it might be those two words rearranged. It was a language he could understand when she explained it to him but he couldn't speak it.

He noticed strangers approached her on the street a lot. She had a straight back, a clear gaze, soft vegan skin – so soft that if you brushed against her arm a shiver ran up your spine – and the peaceful sincerity attained only by those who are happy to spend their Saturday nights working on art exhibitions about Tasmania's forests. She seemed untouchable, treating all men affectionately, regardless of their age and appearance. Andrew started to choose his clothes carefully before each rehearsal, but she never glanced at what he was wearing. When rehearsal was over she would pull him into an intensely platonic, tender hug (Kira dispensed these like tissues, to anyone), and then walk off; she never looked back.

Her lifestyle revealed itself piece by piece. She lived on organic food, supplemented with food she and her friends pulled out of dumpsters during night raids in supermarket parking lots. One time a surprisingly easy-going security guard, oblivious to notions about our tragically wasteful society, tried to give them ten dollars 'to buy real food'. But the guard looked at Kira and knew something else was going on; all the others had the half-dressed, ragged look of the politically-minded, easily confused with genuine desperation. But Kira looked like a female Jesus amongst the rotting lettuces and slightly damaged boxes of chocolates. You could tell there was a mission, and she was on it. Andrew could see it too, but he tried to steer clear of political discussions, it always took only a few minutes for him to find he had nothing to back up his opinions but vague notions and keywords. As a result, he found his opinions changed quite easily in the face of other people's certainty. And Kira made him ashamed of his inane internal monologue, preoccupied always with sex and never with workers in export trade zones.

At night he dreamt of their future together, in settings he lifted from music magazines and peopled with musical luminaries. He read these magazines with compulsive appetite; they were his particular brand of pornography, leaving him feeling guilty and embarrassed but stimulated and excited as well. He read every description of every successful musician's sexy lifestyle, and every sloppy statement about faith and perseverance and holding onto your dreams made by every new darling of the indie press, and he stored them carefully next to his heart, in a secret compartment of belief. Deep down he knew he was special, and his image and thoughts would be immortalised on glossy paper someday. But for now he just put each new NME in a cupboard and shut the drawer.

Kira was not so certain that they were bound for musical enlightenment. 'I'm just very passionate at the moment about art that's about changing the world with your energy,' she said, and took in the pub with a sweep of her hand, 'not just something that is very beautiful for half an hour on a stage in Fitzroy.' Andrew looked into her eyes (so clear of toxins and doubt) and decided he would follow her into any and every project. Eventually, she would come to her senses and he would lead her back to dark country.

*

The rehearsal space was above an empty shop. Stephen the director had broken in with bolt cutters, cleaned the rubbish out of the second storey, and declared it a community art space. He put a new padlock on the door, and started recruiting the cast for his next theatre piece. A small collection of activists, actors and eccentrics came forward to help serve his vision. They gathered in the big room upstairs. It was still dusty but it had the light-drenched, echoing expansiveness of rooms emptied of furniture.

Stephen was in his mid-thirties, had long hair, a good arts-grant history and excellent voice projection. He gave them all a convincing pep talk before starting some of the actors on warm-up exercises.

Andrew slumped in a corner next to an oversized puppet and watched Kira dance across the floorboards in bare feet and a loose dress – the black tattoos on her calves, her lopsided haircut and gleaming cheekbones. He felt doomed to be ever trying to impress this woman. Her hands clasped and unclasped themselves as she spoke and he felt a pang of heat as he imagined those hands on him. He had been watching her so intensely for so long he felt as though he could see her body under her clothes; every glimpse of skin under a short skirt, a baggy singlet or a cropped jumper refined his mental image, and there were now few parts of her body that were hazy when he imagined her walking naked towards him.

Kira had explained that the theatre piece was a movement-based work centring on the theme of factory farming; it aimed to confront our tacit consent to the abuse of animals through physical exploration of the concept of the cage. Andrew found it wasn't as bad as it sounded.

Stephen decided Andrew would perform in the slaughter-house finale, which was a fairly abstract interpretation of the experience of herding and electrocution, but mainly Andrew would be responsible for the music. Stephen said he wanted the play to be a bit messy and undignified, as the meat industry is messy and undignified, and the music should reflect this. Andrew started collecting banjo samples.

Rehearsals rolled on, and the minutiae of the experience pulled Andrew in – arguing with Stephen about microphones consumed hours and obscured the big picture of not giving a fuck. Andrew thought experimental theatre had as much impact on the lives of cows as on the lives of Martians; but he made sure he finished his sausage roll before he got to rehearsals. Whether the show was good or not was not the point, it was continuing and the band was on hold. Stephen said Andrew had an intuitive grasp of the sensual territory that lay between sound and music. Andrew suspected this was a come on.

*

Andrew wondered if there is a word for discovering the woman who you have made the centre of your whole emotional life is fucking a talentless dickhead of an experimental theatre director. There isn't.

*

Andrew would listen to the one recording he had of the two of them performing together and become entranced with the potential. He would listen over and over and each time the songs would seem even better than the last time he heard them. A poor quality recording to start with, the tape became worn and sticky, until he wasn't listening to a song anymore, he was listening to the dreams that came with it: he was forming witheringly clever, spontaneous replies to probing interview questions about his songwriting technique asked by respected international journalists; audiences were breaking into rousing mass applause; his friends were consumed by their amazement and envy; and Kira's head fell on his shoulder as she slept in the plane seat next to him, her hand in his, as they flew somewhere important.

*

As a response to stress, the human automatic pilot is a far more awe-inspiring phenomenon than its more attention-grabbing cousin, the nervous breakdown; the capacity to continue putting one foot after another is almost infinite. Eventually you forget what you are walking away from. Andrew caught a tram into the city to buy the new CD of some middle-rung, American indie-rock band, in order to prove to himself that he was the type of person who cared about such things, and knowing that later at the pub when someone asked him what he had done that day, he could reply 'I bought the blah blah CD', and if they hadn't heard of the band, well, that just made Andrew's moral victory all the more complete.

The Postcard of Dorian Gray
DAVID COHEN

He was my brother-in-law and his name was Colin, Colin Gray, but I liked to call him Dorian. I called him Dorian at least five times before it occurred to him to ask me why. 'You know: *Dorian Gray*,' I said. At the time I was struggling through Oscar Wilde's novel for year-eleven English. 'It's a book.'

'Oh. Right.'

Colin neither knew nor cared who Oscar Wilde was, but the nickname stuck, and before long we all called him Dorian. This was soon shortened to 'Dor', or sometimes even 'Ian'.

My sister first met him at the Perth GPO, where they both worked, and where they discovered a mutual passion for deltiology. It took a certain amount of encouragement on my sister's part, but eventually Dorian invited her home to peruse his collection of rare historical postcards. Until she entered Dorian's life, the acquisition and study of postcards had been his only interest. An avid collector since the age of eighteen, he'd amassed some two thousand specimens, dating back to the 1870s. In addition to his private projects, Dorian had been commissioned to design a series of postcards in preparation for the 200th anniversary of the Australian postal service. He'd already acquired several rare photographs and paintings commemorating great moments in postal history – the opening of the country's first official post office in Circular Quay, 1809; the appointment, in 1841, of the first postman; the introduction of the bicycle in 1898 – and had come up with his own designs to celebrate the introduction of Express Post, the implementation of the barcode, and the advent of bubble wrap.

But Dorian's real deltiological ambitions lay elsewhere. He disclosed them to me at the wedding reception.

'There's this postcard,' he began conspiratorially.

Almost instantly, I started yawning. It was more or less a conditioned response, triggered off whenever Dorian started talking about postcards. He seldom touched alcohol, but on that night he'd cut loose and downed a few Strongbow ciders. Strangely, intoxication made him sound more vapid than usual.

'Yeah,' he continued, as if I'd encouraged him to elaborate. 'Been chasing it nearly ten years.'

'What kind of postcard?' I asked, reaching for a curry puff.

He leaned closer, exhaling into my ear. 'You know Hitler?'

'Not personally.'

'Well, there's a card – done around 1936 – showing Hitler and Eva Braun sitting together on a couch at the Berghof.'

He stepped back, as if giving me room to express my astonishment.

'What's so interesting about that?' I said.

'It's only one of the most valuable postcards in the world!' he practically shouted, going on to explain that it was part of an extremely limited edition, designed by Hitler's court photographer Heinrich Hoffmann, and intended – unlike the numerous official Führer postcards circulating at the time – for private distribution among the Nazi elite.

'Only two known copies left in existence. Guy in Nebraska owns one, but the other one – well, I think I've finally tracked it down.'

'Wow!' I replied, forgetting that Dorian had no ear for sarcasm, especially when applied to postcard collecting.

'"Wow" is right,' he agreed. 'If I owned that card, I'd be famous.'

'Famous?' I said through a mouthful of curry puff.

'In postcard circles,' said Dorian. 'In postcard circles.'

'How famous?'

'Put it this way: the guy in Nebraska is so famous, he actually appears on a postcard *himself*.'

'He's on a postcard because he's famous for owning another postcard?'

'S'right,' said Dorian. 'He's pictured on the postcard holding up his Hitler postcard.'

'And you'd like to be on a postcard, too?'

Dorian gazed into the distance, dangling his empty glass between two fingers. 'Well, it's…kind of a dream of mine. Only problem is, that little Hitler number costs a small fortune.'

*

Prior to the wedding, Dorian had lived in a one-bedroom flat and my sister still lived at home. Once married, they rented an old two-bedroom house in Maylands, where they lived quietly while saving their money to realise my sister's dream of owning a home. Dorian continued working hard on the Australia Post anniversary project, collecting his own postcards and chatting via the internet to fellow zealots around the globe. My sister's interest in postcards was far more low key; it was a hobby to be pursued alongside many others. She simply enjoyed the act of accumulating things, although she gave up shell collecting: Dorian, it turned out, had a morbid fear of the ocean. Apparently when he was eight years old he got caught in a rip at Cottesloe Beach and was carried right out before being rescued by a passing boat. He hadn't been anywhere near the beach since, and wouldn't even discuss the episode, except to say, 'It was hell. Pure hell.'

But, shells or no shells, I had never seen my sister so happy. Dorian seemed happy enough, too, although every now and then I noticed that far-away look in his eyes.

*

It happened just after I'd started year twelve. Dorian had withdrawn all of his and my sister's money and purchased the coveted Hitler postcard. When she found out, there was a huge fight, their first and last.

'I hope you and your postcard will be very happy together!' she'd wailed, slamming the front door behind her. Then she came back to live with us.

A week passed and Dorian didn't call. But not only that, he failed to show up at work for five consecutive days. Maybe he really had chosen the postcard over my sister and was at that very moment on a speaking tour of deltiological society dinners around the world. My sister swallowed her pride and picked up the phone, but nobody answered. This went on for three days. There was growing concern at the GPO. The Australia Post anniversary project, to which Dorian had always applied himself with such fervour, had come to an abrupt halt. So my sister, mother and father drove out to the Maylands house. Everything inside remained more or less as it had the day my sister walked out, except there was no sign of Dorian.

My parents notified the police, whose investigations revealed that Dorian had last been seen entering a newsagent's in Forrest Chase. Then he'd simply vanished. Extensive searches turned up nothing: no suggestion of an accident or abduction; no evidence that he'd been involved in anything sinister or was leading a double life – on the contrary, Dorian barely led one life. And yet none of this came as a complete surprise to me. I'd always felt that if anyone might be likely to disappear, Dorian was the man. But that was just my opinion, an opinion I refrained from sharing.

'Don't worry,' we all reassured my sister. 'He'll be back.'

'Thirty-four-year-old men don't just vanish!' my father said.

'What if he's with another woman!'

'Come on,' I said. 'He wouldn't look at another woman, unless she was on a postcard.'

'Shut up, you!' said my father, adding: 'Wherever the hell he is, he'd better have a bloody good explanation!'

We had no idea if Dorian was dead or alive. A month passed, then another. After six months, still no word, no sign. He had, to all intents and purposes, ceased to exist. The only concrete reminder that he'd ever walked on this earth was his phenomenal collection of postcards, lovingly displayed in a cabinet of wood and glass, which my sister dusted and polished every Saturday.

*

I came home from school one afternoon to see my parents and sister sitting around the kitchen table. Nobody was saying anything. I hovered in the doorway, feeling a strange tightness in my stomach.

My father, sitting with his back to me, was examining something on the table in front of him. He removed his glasses and held whatever it was right up before his face. My god! I thought. Is it a blackmail letter? A ransom note? A finger?

Advancing a few steps, I saw that he was holding a card. A postcard.

'Is it from Colin?' I asked, entering the room. We'd all reverted to calling him by his real name, out of respect. 'Don't tell me it's the Hitler card!'

My sister began to sob.

'It's not so much from Colin,' said my mother, 'as *of* Colin.'

'Can I see?'

'Came in the mail today,' said my father, relinquishing the card to me.

It was a picture of Colin, no question, but not – as I'd expected – a picture immortalising Colin in recognition of his contributions to the field of deltiology. Far from it.

It was a picture of Colin windsurfing.

I studied the image carefully. There was no doubt about it. Wearing only a pair of bright green boardshorts, Colin could be seen in close-up, feet planted on the board, hands gripping the boom, leaning back until he was almost parallel with the ocean's glassy surface. In the background, a few other white sails formed a vague semi-circle, like folded serviettes around an ultramarine-blue tablecloth. I'd never seen Colin in anything but grey trousers and short-sleeved shirt and tie. As I'd imagined, he was as thin as a very thin rake, his white limbs sparsely covered in black hair.

For all the skill with which he manipulated that sail, his expression looked grim.

Yellow lettering beneath the image said: GREETINGS FROM YALLINGUP!

'I don't understand,' my sister moaned. 'Colin absolutely hates the beach.'

I turned the card over. There was no information about the picture except for the words, 'Yallingup, Western Australia'. The card, addressed to my parents, came from some friends holidaying down south.

'Dear Frank and Val,' it read, *'We found this in the souvenir shop. We both thought the guy in the picture looks just like Colin. What do you reckon? Can't be him, I suppose. Weather here is superb and we've just been snorkelling! Terry got stung by something but it's not too serious. See you soon. Love, Joan and Terry.'*

'I think,' said my father, 'that it's just someone who looks a lot like Colin.'

'Then he must have a twin brother,' I said, unable to stop looking at the photograph, 'because there's no mistaking that nose.' Colin had a very distinctive nose. It looked somehow only half-completed, as if the genes responsible had knocked off early, leaving two small nostrils surrounded by a large, shapeless lump of bone.

'Well, if it is really him, at least we know he's alive, though what he's doing on that postcard is a complete bloody mystery.'

'We'll pass this on to the police tomorrow,' said my mother. 'You don't mind if I just stick it on the fridge in the meantime, do you, sweetheart?'

*

Maybe it could have been dismissed as an odd coincidence, but less than a week later my parents received another postcard from Joan and Terry. Again, a windsurfer: Colin, with that same uncomfortable look on his face. The image had definitely not been doctored; it was Colin all right, and he was undeniably windsurfing. He'd also acquired a slight a tan. The card said: SURF'S UP! MARGARET RIVER, WESTERN AUSTRALIA.

'Dear Frank and Val, does this look like Colin to you? Don't want to cause undue alarm but it's a bit odd, don't you think? Must say I never picked Colin for the windsurfing type – in fact neither of us can recall seeing him outdoors. It's lovely down here in Margaret's. You know that TV chef, Ian Parmenter? We saw him coming out of Coles! Bye for now, T. and J.'

The police could do little with either postcard except track down the photographers who supplied the images. It turned out they'd both been shot by the same person, one Geoff Panos. But Panos said that he'd never had any actual contact with the man believed to be Colin. He'd just noticed him out on the waves and decided he'd make a good subject because it was unusual to see short, thin, balding windsurfers. 'Makes a nice change,' he'd remarked.

Police investigators scoured the southwest coast without success. Meanwhile, more postcards featuring Colin came in from other holidaymaking friends of my parents. The images repeated a now familiar theme: he was pictured windsurfing, or making his way seaward to go windsurfing, or sitting on the beach, having just windsurfed. He appeared on postcards from Augusta, Busselton, Mandurah – even as close to home as Rockingham. One card showed him on Rottnest Island, perched upon his board on the sand at twilight and holding aloft a couple of fat crayfish. The caption beneath him said simply: ROTTO! Photographers there and elsewhere recalled that Colin had resisted any efforts to engage him in conversation. He'd appeared seemingly from nowhere and just as quickly melted into the background.

We noticed that on more recent postcards, Colin's physique had developed. At first he'd borne a close resemblance to the 'before' character in old Charles Atlas advertisements. While he hadn't quite made it all the way to 'after', he'd definitely filled out. What's more, he looked healthy and tanned. Over time, he'd gradually come to appear more at home in the sunny, carefree world he inhabited. But his smile always seemed a bit forced. It occurred to me that his dream had come true, in part, and I wondered if that was better or worse than not at all.

It was all my sister could do to cope with the fact of his absence, although she took some comfort in the discovery that her situation wasn't unique. There was even, it turned out, a support group set up specifically for people whose loved ones had disappeared only to be represented pictorially on postcards, calendars and other stationery products connected with the tourist industry. We learned that nearly four percent of the people officially listed as missing persons fell into this category. One group member's mother had inexplicably vanished, only to show up repeatedly in brochures advertising seniors' package tours to Surfers Paradise. Someone else's brother consistently materialised on the *Getaway* website. Even mental health experts were forced to concede that these weren't mere hallucinations. Something else was at work, but what? Nobody could adequately explain it, and even if that were possible, it still didn't fill the gaps in the lives of those left behind. Colin would contact us when or if he so wished. In the meantime we could only offer my sister whatever love and understanding we had to give, and hope that, even if Colin never returned, we might find some meaning in what had happened.

*

After completing my first year of university, I landed a holiday job at a hotel resort on one of the local beaches. Located in its seemingly endless shopping arcade was a kind of souvenir superstore called Down Under Gifts. Passing the shop one day during an afternoon break, I thought of Colin, who had been missing for almost two years but still turned up now and then on postcards from around the state. These days he cut a burly, bronzed figure, and had somehow acquired a mop of sandy-coloured hair. But the nose gave him away every time. He really looked the part these days, but he had never quite shaken off that vaguely pained expression, as if someone stood just outside the frame, barking orders at him through a megaphone.

I entered the store, more out of a sense of duty than anything else. If any of us saw or heard of a card featuring Colin, we took steps to obtain it and deliver it to my sister. She'd got over him, more or less, but had accumulated such an impressive collection of Colin Gray postcards that she felt it would be a shame to stop now. I made my way down one of the aisles, pausing now and then to contemplate the opal-and-koala pendants, the thermometers with boomerangs glued onto them, the images of wattles adorning everything from beer coasters to stubby holders, until finally I reached the postcards. The place was so absurdly large, it could have been a tourist attraction in its own right. I checked every single one, and there were plenty, but I couldn't see Colin.

I left the arcade and walked outside. Standing beneath the awning, I watched beachgoers get out of their vehicles and dash across the carpark, which still baked underfoot even though the sunlight was dimming. Then I too made my way down the path leading to the beach, where I sat on the sand, contemplating the ocean. At the water's edge, about ten feet away, stood a lone windsurfer with his board. On several occasions in the past, I'd seen people who appeared to be Colin, only to discover that, close up, they looked nothing like him. After all, not even Colin looked like Colin. This time, however, I was certain. I leapt up, opening my mouth to cry out, *Colin*! But something stopped me. Something inside me said: let him go.

So I just stood watching as he dragged the heavy apparatus into the water, climbed aboard and hauled the sail upright. Before I knew it he was cutting a neat white furrow toward the horizon, as if being reeled in by someone on a distant shore. And yet I noticed that there was no breeze. The sea was spread out over the ocean bed like a soft blue quilt. The sky had turned from azure to a glorious pink. I kept my eyes on Colin, or Dorian, or whoever it was, sailing further and further away until he'd vanished into a picture-postcard sunset.

The Pudden Olympics
Euan Mitchell

There is naught more pathetic than a friend betrayed who thinks somehow they won. Let me elucidate…

He was an Australian, a natural and deserving target, by the name of Tanner. Like so many others, he's chasing the 'economic miracle' they called Ireland in the early years of this century – thanks to America's software companies being so cosy sweet with the new Irish tax laws and all that business. But Tanner got stiffed by his 'miracle' company only weeks after arriving. At a loose end, he finds his way to an inn at the edge of Dublin's old city centre where he meets the fast-talking Doyle.

It's true the local fellow Doyle *did* like Tanner despite the latter's nasal twang and tall tales of warm sea water. And they contested so strongly with their downings of Guinness that the result remains unsettled amongst all concerned, except the publican profiting heartily behind his counter. It became a matter of national prides, to be sure, but before long they were both shouldering each other in ardent agreement as to whom the 'old foe' is.

On the whiff of this meeting and Tanner's need to earn a Euro or two as winter closes in, Doyle invites his new best friend to join his annual work pilgrimage to the factory of Molly's Traditional Home-Made Plum Puddens.

*

Next Monday morning in the 4.30 dark and drizzle, Tanner and Doyle make their way along wet pavements in a gloomy outer suburb. They round a corner and see the glow of the old brick pudden factory with its front door open to take in various figures emerging from the cold.

Doyle explains to Tanner that the boss's name isn't really Molly, but she answers all the same to this, her nickname, after thirty-four pudden seasons. From late October to Christmas Eve is the duration of a pudden season, and for these two long months of sweat and grind the rewards are handsome enough.

Through the door, they find no-one in a front section that's stacked either side with wooden crates. Tucked between the crates are a small office and a serving counter. But all the chatter and clatter is coming from the back section. The door between slides open. A mature woman of bountiful physical bearing appears in a neck-to-knee white vinyl apron and black wellington boots. She is leading a young woman, clad in similar uniform, to the little office.

'Mornin', Molly,' Doyle calls.

Molly looks over to see who's greeting her. She has an expressive face, lined with a stalwart good humour. 'Doyle, you're gonna go greyer than me if you keep comin' back every year.'

'Tis grand to see you too, boss,' Doyle smirks. 'And this is my *mate*, Tanner from Australia, who's lookin to join us.'

Molly smiles as she shakes Tanner's hand. 'How'd he talk you into this?'

'Too easily,' replies Tanner.

'And I'm Renny.' As the young woman offers her hand, the lilt of her Irish brogue sings in Tanner's ears.

Tanner shakes her hand and tries to say something more than 'hi', but is too struck by her loveliness, despite the apron and boots. Her dark hair is tied up at the back, wisps trail down onto her smooth pale skin. He wants to kiss right down her neck and beyond. He hopes it is not merely his own imagination that has planted what he sees as a twinkle in her eye as well.

And perhaps he *is* right, because Molly suddenly becomes very businesslike in organising the lads into the back section for the morning's mixing. Molly has endured many hardships in her lifetime, but having her daughter Renny fall for an Australian might just determine a mother's absolute limit.

Tanner and Doyle is soon up to their elbows mixing mushy pudden dough in big stainless steel bowls that are nestled into the open tops of old 44-gallon drums, standing mid-factory floor. Half-a-dozen other brethren also mix water into the rich-smelling mystery of dried fruits, flour, sugar, spices and the rest; while around them a dozen or so are teamed up at tables with antique balancing scales to weigh, then tie the raw soft puddens snug into their calico cloths. All workers are hung with aprons of white vinyl down to their black wellington boots. All too tough for hair nets.

The boilers in the steaming room behind are firing up like the Devil's cauldrons to soon be cooking the puddens in big batches.

Tanner drifts into reverie from his round and round mixing – lost dreaming of Renny's hands 'artisticking' all over his steaming-up body.

'You're lucky, Tanner, to be joinin us this puticular mornin,' pipes up Doyle, pointing his wiry finger to a high shelf overlooking the factory floor.

Tanner's dreaming brown eyes follow to where his nose is being pointed. Up on the shelf is an old plastic pouring jug painted in gold gilt. It's shaped like a jug from under a geriatric's bed, but it looks like some sort of trophy. The jug part is gold and mounted on a wooden stand decorated in yellowing stickers for Baker's Brand Brandy (or call it B-B-B, specially after a charge in the cold starts). 'Izat a drinkin' trophy?' Tanner asks.

Other ears are tuning into this exchange, chuckling at the thought. 'No – something you'd have more of a chance at,' Doyle grins. 'It's the trophy for the winner of our Pudden Olympics.'

Tanner don't want to laugh straight out at this idea in case he might be offending some of his fellow workers, so he contains his grin to ask, 'Which is what exactly?'

'A special sort of race,' comes the sincere reply. 'But easier than explainin the rules – better if you watch how the old hands do it first, before the novice event that you'll be eligible for.'

'You think I should give it a go?'

'If y'think you've the hide for it.'

Tanner sets to sniggering at Doyle's too obvious bait, but decides to take him up anyway. Other pudden workers – who till now have been eyeballing Tanner as a suspected tie-wearing type – start into a banter about past great Pudden Olympians, their best times and proudest moments over the whole history of the Games.

'I was there when Shanahan set the Pudden Decathlon record in 1992…'

'My word, that fellow was so fast that – '

'He was lucky we didn't bring in a handicappin' system for the bugger.'

Tanner tries to follow the reeling off of names and feats while he finishes his mixing – amazed by the intensity, but with no real idea about whom or what is being talked up.

When the last of the morning's two thousand puddens are mixed, wrapped and ready for their steaming, all hands set to clearing the wet factory floor. The middle of the factory soon becomes a fifteen-metre course ready for running-type races. At one end of the floor space is a starting line, at the other is a row of four bowls of leftover pudden mix sitting atop their 44-gallon drums.

The experienced contenders are the gabbiest throughout this setting up, with scores to settle from past years and bursting with bluff about their chances this time round. The official timekeeper makes his fuss while undoing the fancy watch from his wrist to hold with two hands as he readies to press the buttons.

The first Pudden Olympians, hardest-bitten by their contesting, swagger up to the starting end of the floor. Molly is at the other end with little rectangular lead weights, from the balancing scales, which she's standing upright in the middle of each of the four leftover bowls of raw pudden mix.

Tanner notices there's money changing hands as the spectating workers hang off the shelves or sit up on the tables at each side of the floor. Renny, with her smooth pale smile, takes up position as the starting official. She gets the nod from her ma when each of the little weights is upright in a bowl's middle.

Renny warns the four competitors to stay behind the line of starting until she bangs a stirring spoon inside an empty mixing bowl she's picked up.

The chatter drops with Renny's crying, 'On your marks.'

The four competitors focus in on their respective bowls at the other end of the room. No lanes are marked. The chattering drops. Tanner wonders what terminal stupidity might follow.

Silence.

'Get set...go!'

The cheering explodes around the scramble of flapping aprons and wellington boots slapping across the wet concrete floor as Renny continues banging her mixing bowl more lively than a screw-loose wind-up. There ain't much between each one's headway, and the jostling seems perfectly legal.

All four lunge headfirst towards their mixing bowls. Behind each bowl are two workers acting as race monitors to ensure no hands are used to brake or prop while bending down to pick up the little weights with their mouths.

All make a clean pass to emerge with a little lead rectangle wedged between front teeth – spitting fury out the sides of their mouths, eyes savage.

They turn heel to charge back the way they came. One Olympian slips on the wet floor and his weight falls out. He pulls up and curses such blasted luck, but Tanner thinks the fellow fortunate that his weight did not fall *in* for the swallow and possible surgery.

The three remaining Olympians hurtle back towards the starting line to drop the lead weights from their mouths into empty flour buckets that have appeared.

The first two land truly, but the third hits the flour bucket's rim and skids across the floor to the accompanying agonised groans of its former bearer, as Renny rings out her bowl banging.

The winner is suitably cheered and lauded, taking a lap of victory around the factory floor to much back-patting while the runner-up tries to breathe through his disappointment, gasping like a fish in a puddle.

Tanner fancies his chances in such an event and is happy to join the next line-up which is being hailed by the madding throng as the year's Pudden Olympics Novice Showdown. An extra mixing bowl is put in place at the picking-up end, since the novices number five this year.

Renny gives all her warnings for the newcomers, catching Tanner's eye about stepping over the starting line. Molly hopes to herself that the event will reduce Tanner to an also-ran for her daughter's affections.

Taking up their start positions, foreheads crease with concentration in order to line up with their bowls at the other end of the concrete floor.

'On your marks…'

Most lift their elbows slightly, in readiness for any bumps or shoving that might be attempted – given that gold gilt trophy is at stake. And boasting rights for eternity cos you only debut once here.

'Get set…go!'

And the bowl-banging and the mad cheering increases the strain on their novice faces and physiques as they slap their boots as fast as they can across the floor. Tanner with red blowing cheeks is neck and neck for the lead. The monitors behind each bowl are calling out reminders to all novices that no hands are to be used for the pick-up. Teeth only.

The five reach their bowls with barely a second between them. They bend over to pick up the little weights with their teeth. They sense hands coming at them from nowhere…

It's too late.

All five have their heads pushed down deep into a mix that looks like mushed-up muesli, before they guess the unleaked conspiracy of practical joking and betrayal that's just been played on them. Well, almost all. Four lift their heads from their bowls and can only join in the gales of laughter from their peers.

But Tanner thinks his dunking is merely part of the event's handicapping system and, oblivious to the joke, he tears with undiminished desperation back to the other end so as to plunge the weight from his teeth into his designated bucket.

It needn't be told you directly here, my perceptive reader, what the responses of all those gathered round were when he stopped to raise his head from the final bucket, displaying a face and wild hair covered so thickly and oozing with pudden mix that it would frighten a New Guinea mudman.

Tanner, with a grin as wide as it was stupid, in that instant declaring – like all the world would toast the pudden season of his initiating – 'I won!'

The Jazz
Paul Dawson

At night the pub's a jazz club and it backs into the under side of a bridge, using part of that vaulting structure as its own. It's dank down there along High where the train meets and then goes over it. Not 100 metres ahead, the line crosses back and then veers, taking a culvert west with it, to the outskirts of the suburb and into another.

We walk along the edge of the road, under the bridge. Anna, my childhood sweetheart and long-time lofty, talks to my mother, arm in arm. My father's ahead of us and his pace quickens across the road to get the door. We've come to see my half-brother play and lately it's all he talks about.

Inside, he looks over the place twice around, puffing for his heart pumping. He sets us down at a table, centre and close to the stage. He brings us drinks and I drink to drunk.

Anna says, 'I love this place.' She sticks a finger down her throat, gags but catches it quickly.

'I could live here,' my mother adds like a barfly, to help her along.

They laugh like leeches on a leg. They're in cahoots.

'Frank comes here for lunch,' my mother says.

He nods and takes in the surrounds. 'Not many folks here.'

'My puppa don't go to pubs,' Anna says. 'He goes to discos.'

We all swallow at our glasses. My father says:

'How *is* your old dad.'

'He gets by.'

'Thank Lucky, it's over.'

Anna says nothing. My father's talking about Jason, Anna's brother, out of jail.

She looks over the back of her chair at the stage, and when she returns my father's expecting more. She gives it. She says: 'I don't think it will ever be over.'

He shakes his head to something he's thinking. 'No, true, these things never go in any final sense.'

Anna drinks and my father watches us both.

'He's haunted by it.' She laughs because it's not funny. She's being candid and my father's good at getting it.

'That's the horror of it,' he says. 'Yours are fine people. Jason's a good kid. My guess is he learnt quickly what some people take a lifetime.'

Anna's not so sure. She looks around the room.

'Only someone got killed for it,' she says as a matter for fact and my father doesn't take it wrong.

'True, things happen. *Things* happen that you don't want to, but they do. And sometimes you feel stupid for them and are humbled by them. He'll remember it by the scar in his head if anything else.'

Anna agrees and my father gives her a knowing nod, enough for understanding between them. My mother's also changed by it and she gives a lost look to her glass, thickened by her lip.

I say, 'Where the hell is this Brother's Band.'

Anna pokes at the ice in her drink with her straw. 'He's changed but it's as if he's always been that way.' She stirs and looks lullful.

'How, love?' my father asks.

'It's like he's always had it in him, the ability to get off track and then hurt someone because of it.'

My father and mother don't flinch. My father says: 'He's adjusting.' He says it as if he knows from practical experience. Jail time. 'It's a man's world in there and when there are only men-'

My mother's pushing at him under the table. It's in her eyes. Her mouth drops slowly. 'Frank,' she says. He ignores her and continues: 'Men need women around more than women need men. That's been my experience. Men get mighty serious when there are no women.'

She lightens.

He looks around from table to table to stage behind me, and says, 'Nick-o! Where *is* this be-bop.'

A few people come through the background. Band members mill about the stage and tap microphones. Blow horns. Tighten drums. Dave's piano is a coffin closed.

We drink.

My father says, 'Where's David?'

I get a round of doubles, a triple for my blood. I draw hearts on the table, ink from drink rings. The musicians step to the stage and my father says, 'Where's David?'

They breathe in and then play. The music's quiet, and they all play the same one note at once.

'This is not jazz,' he says.

'It is jazz,' says my mother.

'Where's David?'

Anna looks at me and says under, 'Nick, tonight, I need to-'

My father says, 'David's playing tonight.'

The music stops and the band breathes. The snare snaps and they play that long note again. My father says, 'Nick-o, go ask the publican. Say you're family.'

The band breathes. Snap. The note.

I lug-it to the bar and say to guy behind, 'The piano player. You know where he is?'

He grunts for all the goodness in him. 'There's no piano tonight, just those horns and those drums.'

He has cauliflowers for ears. Pits in his nose.

'My brother, David Morrow, is the piano player and singer for this group playing tonight. They're his buddies.'

'Ask them.'

'They're playing.'

They snap the note and the barman picks a glass and polishes. It's what they do when they couldn't care less.

The note disappears and players play a tune of tuning.

He spits, the glass squeaks, and I stare the best deathly.

He stops his polishing.

'I'll take a triple,' I say, and I pay with a pocket full of coins. To pain him.

Back at the table my father says, 'These guys need our David to keep them together.' He turns to me, 'What's the word, Nick-o?' Like a jazz man.

'Says there's no piano.'

'Where's Johnny? Johnny'll know.' He stands to get a look. 'I know him from somewhere not here,' he adds, but is drowned down as the music sets to a chug, lowered to a misery minor. Someone has opened the lid on the piano. The trumpeter points his bugle above us into the black like it's the night and he's a wolf wet-breathing into the room back behind us.

Next thing Anna is close. She says, 'We need to talk.'

'Speak, baby.'

She pushes a nail into my neck. Across the table my father's gritting and staring at the bar. My mother's saying, Frank Frank Frank, as he gets up, struggles with his chair back against the table behind him, and is gone. And the horns are blowing a-pushing against me and the drums are bouncing across the room. And I can't hear anything except for the horns' long fog fingers and the drums now car-rolling, roof to side to wheels to side, down, down a rock rocky decline.

Even Anna's into it, although she keeps the point of her elbow stiff in my side. She's settled in for the set. I give her a wink and whistle whistle-e.

My father comes back and then is gone again. My mother gets up and is gone. I close my eyes for listening's sake. The drummer rolls his sticks over everything he owns trying to touch it all. He plays the glasses on the table we sit, chairs, the walls, my head. He has tambourines and bells, and over it all he rides a cymbal and taps a cow-down on my thighs.

And then the piano is old-time upright rollicking so I open my eyes, and my father and mother are at the table and Anna is drinking and they're all looking at the stage. I twist in my chair, and there he is in a cream suit. Dave at the piano. Wig-less.

My father clicks his fingers. My mother fusses over a cut above his eye as he taps the table and nods his head.

'Frank-' my mother says above the music.

'Yeah-' He yells. 'Now that's the jazz!'

And the piano tucks under everything. The drummer is all crabs and claws. A sax honks, and then another, a smaller one, honks like a bubba. And together they honk honk on the winds of trumpets. The piano has sharp chords. I sit up in my seat, nodding beats, looking like my father grin-grinning.

And Dave's piano is messing it with the drummer. Cuts in at the gaps. Pokes through to let us know he's there. His comb-over flaps a wave hello. He fists at the keys: Who?- Dave on the bar. Dave? Hi- under your chair! Where? Hey!- lifts that lady's hat. Tickling the tummies at her side.

And people are talking. Glasses ting-chinking. Smokers blowing clouds, misting the air above us. A laugh behind me.

Read my father's lips:

'Yeah, Nick-o!' he says, 'Now this is the Jazz.'

In the break Dave comes over serious, takes a chair from a table by us and sits saddle next to my father, who nods to him likewise. Dave smirks to strangle a smile and my father mirrors him. My mother's talking to Anna and then Anna's talking to me and Dave is talking to my mother. Everyone's trying not to look at Dave's hair. Then my father is gone.

My mother says, 'It's good David.'

'It doesn't really matter what you think.'

'I said it's good. And that's all I really need to say.'

'I'm saying I know it's good and I don't care what anyone thinks.'

Anna tugs. 'Now, Nick,' she says.

'Saying doesn't mean anything, David. It's good. It was a compliment.'

'Nick, please let's get out of here.'

'David I can't see why you're like this. Don't mess with me. Don't mess with your father. He's sick. He doesn't need it, I don't need it.'

My father comes back and sits next to them. The cut above his eye is bleeding again. Dave turns to him and my mother gets up and goes to the bar. Dave says to my father, 'Good?'

'Great.'

He asks me, 'Good?' His eyes squash at his brow. He says, 'What are you so drunk about?'

But we're looking at my father, so Dave looks too. 'For fuck-'

My father touches at the cut. 'It's nothing.'

'Are you trying to stuff this whole thing up?'

'I had a little altercation with the barman, that's all. It's fine. Mae's over there now.'

Dave turns from my father slow-shaking his disgust.

'It's a good gig Davo, nice crowd. Everyone loves it. I can see it.'

Dave won't look at him, instead he mumbles to sorry himself. He can't believe it. My mother comes back with a cloth of ice she's suitably sweet-talked the barman into letting her have. She touches my father's head with it and he doesn't move. 'But, I'm not so happy, Frank,' she says. 'We're supposed to be good-timing not tending to cuts and bruises.'

Dave stiffens, 'Bullshit. Fucking bullshit.'

He stands, drinks my drink and takes my father's with him.

'Now we can go.' Anna pushes at me. 'We're out for a breather,' she says.

My parents are fussing at each other, and Anna pulls at my arm for out, and for some fear in our futures creeping.

Outside, water drips drop from the bridge above, and Anna is sick in the gutter. She forces it out with her fingers.

'Too much?'

She looks at me ruthless and cleans her tongue and teeth with the sleeve of her jacket. We walk along the road for a time, and then turn into an industrial estate where factories are built like boxes. We turn down a dirt track and keep on walking, off the road towards a group of trees froze for spooking.

It's a quiet moon for a hole in the dark and everything is lit dusty by it. At the end of a stumblesome block we come to tough grass under our feet, and then shrubs and then trees about us and over us and the ground soft and thick with pine needles. Anna's in my belly beside me. A big face of her faceless.

Down a small hill into a gully, we let the slope take us to a tree where I pull her to me and we kiss, but she stops for the acid in her mouth.

She says, 'I don't know what's happening to me. Can you see it? Nick?'

I say nothing but breathe her breath.

'Nick, I don't know. I'm-'

I pull her to me with a fist of her hair at the back of her head and she stops me, then lets me, and I push at her and she pushes back. We hold our respectives in cold cups. We kneel to the damp ground, and then lie on it with papers and bottles under us. A stinking blanket bunched up as our pillow. By my head is a tin can. Out of the corner of my eye, a chest of drawers.

She undoes my pants and I pull her tights below her hips. I lift her skirt up insideout, and we come close together to burn holes for heating through plastic bags.

We slow and then stop. And I don't move because I have no bones.

Baby.

Anna lies heavy on me and sleep changes her breathing deeper. For a time I look up into the canopy of branches, the cold coming up through my back. I sleep. When she wakes she rolls away and pulls a boot from under her back. She looks up at the trees and says, 'Nick, I can't do this any more,' then stretches her tights up as she lies there, pushing her pelvis nightwards.

I don't say a thing.

'I'm sorry,' she adds. She looks at my middle and then stands and bends and kisses my forehead. 'I'm sorry, I can't be here.'

I don't say a thing. I say:

'I know.'

We walk a long lonely back to the pub, and outside the front my father is sitting on a chair jacketless. He shivers. He says, 'Where you been?' His hair has blown windy to one side. The cut above his eye has blood coming from it, a smash in his cheek down from it, it shines black in the light above the door.

'Where have you been?'

Water drips around him from the bridge above. His arms are crossed. A drip drops on his leg and he looks to where it landed. The light goes off.

'Where's your jacket?'

'Everyone's gone,' he says, 'I can't find your mother. Dave fell into his band and they shut the whole thing off.'

'Mum's probably home.'

He looks at Anna. 'Sorry, love.'

'We'll get a cab.'

'We'll walk. Walking's for thinking. Ring your mother see if she's alright. Then we'll walk.'

'Walking is good,' Anna says.

'That jazz! The craziest thing I ever heard.' He shakes his head, his back straight in the chair, arms crossed for the cold.

'Maybe we should get you checked out.'

'Don't even think about it,' he says so I never suggest it again. 'Ring your mother. Find my jacket.'

'Mum will be fine.'

'Ring your mother, then we'll get gone.'

I go to the door of the pub but it's locked. There are no lights on inside. I overhear my father say to Anna: 'They tried to take the chair, and then I don't know what happened.'

'You got to keep your chair,' Anna says, watching at cars going by. A taxi slows to see us and she hails it. She kisses my father and gets in, looks at me and closes the door.

When she's gone my father laughs a cough that looks like it hurts and everything relaxes just a little.

He says, 'She forgot to kiss you goodbye, Son.'

Eagle-eyed.

He takes the first step as a shuffle and I join him in his hobble towards home like a couple of old sticks stickless. And our shadows in the streetlights go from long to squat, from forward to behind.

He says nothing for a time, but as we leave High he starts, fixed ahead, 'Don't get to thinking things will change, Nick, that life will get easier, or that your person will become new or different.'

'I don't think it.'

'That low you might sometimes feel will always be with you. I promise. Get used to it. It comes creeping and will be the same throughout your days.'

He looks ahead and now knows the way home, can see the train line, and the boom gates waiting. He continues: 'It's a reminder. It will let you know you're still who you are, even if you think you've changed. Even if you think the things around you have changed. Little *d* despair knows your name, even if you've forgot it.'

We step a few paces in silence and then I say, 'I think the train's coming.'

He ignores me and rolls up his shirtsleeves, unbuttons a bloody collar.

'Son, the thing of it is, in my head I'm still twenty-odd, and that sensation, when you get to my age, is a great tragedy. I've talked to many an old man about it. They've all said it. All the decisions I made back then, were decisions I could make now. There's no maturing in that thing that makes you who you are. I've got better at managing my affairs, but there's no difference between me now and me at any time in my life, short of the physicalities of it all.'

The bells start from south in the distance, and get louder as each crossing starts and then ours starts and the boom gates drop. The train's lights lurk. A slow mover. We stop at the gates and when the diesel comes it drives its mile-long weight and blows its horn for the crossing. My father waves to the engineer, whose face is lit ghoulish from below, dragging the greasy diesel and its tail behind it like a cloak.

Above the train my father continues:

'And it's worrying that I'm going to feel like this on the day I die. And I don't want that Nick. I don't want to be lying in a hospital bed, saying, Frank Morrow, same as I ever was. I want to be saying, *Frank Morrow?* Now there was a chap. And then I'll off into an afterlife.'

He looks at me and smiles his sweet sorrow. The train rattles interstate and a few people sit in the yellow windows. Reading newspapers. One sips at a tumbler. Carriage after carriage.

'It's not about God, Son, although I wish to Him I had one.'

We both look for the train's end, the freight now following, and when we see it coming he says: 'It would make it easier to leave the memory of myself behind and get a godly handshake of welcomes, arm over my shoulder, Now Frank, you did well looking after that Morrow.'

He laughs for the thought of it and follows the last carriage as it's taken past us and then starts to disappear along the line the track takes. The boom gates rise and we look at each other, say nothing and walk on home.

Byron's School of Method Reading
CAROLYN COURT

Byron likes to get into the spirit of the books he's consuming, he calls it 'method reading'. When he read *The Three Musketeers* he had to shoplift a plastic sword and cape at the $2 Shop and wear them until he'd finished the book. When he read *As I Lay Dying* he bought a huge fish at the fish shop and walked around the shopping centre with it in his arms, saying 'my mother is a fish'. He didn't mind that this brilliant idea was lost on everyone but himself. When he found *Fight Club* at the op-shop I stayed with my folks for the week, just in case.

I wondered how far he'd go, I mean what would he do if he read *American Psycho* or *Silence of the Lambs*? What would he do if he read *The Shining* ? He says he's selective about what he reads. I taunt him and say that really he's gutless about this whole thing but I'm not sure why I'm going along with his fantasies at all.

One thing that bugs me is that when we're sitting on a tram together I attract all the crazy people and Byron is left relaxed and peaceful. I would have thought that other strange people would be drawn to him but maybe they sense Byron's self-containment. Perhaps they know that he will launch into his own stories and block out their worlds. Me, I must look like a vessel that needs to be filled.

A woman got on the tram last night when Byron and I were coming back from town. Of course she sat next to me. She had cracked glasses and bad teeth and she looked at me intently. She asked me if I thought communication between people was going *forward* or *backward*. I thought maybe she had a point, even if she was clearly crazy. There did seem to be days when communication with other people went forward or backward or straight down the toilet. She seemed to place a lot of importance on my answer so I decided to play it safe and say that communication today had seemed neither forward nor backward, just normal. Actually I think she just wanted a chat. She wanted some forward conversation.

Some dude was walking down the aisle of the tram, asking for money. *Leave me alone*, I was thinking. *Do I look like I've won lotto?* He smiled in my face like he was my best mate.

'Come on,' he said, 'just five bucks. Come on mate, only five bucks for my dinner.'

Why wasn't he leaving me alone? Why wasn't he hassling the forward conversation woman? I looked at Byron, sitting there with a smile on his face. He was humming to himself while reading *Trainspotting. Come on, Byron, try some method reading on this one, you slack-arse, up-your-own-bum-hole, method-reading weirdo.*

I envied his elephant-hide world. When I thought about it I wanted to be in *The Great Gatsby* and cruise away right now in a sleek limo, hermetically sealed from the piss smells and the depressed winter faces. I wanted to drink brandy and soda from a crystal decanter in the car's minibar with the sun shining through, and be able to keep to myself.

'Sorry mate, not that flush myself.' The guy turned from smiley to narky and moved on. For once I didn't take it personally; I was still in the limo.

At the next stop the conversation woman was getting up. I told her that I'd changed my mind, that perhaps communication had taken a turn for the worse and wasn't going forward at all. It was stuck and kind of strangled. She nodded seriously and said 'I'm so glad you said that'.

Byron and I were off at the next stop. I told him how I was going to read Bukowski and how we'd have to get smashed and scream at each other. He was pleased that I finally understood. Things were starting to make sense and it had been a long time since I'd thought that they did.

The Little-Big Soldiers
MIRA CUTURILO

There are many of them in town these days, but we don't see them very often. They work very hard and very long and after work, they come with their big cars and buy their food at Choitrams, the Lebanese supermarket. At night times, they go to Sweeties and Sweeties, the bar, to drink much beer. So you could imagine how Emmanuel and me were very excited to see them again. One was older, older than my grandmother and the other, she was beautiful; she was young and tall with chocolate skin. You don't get chocolate skin like that unless your mother is together with a white man or one of those soldiers. Emmanuel's mother did that, but she dead now. She got the big sickness. People say those soldier are no good, they poison to a woman, still they give Emmanuel some money, and they fix Emmanuel's house. Mariama, she Emmanuel's sister, she works for white family, she clean their house and cook their food. Mariama says white men like sweet talk, white men like sweet things, but they mean. They only nice when they want something.

It was the second time the women come down to the gardens. First time they came looking for Mama Gatare, but she was not there. She was in the mountains with the girls that need to be cleansed. Mama Gatare a doctor as well, she clean all the women in the village. Mama Gatare is very wise, she know everything. The white people come in their big cars and have meeting with village and say she must stop what she doing because it no good for a woman, they say not fair to a woman, but nobody listen to them, they only listen to Mama Gatare. White man brings cake and soda drinks, they kind to us, but nobody listen. Mama Gatare, she prepare the whole garden as well. She is like a man, telling all the other women how to grow – except she no yell like a man. Mama Gatare she talk sweet, sweet like mango juice, all the children love her. This season we had best harvest since the war. We had big feast one night, lots of sweet plantain and cassava and three chickens and the small, sweet tomatoes, like little red balls. I remember that night for all my life.

Next time the chocolate girl come, she come with the same woman, the woman's name is Sue. Mama Sue's hair like maize, so beautiful, but the chocolate girl, she more beautiful. They came to give seeds to Mama Gatare. The chocolate girl, she walk around the garden looking at the cassava growing and then she sit down watching the little children wash themselves in the water that come down from the mountain. She seem sad. She so beautiful and seem so sad that I want to make her happy. She look at me and smile and so I say,

'I'm an albino boy.'

'Yes you certainly are.'

'I almost like you, except you chocolate.'

She smile at me. I open my shirt and point at my chest. I point to her and then to my chest. I move my hips the way they taught me in the Rebels, around and around – the way they taught me to make a woman feel like she with a real man. The chocolate girl, she just sit there and look at me. She say nothing. I raise my eyebrows and make sound of a soft whistle; they say that's how you call the woman in. They say women are like dog, you whistle, they come.

'How old are you?' she ask me.

'I'm twelve.'

She surprised. She probably thinks I'm older. I am a little-big boy. I tell her I am a little-big boy, but she say nothing. I'm like the men down on Banja Street. I know them men, they used to be my leaders. They took me when I was eight years old and teach me how to be a man. They gave me everything I want. They gave me food, gun, they give me women. Sometimes the women not like it, sometimes they scream, sometimes blood comes from the little ones, but they told me, 'just keep them quiet and they really like it.' So I try to keep them quiet. I tell them they really like it, but still they scream. Sometimes they scream so hard, I had to hit them. My gun was good for that, I just take my gun and hit them across the head until they stop screaming.

'Do you live around here?' the chocolate girl ask me.

'Yes.'

'Do you live with your mother and father?'

'No. They die in the war. I live with my friend Emmanuel and his sister Mariama. He that one there. I live with him and his sister.' I tell her and show her who Emmanuel is.

'Do you go to school?' she ask me.

I tell her I sometimes go to school, but sometimes I no go to school. Sometimes my brain don't work properly and I wish I get the gun back, I wish I get the gun, because my brain screams like one of those bleeding girls and it won't stop all day long. Mariama, she says my head hurts because of the war. She says the Rebels shouldn't have given me those things to take; that white medicine. She says medicine bad news. But the medicine it make me brave, make me a strong fighter. The more I take, the better fighter I am. She said I'm *done-done*, my brain *done-done* from that medicine. She says only take medicine from hospital, not Rebels. Mariama don't like Rebels, she says they are bad. We fight sometimes about the Rebels. She don't know, she just a women, she not like Mama Gatare.

The chocolate girl she seems more sad. She ask me if I have seen a doctor for my headache. I say no – I have no money for that. She tells me she is a nurse at the hospital and I should come to see her. I say they will ask me for money. She says it cost nothing to come to the hospital. It no matter, they will come to my house after she goes and they will want money. She says that is not fair. Nothing in Salone is fair, I tell her. Only good time I had was in the war, when I was a fighter, then I had everything. Now I have nothing, just headaches and no gun and sometimes my bad, bad dreams where the juju comes and I can't sleep all night, I am so scared I think I am going to die.

'You my friend,' I say to her.

She smile at me and say, 'Yes, I am your friend.'

'You my special woman.'

She laugh at me. She so beautiful when she laugh, I no want her to stop. She laugh like the angel of heaven. She call over the garden to Mamma Sue and she yell something to her. They both laugh and laugh. Then I laugh, Emmanuel laugh and all the women in the garden laugh. The children slowly laugh, the dogs laugh, but the birds don't laugh, they fly away.

'You are very beautiful,' I say.

She say thank you. She ask me if I have had a special friend before. I say I had Josephine. But that was different. Josephine had chocolate skin, but her Pa was African, because I saw him when we came in the hut. We found Josephine after we kill her family. She was hiding under the bed, crying like a hungry dog.

We made Josephine our special woman that night, one, two, three, four, I was number five. But she no scream, she keep very quiet. One day Josephine try to run away, but we found her. Uncle Simbo he gave her some medicine and she became a fighter just like us. Josephine kill more men than three of us boy-soldiers together. She kill them like the juju had entered her blood and then she laughed, only time Josephine ever laugh was when she kill men. Uncle Simbo said Josephine was a true soldier. I afraid when Josephine laugh, she not laugh like an angel, she laugh like a crazy woman.

'Where is Josephine today?' ask the chocolate girl.

I don't know. The night of the bad trouble, Josephine disappeared, only Emmanuel and I survive. We went into the jungle to hunt for monkey and when we return, all our brothers were dead. Their bodies were lined-up straight, one, two, three, and four. Bad Rebels, they shot them in their manhood, and then afterwards they shot them through the mouth. We think they came to steal the white medicine. Emmanuel and me think Josephine kidnapped by the bad Rebels – no Josephine, no medicine, no brothers. After that, Emmanuel and me were very sick, we had no medicine and our body shake so much we think we're going to die.

The chocolate girl she listen to me and then she get up and tell Mama Sue she want to go home, she no feel good. Her face no longer chocolate, she look very white, very sick. Before they left the garden, Mama Sue she gives Emmanuel and me some seeds. She says they are seed for big tomatoes; she says we should grow them and give them much water.

When I went to the hospital the next day, my chocolate girl was not there. But Mama Sue she help me, I don't pay nobody and she give me clothes and good medicine and even books, big books with names like *Repatriation* on them. When I am bigger, I will read them all.

The chocolate girl she don't come back to the garden. I am very sad because I love her very much and know she is my special woman. When the rains finished and the sun stay all day, the tomatoes they grow so big, almost big as an avocado and I am so happy, I want to show the chocolate girl. They so big and Emmanuel and me have much money.

One day I walk to sell my tomatoes at the market and I see a woman walking towards me with chocolate skin and she African and look like somebody I know. She has a big white turban on her head. It is very dusty so she cover her face with a scarf, but when she walk past, she look straight at me and I see her eyes – they look like the juju was inside of them. That night, the juju come to me in bad dreams, the juju is laughing like a crazy woman and then I remember who the woman look like.

Upside Down in Parallel
MELANIE JOOSTEN

Ella Fitzgerald sings love on and off. We lie on our backs, staring at the fairy lights that are standing in for all the stars we can't see above the city. Alex is teasing me again, asking the age-old question levelled at us antipodeans – what is it like to be upside down?

'The light fittings are the most dangerous. They stand there, straight up in the middle of rooms, like Van Gogh sunflowers all bright and cheery. And then they burn like hell when your knees knock them!'

He takes my answer into consideration, nodding seriously, which is quite difficult to do when lying on your back.

'But what about the doorways? Surely they're a little difficult to climb over?'

'They're not so bad. That's why they made us Aussies tall, not like you short-arse Scots.'

*

Sometimes we lie on Alex's bed and stare out the window waiting for the moon to come up. We fall asleep before it's fully dark, seven years old again when daylight savings has just kicked in, all freshly bathed in our picture pyjamas. When we wake to the morning light, the moon has become a faded memory so we make up stories instead. We discuss the logistics of Moonface actually building the slippery dip in the Faraway Tree, choose colours for our cushions should we ever be lucky enough to get a ride.

Alone later, I wonder if the moon ever feels like an impostor, always on the outside looking in, more reliable but never as anticipated as the sun. The odd one out at the party, reflecting everyone else's sparkling wit. And never anyone to compare himself to. I can see him now, waking with a mouth like an ashtray, stumbling from room to room of sleeping bodies after late night parties and having nowhere to go.

*

'There it is.' He points. 'The apple orchard.'

We wheel our bikes along the verge and lay them in the long grass. Apple blossoms are the poor sisters of cherry blossoms, I decide, looking around. Even though they're white, they have that hint of greenness showing where they'll end up; not quite as beautiful or daring as the pink cherry blossoms that bring to mind calligraphy and willowy silhouettes. Somewhere between Eve and Granny Smith, apples lost their temptation, their desire, became instead a dishwashing scent, a school-lunch staple.

'If you were an apple, you'd be a Golden Delicious,' I declare, looking sideways at him as we settle cross-legged beneath the low boughs. 'You're subtle and delicate, always surprising, a matte finish and no tan.'

'Fuck off!' He counters, laughing. 'Golden Delicious are nearly always disappointing and have no kick… I'm a little concerned what you think of me.' He pauses, calculating.

'In which case, you'd be a Granny Smith, waxed and refrigerated, so cold that anyone taking a bite can feel the ache in their teeth as they make contact with your sweet white flesh.' He leers at me, like a B-Grade pimp but I'm not laughing anymore, I can feel the red creeping up my neck. He's only joking, he's only joking.

'Hey, come on, I'm just messing with you.'

He looks concerned and I blink rapidly, feeling stupid. Why can't I have any control over my emotions? It's always been that way with me, I cry too easily. When I'm really happy, or really angry I find myself not being able to talk properly and having to clench my jaw to stop from shaking.

'I know, I know.' I rummage in my bag for a distraction, pulling out my camera.

'Smile.'

But he never does, pulling smouldering model-like poses instead, always turning away as I close the shutter. He winks at me, an apology, and we roll over, lying in the grass, reading our books as the day wears on.

'Apple blossoms are a symbol of unconsummated love.' The sun is warming up now, and we've tossed the books aside. He stares at me with those fucking dark eyes, and I can't tell what he's getting at.

'Plucked before the fruit has time to ripen, perhaps?' He nods in agreement.

I reach up to pick a blossom from the tree.

'Try it. All promise, no flavour. Just like herbal teas. No wonder it's never consummated.'

We know we're talking in riddles now and as he makes a face, chewing on the blossom, I think about kissing him. But the afternoon sun is making me all warm and lazy so instead I swivel around, placing my head in his lap.

'Draw me a map.'

*

Alex has a thing for maps. Atlases, street directories; the walls of his room are covered in them. On Saturday mornings we trawl through the second-hand shops around Edinburgh looking for anything new to add to the collection. His favourites are children's atlases. When he finds one he's like a kid himself, hopping from side to side as though he's about to wet his pants. He loves the ones that devote a page to each country and fill the borders with quaint little facts about literacy rates and population, all very concise and factual, as though no one was born or will die after publication. The Third World countries have photos of smiling kids dressed in bright traditional dress, no slums or malnutrition. And Japan is always depicted alongside a pale-faced geisha and business men tucked liked sardines into a high-speed train.

My favourite map is one we found in an old *New Internationalist* magazine. It shows the countries as their actual size, rather than the politically motivated ones on the maps we're used to where Europe is as big as South-East Asia, whilst North America looks set to crush Alaska. And always Australia, stuck on at the bottom looking like it will float away.

*

Alex is running late. It's Open Mic at the pub tonight, making me think of my guitar-playing ex-fella. It's six o'clock in the morning back home. He'd be dead to the world, my boy and I remember in those first few months we'd wake ourselves up in our excitement, couldn't get enough of one another. All we wanted was to hear our voices disembodied by the dark, our hands running up and down our bodies, our love was new and exciting then, our love was.

Gone. Love just disappears like that.

*

We meet at a party of a friend of a friend. Whose friend? Who knows. The stars are out and the smell of honeysuckle hung in the air. I sit out the front smoking a cigarette, a six-pack by my feet and a long night ahead.

'Can I join you?'

I nod without looking up and he sits. Silence.

'So who do you know here?'

'Caitlin. She works with my housemate.' I look sideways at him, trying to size him up.

'You?'

'I came with Pete, we went to school together.'

'So he's a friend?'

'Sort of.'

'School's a long time ago.'

The stars watch us, wide-eyed children of the world.

That night we fall asleep, curled up on the beanbags in the lounge room of someone neither of us had ever met. Is this going to be love? My mouth's all furry and I've got a cramp in my calf. I don't think I want it to start like this. I don't think I want it.

So we keep it to long afternoon beers, morning coffees. Lying in bed, staring at the ceiling, not touching and talking ourselves to sleep. And it's always about sleep, isn't it? I'm beginning to think that when we say 'sleep together' this is what we mean.

*

'I think I'd like a dog.' Alex announces this with a decisive nod, looking up from the newspaper, squinting because the steaming tea has misted his glasses.

'What sort?' I ask, not because I really want to know, but because I like to hear his morning voice, all crumpled, and the way his thoughts jump over one another, jostling for attention.

'I don't know. A mongrel probably.' He puts down his cup of tea, focusing on the proposition at hand. 'I think pedigrees have too many problems. And I'm not pedigree, I might get jealous. No good having someone around the house with pretensions, is there?'

'What about a black one? A black one with brown eyebrows and feet. And it would have to be a snorer, so it would keep you company even when it's asleep.'

'Paws, not feet. Dogs don't have feet.' He looks at me pointedly. 'I hope you are giving this your proper attention.'

'Where would it live?' I ask, acting interested, as though we might perhaps go out and buy the dog today.

'Here. It could sleep on my bed and in the morning I'd take it for a run. Then we would go by the butchers and get strings of sausages and T-bone steaks for special occasions.'

'But you don't run, Alex. The poor dog would get all fat and sad.'

There's a pause and the hum of Edinburgh floats through the window on a cloud of bus exhaust. I take a gulp of tea and stand to pour some more.

'But you do.' He looks at me. 'And I don't see you going anywhere.'

*

From a phone box on Leith Walk I call my ex-boy, wondering if there is anything I missed. We speak about the little things in life, his new haircut, my old shoes. As we talk, on and on, feeding in the coins like worms into a baby bird, a drunk guy wanders up the street, haphazardly swerving around the people on the pavement. All hairy and dishevelled he swerves on, eyes no older than mine, eyes that see none of my world. Calmly and with a strange amount of concentration for one so unfocused on the world around him, he opens his fly and proceeds to piss on the Perspex wall of my phone booth as I stand back, startled.

'Are you still there? Are you? Hello?'

I watch as the yellow waterfall continues, my own little urban water feature, splashing all over his feet and I want him to stop – does he even know I'm here? But I don't want to anger him, this unpredictable boy. And then he stops, nods politely and moves on.

We talk as I keep feeding in the coins, some of them falling straight through to the return chute, neither of us wanting the conversation to finish even when we have nothing more to say, this false intimacy across the oceans.

A woman is banging on the door now, pointing angrily at her watch. She wants me to get off the phone, wants to call Mexico and I explain that I will be awhile. I don't speak Spanish and she doesn't speak English and I try to tell her I am calling Australia. She nods and then keeps on banging. I make wildly exaggerated hand signals at her, indicating the banks of phones up and down the street. But she shakes her head and stands there staring as I keep talking to my boy. I don't tell her about the yellow pool that is bathing her feet. And when she finally crosses the road to use another phone, our conversation dwindles anyway.

He asks me if I've found anyone new. He laughs but I don't. He once told me that it was my body he was in love with, not my mind, though he quite liked that too. I think what he liked is that my body would respond to him, it didn't argue and it didn't try to deconstruct his useless utterings of love in words he didn't understand himself.

When I hang up I feel exhausted. When you're not being pulled in any direction, it's hard to decide where to go.

*

The smell of freshly laundered sheets is euphoric. I feel in control when my sheets are clean. At least I've been able to look after that part of myself, I think. And it's different, the smell of sheets warm from a tumble dryer, all that lint miraculously escaping forming its own being. Different to the smell of sheets that have dried in the sun and a warm northerly wind. Sometimes in summer, even sheets hanging in a tiny, sheltered inner-city Melbourne courtyard can dry within ten minutes. Yet all it takes is one night of sleep for the fresh coolness to disappear silently out the window and be replaced by the warm, slightly sour smell of sex, or just the gentle tedium of sleep. On a still Melbourne day the sheets lie, no they hang, so inert and flat, not giving away anything of their tumultuous lifestyle once darkness falls.

In Scotland though, the sheets flap about with a dominating authority. It reminds me of my brother flicking me with a tea towel in the kitchen, all twisted up tight and slightly damp to give it enough weight to inflict pain as we sulkily dry the dishes.

*

So strange that it should be called a curse when it's so often a blessing. Or a period when it's not still and small like punctuation, though sometimes it does seem as endless as a Friday afternoon maths class. I feel like a puffer fish today, all bloated and irritable. Once a month and it all comes crashing down.

I swim through the day, my cramps coming on in waves, on and on, the tide refusing to go out. I used to think the tide was a tiger and would run terrified up the beach as the frothy waves nipped at my feet, screaming, 'The tiger's coming in, the tiger's coming in,' just as I heard Dad say when he played with me and my sisters. And I couldn't understand why they would all be laughing as I lay terrified and gasping for breath on my scratchy beach towel. Now I wonder why no one ever told me.

It feels like a tiger now, gnawing at my belly, my womb rattling around with nowhere to go. When I lie flat I isolate the pain too much, curled up in the foetal position it softens and ebbs out over my entire body. For two days, sometimes three it takes over, rolling me bruised down grassy hills before picking me up and letting me spiral away again.

Alex comes in with a cup of tea and I feel so small right here. He rubs my back, his hands running up and down, if I were a cat I think I might just purr.

*

We talk nonsense all through the night as the rain drips from the ceiling into the aluminium saucepans and plastic bowls on the floor. I ask why he has material hanging from the light.

'It used to be a red tulle petticoat, but now it's a vortex,' he says, eyes closed. 'It sucks up all the bad thoughts.'

I lie awake for hours after he has dropped off to sleep. Dropped off what? I wonder, or did he jump? Listening to his even breaths, deep and so calm, I wonder how he could sleep at a time like this. I think I'm falling for him but I'm not sure that he'll catch me. I want to smother him with my whole body to be all over and under him all at once but instead I lay, arms by my side, headlights folding the night outside and through the bedroom wall I can hear our other housemate watching television.

*

And finally, drunk at a party of a friend of a friend, I throw myself at him and he turns me down.

'I don't want to do this,' he says, not looking at me.

Later, lying in my own bed, next to someone whose name I can't remember, I wonder if he actually said, 'I don't want to do it like this.'

My blurry-eyed, hungover brain, mulls this over, again and again and begins to panic. Maybe he wanted me after all, maybe just not within a cloud of beer. And when Alex bounds into my room with a morning cup of tea, I realise the look on his face as he takes in this boy's body, might just be disappointment. And things aren't the same after that.

Gone. Love just disappears like that. I think I'll buy a dog.

Lights
Claire Thomas

Jamie leant against the wall of the caravan, watching. She was wearing her white sneakers, the ones with the lights on the back that flashed with every step, like a rhythmic blister on her heel. The problem was that she'd almost stamped the light away, lifting and pressing her feet down on the ground to test it out, twisting her head back to see the plastic globe embedded in each shoe. Her dad had offered to cut them open, find a battery, but Jamie screamed her refusal to that suggestion. Her mum had just said it was her own fault for wanting the silliest bloody shoes in the whole store.

'They were *not* the silliest,' Jamie replied. 'Those blue thongs you got were way dumber.'

They'd bought them in the summer holidays at the end of Grade One and sometimes, even months later, the lights still came on when she made them. Sometimes, the shoes still worked. She was wearing them as she watched the hordes arriving, like they did every year.

She hated the Easter break. The way she'd have to stand in a queue just to have a shower when usually she could walk straight in. How she couldn't go to school for a whole week. All the people everywhere, arriving at the place like it was fun, like it was some kind of a resort. She hated those huge high cars that'd roll into the dusty drive, radio shouting over the birds as they parked. And then the unpacking. The men, wearing their shorts and caps like kids, opening the boots of their cars and pulling out so many shiny things, so many balls and pans and folded BBQs, so much *stuff*. She liked to watch them – the carloads of people pouring into the grounds all day Friday – just watch the way they'd pace around and around the boundaries of their site, assessing the area before the big set-up began. Some of their tents were like small houses, she thought, with plastic flaps for walls. She'd watch couples fighting over how to pump up a mattress or where the last tent peg went or which pot they'd hide the dunny key in. She'd watch pretty girls in hooded tracksuits snuggling into the bright spotted doonas they'd brought from home, while their boyfriends arranged brown stubbies and extra large cans into enormous, icy eskies. She'd watch as people would carefully, methodically find the perfect hook to hang their rubbish bag from, swapping it with an orange plastic torch a couple of times – bag, torch, bag, torch – until they finally decided on the ideal positioning for both items.

And every year, for something to do, Jamie would pick a person to watch the most. She saw the girl straight-away, picked her out without a second thought. Big, trendy jeans and long dark hair like chocolate sauce. Jamie liked the way she pitched her tent right in the corner of the site, shoved up against the row of ti-tree that had seen better times, as though she wasn't quite sure whether she wanted to be there at all.

Inside the toilet block, a group of teenage girls was getting ready for a night on the town. There were four of them, already dressed in their matching outfits, nudging around the grimy mirror, putting on make-up. Four neat bodies sealed inside four pairs of skin-tight white trousers and four tiny tubes of sky blue lycra stretched around their torsos. One of the girls was a little bit taller than the other three, so the strip of brown tummy between her top and her pants was bigger. She'd made a feature of this by clipping a tiny pink flashlight to her belly button. They were wearing high-heeled strappy black shoes, all a bit different, largely concealed by the flare of white material at their ankles. Their hair was uniformly dyed peroxide blonde and pulled straight back into thin, high ponytails. And on top of all that, they wore silver bunny ears: a special Easter touch.

Jamie stood inside the door and watched them.

'What are ya staring at?' The tall bunny suddenly looked at her, all aggro.

'Your ears are cool,' Jamie told her. 'And that light thing in your belly button reminds me of my shoes.' And then she turned her back on the bunnies, did a couple of quick stamp-stamps with her shoes, checking over her right shoulder that the globes were lighting up and relieved to see that they were. She turned back to face the bunnies, all standing in a row and smiling.

'Do you want some glitter?' said one.

'Shit yeah,' said Jamie. And she jogged over to the mirror, hoisted herself onto the one bit of dry bench and shut her eyes. With her legs dangling towards the sticky cold tiles, she beckoned the bunnies towards her face. 'Eyes and cheeks only,' she ordered, as a glitter-coated fingertip smeared her skin.

Later, when the girls left the camping grounds to go to the pub, Jamie and her new sparkly face went back to the van. Her dad was sitting on the outside step, drinking a beer. Jamie passed by him, squeezing herself between his fleshy knee and the doorframe.

Her mum was inside, stirring white strands of spaghetti around a boiling pot of water. 'What's all that?' she asked, flapping her hand in front of her face.

'Glitter, mum,' explained Jamie. 'From some girls in the dunnies with bunny ears.'

'Oh yeah, I saw 'em,' said her mum. 'Why'd you wanna look like those little sluts?'

Jamie shrugged, pulled the hem of her T-shirt up and began to rub at her cheeks with the cotton.

Later that night Jamie was in bed, head under the blanket, with a big torch wobbling some dim light over the pages of her book. She was reading the copy of *Little Women* her gran had given her for Christmas.

'Don't know much about it,' her grandma had explained, 'but the lass in the bookshop thought you'd like it. I told her you were pretty clever.'

'Go easy, mum,' Jamie's dad said. 'She's already too big for her boots.'

Jamie wasn't thinking about that, though, as she struggled to hold the pages open and breathe. She was thinking about getting her torch on the perfect angle and also how funny it was when a character said *truly superb* and how weird it'd be to have three bonnet-wearing sisters, pressing pansies for a hobby.

And then she heard it. The unmistakable sound of a stream of piss hitting the wall of the van.

She threw back her blanket, dropped her torch and stormed over to the door. She opened it and walked outside, stood there in bare feet and her pink elephant nightie, glaring at the culprit.

'This is *my* van,' she said to him. 'Don't piss on it.'

'Ah, fuck. Sorry, sorry,' he looked down at her fierce little face. 'Sorry.'

She waited there with her hands on her hips like some old rural wife defending her verandah, as the guy shoved his dick back into his pants.

'Get lost,' she shouted, as he stumbled back towards his site.

She watched him walking back into a circle of people crowding towards their fire, the one they'd practically organised a working bee to get going six hours earlier. And then she watched as he tried to sit down on the only vacant chair. He missed the seat, whacked it, and grabbed one of the arms as it folded into itself. The beer that'd been wedged into the chair's super-handy stubby pocket bounced across the grass, coming to a stop against a boy's beige sneaker.

'Lost your beer, buddy.'

The pissing guy fumbled with the chair. 'Hey, hey, guess what?'

Most of the others turned to him and waited. Jamie saw the girl she'd chosen to watch earlier; she was looking out across the grounds, towards her.

'I just got told off by a kid,' he continued. 'For pissing on her van. Silly little bitch.'

They laughed at that. They thought it was so hilarious. Typical Thommo to get told off by a little girl. Ha. Ha. Ha.

Jamie squinted into the dark and listened. The noise of them rushed across the camping grounds and hit her in the face like spit.

She turned and went back inside. Her mum and dad were still snoring as she picked up her torch once more.

Next morning, Jamie was outside under her favourite tree, beside her mum as she had a smoke. They weren't talking, just thinking about stuff, side by side. Jamie was writing her initials into the dust with her big toe; her mum was staring straight ahead as though she was still a bit asleep.

Just then, the bunnies appeared, walking in a row from the front gate of the camping grounds, towards the toilet block. They had the same outfits on as the night before, except one of them was also wearing a red windcheater that was much too big for her. A couple of them were clutching their shoes by the straps, the black high heels banging against their thighs as they wandered along. Only one of the bunnies still had her ponytail; the rest had shoved their ears on top of loose, matted hair. Their eye make-up was smudged into their cheeks, the glitter was almost entirely rubbed off and the belly-flashlight was gone. They all seemed to be really cold.

'Gee, they look fan-fucking-tastic, don't they?' Jamie's mum took one last suck on her fag and threw it into the dust as another couple of campers walked by. A hippy-looking guy with large, purple 'happy' pants and a nipple ring glared at the ground.

'They're places for those to go, you know,' he said.

'What?'

'Your butt. The bin.'

Her mum sneered at the hippy. 'Jesus Christ,' she said, as she stormed back to their van.

This isn't going to be a good day, thought Jamie. She followed her mum into the van, got herself a bowl of cocoa pops and took it back outside where she sat down on the edge of the fence with the cereal balanced on her lap. Jamie was staring into the bowl when she heard her.

'Hi.'

Jamie looked up. The girl she'd been watching the most was standing right there. She looked different up close, with her hair mostly hidden by a beanie and just dribbles of chocolate sauce falling out. She had lots of freckles across her nose and a big smile.

'Hi,' said Jamie.

'Sorry about my friend.'

'The one who told my mum off about her ciggy?'

'No,' the girl laughed. 'The one who weed on your van last night.'

'Oh, that's okay. I let him know I wasn't happy.'

'Yeah, so I heard,' the girl said. 'I'm Tiffany. Tiff.'

'I'm Jamie.'

'Jamie.'

'Yeah, named after Lisa Curry's daughter. With the iron man.'

'Wasn't their kid a boy?'

Jamie frowned at Tiffany and decided not to be offended. 'Probably,' she said. 'My parents are pretty dumb.'

'Do they hurt you?' As soon as she said it, Tiff wanted to take it back. She sounded like a social worker or something.

'Nah,' Jamie said. 'Just each other mostly. They mostly just hurt each other.'

'Oh,' said Tiff.

'You hate it here, don't you?'

'Yeah. You?' Tiff asked.

'Yeah. But I live here, so there's no point hating it.'

'Sorry.'

'That's okay,' smiled Jamie. 'So, why are you here?'

'My friends. They like it. They've been coming here for years. It's my first time.'

'And last?'

'And last,' laughed Tiff. 'They reckon they're camping.'

'Whaddaya mean?'

'They think they're being rugged, getting in touch with the *great outdoors*. And they're sleeping in fancy tents with the arse end of a supermarket on one side of them and a dirty big shower block on the other.'

'You're funny, Tiff.'

'You're pretty funny yourself.'

'I can take you to a pretty bit near the water, if you like,' Jamie said. 'Dad showed it to me when we first moved in. It's nothing like round here. There's no one there.' And she threw her cereal bowl onto the ground, jumped up and grabbed Tiffany's hand.

When they reached the pretty bit near the water, the first thing Tiffany saw was a used condom on the edge of the dirt path. There might've been a couple of them. A pile.

'Hey, let's not go down there,' she said, reaching her arm out towards Jamie, trying to veer the little girl away.

'Why not?'

'I want to go down there instead,' Tiff tried, glancing again at the shrivelled pieces of latex, both dusty and sticky on the ground. She quickly averted her eyes, but it was too late; Jamie had seen what she was looking at.

'Cos of the dingers?' laughed Jamie. 'Were you trying to keep me away from the dingers?'

'Yes,' admitted Tiff, all embarrassed.

Jamie giggled. 'You know, it's very important to use protection, whatever the circumstances,' she said in an earnest, grown-up voice.

Tiff laughed and looked at the tiny kid beside her. 'Where'd you learn that?'

'School, of course.'

The two walked on, stepping over the condoms.

'Toffy Tiff?'

'Yeah?'

'Do you always practice safe sex?' Jamie asked.

Shit, thought Tiff. 'None of your business,' she said.

They spent the rest of the afternoon together, with Jamie continuing her tour of the best areas around. When they reached the beach, she told Tiffany about how she really wanted to be a writer when she grew up.

'I write stories,' she explained. 'And I won a competition against everyone at school even though I'm only in Grade Two. There was a picture of me in the local paper and everything. I sent it to my gran.'

'That's great,' said Tiff. 'You must be really good.'

'Yeah, I am,' Jamie shouted, running down the sand. 'Reeeeeally good!'

That night, people were lying on their thin mattresses in the dark, listening to a woman screaming. She began by yelling at her friend – teary hate-filled accusations of betrayal – before extending her abuse to include everyone staying at the camping grounds. 'This place is just full of fuckers, you're all dumb fuckers and I'm going to kill ya all. I promise, I will, I really will.' The words warbled through the darkness. 'People are shit. People are really *really* shit.'

Toffy Tiffany woke up in her small tent, feeling tense. What if she means it? she thought. What if she just starts killing us? I bet Jamie's terrified too. Tiff sat up in the darkness, refastened her hair and hugged her knees.

After almost an hour of ranting, the woman's voice became so muffled that it was obvious she'd finally collapsed into sleep. And soon after, the rest of the campers were able to as well.

The next morning, Tiffany crept out of her tent very early, unlocked her friend's car and retrieved a bag of Easter eggs. She deposited two of them, wrapped in nicely contrasting coloured foil, at the entrance to each tent on her site. She tiptoed around the damp grass in her baggy trackies, rubbing the sleep from her eyes. Then, once she'd delivered all her friends' eggs, she slid on a pair of thongs and made her way towards Jamie's van. There were four eggs left in her bag and she put them in a row on the bottom step: blue egg next to green egg, next to yellow one, next to red.

'Boo,' shouted Jamie, appearing at the door in her elephant nightie.

'You saw me,' Tiff sighed. 'I wanted you to find these later.'

'It's lucky I saw you, otherwise Dad would've stood on them when he got up,' Jamie said, leaning down to pick up the eggs. 'Thanks.'

'I was worried about you last night,' said Tiff. 'That woman shouldn't have been saying stuff like that when there are so many kids around.'

Jamie started giggling. 'Yeah, she was pretty gross, pretty pissed. But I was worried about you.'

'Me? Why?'

'Because I knew you'd be scared. I was thinking that she shouldn't be saying that stuff when there are so many Easter people here. They'll freak.'

'Yeah. One of my friends called the cops.'

'Did they come?'

'No.'

'See? There's much worse stuff going on.'

'Yeah,' Tiff nodded to the ground. 'Sorry.'

'It's not your fault,' Jamie said. 'Hey toffy Tiff, we can be pen pals!' And she bounded back inside the van. Tiffany didn't go in. She waited on the grass, instead, next to the step. Jamie didn't take very long to find a piece of paper, presenting it to Tiff on top of *Little Women*.

'Good book,' said Tiffany.

'Yeah. Something to lean on.'

Tiff sat down on the step with the book on her lap. She wrote her address in her best impression of neat primary school teacher's handwriting, even including a small flower on the bottom, underneath the postcode.

'You can just send me your letters here,' Jamie said as she took the paper.

'Will they get to you?'

'Definitely,' she grinned. 'They know me in the office. No worries.'

'Maybe I'll see you again next Easter,' Tiff suggested.

'Well, maybe we won't be here anymore,' Jamie said. 'You never know your luck. Dad's been talking to some people about working at their guesthouse. I could be living there in a couple of months.'

'That's great.'

'But don't worry, Tiff, I won't forget you. We can still be pen pals, wherever I go.'

Tiffany stood up and looked down at Jamie's face as her small arms suddenly flung around the legs of her jeans in a hug.

And that was it; the promises were made.

A couple of hours later, Jamie watched Tiffany-with-the-chocolate-sauce-hair drive away with a carload of friends.

Tiff was in the front seat, leaning out as she waved and shouted goodbye to the little girl, who stood beside her parents' van in a pair of cute white sneakers. The pissing guy was in the back seat with a couple of other people who joined in with Tiff until the whole group of them were farewelling the park.

Jamie waited until the four-wheel drive had whooshed through the gates, and then she swung around, stamping her feet on the ground and checking for the light in her heels.

A Raga Called Milk and Honey
PETE NICHOLSON

I had printed out a sign, but it was two inches too short to fit across the entrance to the living room. It said, 'WELCOME HOME JUSTIN'.

Dad was off work early, picked Mum up on the way, had an argument with her about how Justin was getting home, saying that Justin had to learn responsibility, to do things himself, that it was outlined in the institute's literature on the subject. Mum became hysterical as the car pulled into the drive, lost in her imagining of the distance between the facility and our house. The argument continued into the house where mum started work on what used to be Justin's favourite casserole – a steaming, dense mass of cheese, mince, macaroni and tomato – with Dad behind her, scooping up alcohol to hide in the cellar, and moaning to her about how Justin's palate would have changed, become 'institutional', as he called it, but by the time he'd got to 'institutional' he'd stopped talking to anyone in particular and was continuing his monologue to the bottles under the house. When he ascended, the casserole had been abandoned.

The bus stopped two streets from our house and Justin was drunk by the time he arrived. Mum had disappeared into the cellar to get the alcohol again, to put it back out in its usual ascending order on the shelf above the table. If Justin was strong enough to make it home by himself, she said, he could withstand the sight of a few bottles of wine. Dad followed her, mumbling into his chest.

They'd been down there for a while when I walked out to the front patio, the door thrown shut behind me by the wind in a way that sounded dramatic, final. I reached up and hung the sign from the veranda. It fitted alright, but I couldn't get rid of the potted plants in front of it that obscured the words. It read 'W— ome—ome'. I sat down on the landing, sign scrunched in my hands, when I saw him appear as if by conveyer belt on all fours in the drive, acid dripping from his mouth, a mustard-coloured vomit stain spreading across his shirt.

I had this one song in my head for the whole week since we found out Justin was considered stable and would be released. It was probably a folk song of some sort – I could almost make out the words 'honey' and 'autumn' – but it played at half speed, so the voice was slow and weary, with an almost inhuman depth.

It was the second song on a tape I found at a bus stop a day or two after Justin had the attack and was committed the first time. The tape was covered in thick black texta and labelled at random with the generic stickers from blank cassettes – RAP, REGGAE, MASTER. The day I found it my stomach was liquid, and I left school early. The bus didn't come and I ran cursing through courts and gardens, screaming at dogs. I didn't make it home in time, and, embarrassed – who, at my age, shits themselves? – I left the pants there in the spare block at the foot of our court, the tape still inside them.

The letter arrived, another photo of Justin, dates, times, buses. I remembered the tape in the block still empty, walked down at dusk, walkman in hand. Grass had grown in yellowed patches between the legs of the pants, which were hypercolour™, and now, somehow, three colours at once. I persisted through the first song – a saxophone, bleeding – to the second: a glacial supplication, I thought, to Justin. I sat there for a while, at a safe distance from the pants, until the sun went down.

I was singing this song, this song where the acoustic guitar is so slow it sounds rusted and submerged, singing in the frail and uncertain manner of people ashamed of their own poor voices, when I went out to Justin on the driveway and pressed his chest against mine. I felt the vomit seep into the cotton of my shirt, nuzzling my head into his shoulder and neck, noticing that I had missed him more than I ever realised, that the smell of vomit was just an accent to the talcum in his pores. He let me hug him, though his hands remained limp by his sides. Brandy leapt from his skin.

'Let's walk,' I said.

'Where!' It was an exclamation.

'You're not going inside like this.'

'Like what!' He looked at his chest, noticing the stain as if for the first time.

'Like that. We – you – can walk it off.'

I put my hand on his back and felt it stick there.

'It's great to see you,' I said.

There was a milky film over his eyes, and he didn't say anything. He followed me out of the driveway and onto the street, taking care, it seemed, not to look up at the house. Was he twitching?

Waiting for Justin, I'd read a pamphlet I bought at an anarchist bookstore about electro-shock therapy, about the 'system', synapses and mental health. I looked at his temples, trying to find some evidence, some burnt skin or a stray electrode. Instead, I saw red lines fanning out from his pupils, lines that spread across his face to connect with blotches on his cheeks, and I wasn't sure whether it was Justin that came home, or whether he was still bound up in a skinless ball somewhere in the corner of the Fairfield Institute, unable to be put back together again. I wanted to ask him about this, and what was done to him while I finished school and began having sex, but instead I updated him on football scores and talked too fast about people we both knew whose lives had gone even worse than his, trying to raise a smile in him at first but after a while even a twitch of the eyebrows would have done, or a cough or a scream or –

We cut through the commission flats and Justin looked up at me for maybe the first time, and tried to speak.

'The pastor, Jaryd, told me about…he told me about…the castanets, Jaryd, the cass…ta-nets.'

I stopped walking suddenly, my legs refusing to work in concert with the questions I now had of him, questions I knew there was no point in me asking: Justin, did they-? Who have they sent home instead? Didn't we used to laugh at people who spoke like this, marooned in shopping centres with our parents? I turned away, half expecting him to crack up, telling me of the joke he'd mastered, so long in planning.

Most of his sentences took on that staccato pattern at first, as if he was suspended, frozen almost. The Institute had sent us a letter, telling us patients were encouraged to find their own way home. The letter said that hope was not to be abandoned, and illustrated this with a sun-drenched picture of a family lying on a picnic rug in a meadow. The children in the picture had skin the colour of whipped cream. None of them had red hair.

I took his forearm, which was cold and thin, and led him across the grass. I had faith, if not in the literature we had been sent at least in Justin, and believed that as he thawed sentences would come, and the life he had led alone across town in the building with the three stripes would unravel itself as we walked along.

But I was blank – nothing from our previous intimacy to find out how far gone he was – You remember the time? – no mind of how to simply talk like brothers, lost but now reunited, young still, alive. How would such brothers talk? Ecstatically? About everything possible? Any thought that comes up? Topical things: new foods? Pop trends? Have you lost weight? You have lost so much weight. Could he even talk? So far, I had not heard a full coherent sentence, no acknowledgement that he even knew who I was.

We'd only really started getting close around the time that he began to fall apart. I could never explain it to Mum and Dad, and several dinners were ruined trying, but there was something in him all along that only began to come out when he got sick. I maintained – earnestly at first, ridiculously towards the end – that if he had been treated with love and simple compassion, rather than worry and private health care, the result might have been different, and I would not be walking him through streets he had known all his life explaining where they go and how to use them safely.

Justin was found a few days after my sixteenth birthday hunched over a dog behind our high school. He had stabbed the dog several times with a screwdriver he had taken from metal work class. He was whimpering, and as he said later, doing his best to bring her back to life. He had learned mouth-to-mouth just weeks before, and was holding the holes in her belly, trying to force air back into her. The dog's name was Mohammed, and she was a favourite of the school, a regal old scotch collie whose hippie owners let her wander out the gates and play with the students most days.

Kids had gathered around, then made way for teachers, who made way for police, who, a little later in the day, made way for mental health professionals who introduced my brother to beige and tagging and two-tone apparel.

It turned out that Justin had been drinking an enormous amount up to the time of the stabbing, and had been doing so for a number of years. He had hidden this exceptionally well from my parents, who thought he had become erratic after his earlier bout of glandular fever had rendered him tired and inert. They thought that the end of his tennis career had made him moody and distant. He would need some new hobbies, they said, some time to adjust. Kelsey, his girlfriend at the time, and the only reliable source of information during the whole ordeal, said that she never saw him drink, though she was smoking a lot of pot when they were going out. She said the only hint was his going to bed half an hour earlier than her each night, no matter when that was, and that on the odd occasion she would want to wake him for comfort or sex or so they could fall asleep together, she would be unable to rouse him, even when she was blown and cruel and would pour coffee on his head and pick at his bones and curse him.

The first facility was considered progressive, a colonial-style mansion set back in the hills, donated by a philanthropist whose son died of schizophrenia there in the seventies. The inmates were instructed not to think of themselves as patients but as part of a community. They were told to speak only in the present tense and were encouraged to take responsibility for a small farm at the rear of the centre. They fed cows each morning and sat in concentric circles after dinner and listened to ambient drone music and talks on the cosmic mandala.

Justin did well there for a while – he was made head of the kitchen roster and was allowed to ride horses in the neighbouring paddocks without supervision. He mastered the djembe in a few short months and began negotiations to have a festival, open to families and the public, on the facility grounds. There was never any precise reason why he was moved to the 'sister' facility back in the city before a year was out, just a letter on recycled paper repeating itself in sentence after sentence using words like 'recommended' and 'unstable' and 'understanding'.

The sister facility did not encourage families to visit for a reason they couldn't properly articulate, even in their pamphlets specifically designed to answer such queries. We went once, about a year ago, and following their advice, never went back. Everything was fluorescent, the patients scrubbed and quiet. Justin sent a message from his room that he would have really liked to see us, only in a year or so.

Letters made from templates arrived with unnerving regularity to tell us of Justin's continual improvement. Occasionally, photos of Justin in front of a painted background with what looked to be stage make-up on his face accompanied them. Mum and Dad, so tired, would look at the photos briefly, comment nervously to one another, and then put them in a drawer designated for such things. After a letter arrived, ordinary things in the week – dinners with relatives, bills, school fees – took on a profound and urgent significance.

I held his arm across intersections, with no thought as to the direction we were heading, as far as necessary, to the docks if need be, into one of the massive empty apartment towers where we would sprawl about on carpet and start a new life. Through quieter streets and shapes of sunlight he started spluttering something that sounded like garbled scripture, the same fragment over and over again, eyes narrowed from struggling with it.

'Seasons,' he said. 'One…two…three. '

We moved toward the underpass, where the trees thinned out and gave way to traffic. Each elm looked more pained than the last, the colour of rot spreading up and through the limbs to the rusty warehouses they overlooked. A hot-air balloon hovered above us, the colour of morning urine. I imagined the couple inside the balloon looking down and appraising us, as everyone soon would:

WOMAN: That boy is retarded.
MAN: Which one?
WOMAN: The red-haired one. And maybe his brother.
MAN: They walk funny.
WOMAN: They have no idea where they're going.
MAN: Are they joking?
WOMAN: If they're impersonating disabled people, they're doing a rather poor job.
MAN: Have you ever met a retarded person?
WOMAN: Of course I have.

I spent a lot of my youth hanging out at football games and suburban shopping centres making fun of retarded people. My friend Trav and I would take turns of being carer and patient, though I was usually the patient as I had a natural performing streak and Trav didn't like to animate too much in public. My name was usually Sebastian and I veered between cerebral palsy and a peculiar condition of my own creation – a sloppy mixture of saliva, atrophy and barely concealed laughter. We shaped people's sympathies into an endlessly renewable theatre that celebrated our health and good fortune. It lasted for about a year. I was found out one day walking to the milk bar, thinking how well I had the impression down, when a shabby man in his thirties looked straight into my eyes and told me a number of things about myself I hadn't yet slowed down enough to realise. I had never since impersonated a retarded person. They fill me, these days, with a quiet sadness.

It was out of frustration, I think, that I started singing to Justin, on a street corner in front of an auto-parts factory as the clouds rolled in politely, one after another. I had asked enough questions to know from his responses that we would not be talking, or at least not in the way where any sense would be made of his absence. I tried to speed up the song, to sing it tunefully and beautifully, because it reminded me of Justin and was the only song that came to mind. I started singing about the cycle of the seasons, about milk and honey and gold and silver, making up words in the chorus where the tape had rendered the singer's pipes a ship's horn, all fog and reverb. I was singing, even though my head was blank, about Justin, and the fact we had walked some five miles and were way out of our neighbourhood, down by the docks where we were never meant to go. I have a terrible voice, but hearing me Justin stopped his twitching and grabbed my arm and made us both stop. He was beautiful when he stood still. His ginger hair was re-emerging from the colourless base of the severe crew cut he'd been given, and it matched the colour where the whites of his eyes should have been.

He began walking ahead of me, though just slightly, and the twitch of his eyelids, blinking, blinking, had been replaced by a restless need for movement, his eyes now straining in their sockets. He had sudden cause for gesticulating about everything – a burnt mound of tyres, the tattoo on my forearm, his own wasted body. His movements became grand, sweeping – he pirouetted across the road and embraced a kebab truck, hands splayed on its window. I pried him from the truck and we walked, faster now, down the alley past the pathology centre and the old men waiting in line.

He was as happy wandering in this alley in West Melbourne as I had ever seen him, happier than I can remember being. He began grabbing me roughly around the back of my neck and telling me about geometry and God, and how there were lines throughout nature that spoke to him of various things, none of which he stayed with long enough to explain very well. He spoke in clipped phrases, punctuated by spit, always so excited about the next idea that none was ever finished. He began emptying his pockets, as if, once empty, they could explain everything. I smiled at him.

The highway stretched out before us, a snake split in two. Mum and Dad would be driving around frantically, their two children merging seamlessly into one unsolvable problem. The vomit had almost dried on Justin's shirt, but the sweat on his chest – we were moving like wind – was giving it new life. The smell was like nothing I'd ever known, somehow a mix of aniseed and car tyres.

We walked across the bridge, out onto the grass toward the football stadium. Justin was exhausted now, the energy from the drink spent and replaced by a torpor that dropped his head into his chest. I slowed until I was again alongside him. We lay down on the oval. The grass was wet on our backs.

'Jaryd,' Justin said, rolling over. 'What…what was that song?'

So I started singing.

Downsizing
ADELE SMITH

My mother had drawn a series of important-looking numbers on the back of an old receipt, remarking in a timid voice that I should 'use this information wisely'. She had a way of never saying much with words – sometime after dad had left she'd taken to speaking directly into her chest, letting the short sentences drip quietly onto her blouse as if no-one would really notice them anyway.

Aside from a cheque or two, my father had made no attempt at contact for twenty years. What I knew of him came in the form of pauses, coughs and ellipses during conversations with Mum about childhood, responsibility and the self-help market. His first book, *Be Your Own Boss* sat on my desk for a week after I moved to the same city as him, its pages flanked by a well-built man in beige slacks and a cautiously flowered tie. It was the first clear picture I'd seen of my father, who for some reason always appeared out-of-focus or half-obscured on film. The book consisted mainly of buzzwords like 'championing', 'lifestyle-zero' and 'downsizing'. It took me two weeks and a marketing dictionary to read. Afterwards, I took out the old receipt and dialled the numbers. Yvonne, his second wife, answered.

'Who's this?' she said, her voice as stern and nasal as a swimming instructor's.

'It's Susan.'

'From the publishers?'

'No. From Bendigo.'

'Oh?...oh.'

'Is William there?'

'No, he's, ah, unavailable.'

'I want to arrange a meeting.'

'Regarding...?'

I let the receiver fall slightly down the side of my neck, and ran my tongue along my teeth.

'Tell him I want to talk about downsizing,' I said, and placed the phone carefully back on the hook.

I had already decided that Yvonne would not be pleased about my visit, despite the fact that she would vacuum the carpet and dust the piano and politely give her husband and I some 'time alone'. I knew that my father's new wife was different to my mother, and that our simple rural life was more than likely the inspiration for my father's bestseller *On The Upside: Moving Up The Ladder Of Love*.

The morning of my visit I threw a few things together and caught the bus over to the eastern suburbs, where everybody looked like extras in a daytime soapie. Alongside *Be Your Own Boss* and *On the Upside* I had bought a copy of *Get Involved...Now!* that I had found in the 'Inspirational' section of the second-hand bookstore. The cover was faded and seemed to accentuate the shadows around my father's eyes. I traced my finger over his nose and skimmed my own reflection in the bus window. His mouth was small and our faces shared an asymmetry that was heightened by bad lighting.

I wasn't entirely sure how I was going to greet my father, whether we would hug awkwardly at the front door, shake hands over the kitchen table or nod sternly at each other with our big chins. I practiced my smile at the dust jacket, first cautiously, then angrily, then with my lip curled up at the corner as though I were aware of some sort of crass and hilarious in-joke. I pictured my father receiving me, in an armchair or, no, reclining at a desk with some sort of well-groomed Siamese at his feet, talking about my mother and the sacrifices – oh, he would emphasise that word and put it in italics and make a success of it the same way he had with 'downsizing'.

His street was clean – a white-with-two style affair framed by expensive-looking vehicles competing silently along the curb. Evidently, this was the product of 'championing'. I pushed the buzzer, listening avidly for the sounds of success. Nothing. I tried again, this time wedging my fingernail in the button so that it rang until my ears hurt. Against my thigh *Get Involved...Now!* pinched into my skin.

I walked around to the side of the garden where a potted plant with sickly arms reached out from the cement and a deflated soccer ball sat quietly in the sun. I was suddenly unsure about this; nervous that I'd missed one of my mother's mumbled pieces of advice or overstepped some invisible line.

It was the newspaper I saw first, flapping in the breeze like some flightless and itemised bird. The front page rose and fell back onto the unmowed grass of the backyard, and I stared at it for a moment, trying to read the headline as though it might offer some vital information. Next to it, a man lay long and still in the warm sun, his hair dishevelled and his feet splayed like the bottom of a Pez dispenser. He turned his head towards the direction of the footsteps and his eyelids fluttered, beating away the afternoon light. The newspaper blew across his chest and he flinched for a moment, reaching out and tracing two fingers along the length of his sternum. He looked up.

'Hey.'

'Hey,' I replied, biting my lip and holding onto the taut straps of my shoulder bag. 'Nice place.'

'You look like your mother,' he said, but from where I was standing it looked like he was staring at something over my left shoulder. He let his hand drop to his side and traced his finger over something in the grass. 'You look like your mother,' he repeated, although we both knew that this was untrue, and the statement made a mockery of everything.

'Are you drunk?' I offered. The unmistakable smell of whiskey shrouded him like an old coat.

'A little…' he said, trying to sit up, '…sure.'

It wasn't exactly a revelation. I'd known about his little problem with the bottle from the way my mother mumbled about him 'not always being present' at family gatherings, important dinners or even during the evenings they stayed at home and watched the flickering images on TV after things got difficult between them.

'I need to get up,' he said, and the wind picked up and blew his collar against his neck. He paused and looked up at the clouds that were skimming excitedly through the blue sky. 'I want to show you something.'

'Yvonne did tell you I was coming?'

'In the garage, Susan, there's something…great.'

He dusted off his shirt and stood up. Underneath each armpit, sweat had pooled to form two large islands on the beige sea. He was taller than I had imagined. Through his pants I could see the outline of the long and knobbly legs I spent most of my childhood trying to cover up.

We walked across the lawn to a garage, where some sort of creeper clung desperately to the bricks. He turned as he opened the door, his eyes squinting and bloodshot underneath his smeared glasses. For all his success, my father was about as intimidating as a cork. He clicked his fingers and cupped his hand over his mouth to smell his breath.

Inside, the garage was grimy and reeked of oil and escapism. Amongst the discarded bike helmets and kids toys was some sort of old car, half-finished or half-started and covered with an expensive-looking sheet.

'See? She's beautiful huh?' he said, pulling at the edges of the cotton and revealing a shiny red Mercedes.

I had compiled a mental list of my own buzzwords that I wanted to give my father for his next bestseller. They were a) 'critical abandonment,' which referred to the severing of ties that bound you to certain people or places you found restrictive or underwhelming, b) 'emotional blacklisting,' a dysfunctional response to conflict whereby an individual refrains from showing any emotional attachment or remorse, and c) 'slash residue,' the deposit that forms after a particularly aggressive downsizing project has been undertaken. I ran a knuckle lightly over the car window, wanting to trace these words in the dust before I lost my nerve.

'Hop in.'

I swung open the car door. Inside, the vinyl was the same cold beige as his shirt and I noted this on the other list I had drawn up for my father in my mind. On one side, 'beige' now followed 'success' and 'patios'. Directly opposite them, in another column were 'mum,' 'me' and 'tapioca'. It was almost enough to build a case.

In contrast to the surrounding garage, everything in the car was clean and orderly. The smooth panelling seemed to come from all directions and every surface I tried to rest my hand on was cold and smelled of expensive polish. My father reached underneath the seat and produced a bottle of whiskey and a ream of paper cups. Apparently this was where he spent his leisure time.

'I'm all outta ice,' he said, and a smile crept up the left side of his mouth.

From the glove box he produced a packet of cigarettes and a hat with a peak, which he placed over the hair that had started a pilgrimage to the back of his head. Sprawled across the hat was an advertisement for an aftershave, with the caption, 'Because It's You'. Underneath the title, an embroided yellow swan pointed a wing towards the sky – although frequent wear had caused the stitching around its beak to come loose.

'What should I call you?' I asked, unable to take my eyes off the wayward threads.

'William. Will. Billy. Whatever.'

'I read your books…William.'

'Which ones?'

'*Be Your Own Boss, Get Involved…, On The Upside.*'

'What do you think?'

'Honestly?'

He sighed, and ran his finger across the rim of his cap. He lit a cigarette with the car lighter and wound down the window just enough to let the smoke escape. He took a sip of his whiskey and bit down on the side of the paper cup.

'You know, my wife writes most of them.'

He coughed, and his wrists fell limply on the steering wheel.

'That is to say, all of them, for the last few years.'

In the windscreen I could make out both of our tight mouths, the dry lips curled cautiously in the dull light.

'What about *On The Upside*?'

'Huh?'

'*On The Upside: Moving Up The Ladder Of Love.*'

'Oh. No.'

I took a deep breath and scratched at something on my skirt.

'Did you hate us that much?'

'No. I don't think so…Yvonne proofread it…heavily edited.'

Between us, a crystal pendant dangled off the rear-view mirror, twisting in some invisible breeze.

'Do you love her?'

'In a way.'

I tried to imagine my father telling his wife he loved her, hugging his kids close to his stained armpits or even being sober enough to string a sentence together about how he was sorry – how things had got out of hand and he'd overestimated the significance of his downsizing project. But listening to his voice was like fumbling between stations on the radio, and even though we were here, in an incomplete Mercedes with our hands limp like stunned birds in our laps, I wasn't sure if we were talking at all. I shifted uncomfortably in my seat.

'Does this car work?'

'Like, move…go? I don't think so.'

'Can you drive me home?'

'I've…had a few today.'

My father called a cab from the phone in the corner of the garage. He said that it shouldn't cost more than twenty-five dollars, and if it did, to call Yvonne and get her to talk to them. He shook my hand and told me he was moving house in a few months and that he would call me with the new number.

'Come again,' he said, slowly raising the roller-door so that light rushed into the musty garage.

'Maybe,' I replied, standing awkwardly beside him in the doorway as our eyes readjusted to the light.

'I'll take you for a drive.'

'Where to?'

'I don't know…Kununurra.'

He blinked a few times then closed his eyes. He seemed pleased with the way the word rolled off his tongue.

'Kununurra.'

Electric Cherub
ANDREW MORGAN

Yesterday afternoon as I peeled myself from my spit-encrusted uniform, I noticed an Unfamiliar Shirt in the laundry basket. It was a shock; I hadn't realised the situation had degenerated so far. Something had to be done, and quick. Fortunately, I've become adept at keeping my presence of mind in difficult situations and there was enough time before the shop shut.

My lipstick collection is selective rather than extensive. Still, the new tube of Warm Plum sits inconspicuously enough amongst the rest, like that letter in that Edgar Allan Poe story. And this morning, school day or not, I am transcendent. So far above and beyond this shit-house world that the choice is obvious: on this morning it would be sinful to consider anything but Electric Cherub.

The result is indeed so magnificent I can overlook the haze of stubble above my upper lip. (Thank Dionysus for fair hair. But even if I shave only every few days, how long till the follicles toughen?) Having carefully retracted the stick and re-capped the barrel, I slip it into the back pocket of my trousers along with the Warm Plum.

Of course my grand entrance into the living room goes largely unappreciated. My darling sister, Georgia (her blouse apparently retrieved from beneath a herd of stampeding buffalo), is engrossed in a debate with Hermann. That is, she's engrossed in delivering one of her rants about some Issue or other. Georgia's determination not to be just another self-obsessed teeny-bopper is rather touching and entirely to her credit. But I do wish she wouldn't get so carried away. She is seriously losing half the contents of her mouth in an arc over Mum's new tablecloth (left out after last night's banquet). Though I daresay, given the nature of that content – some sugar-based, nutrient-free chemical engineer's wet dream – it's better out than in.

Hermann is doing his best to appear simultaneously fascinated by Georgia's spiel and oblivious to her grotesque manners. However, he cannot help but register my presence. Keeping both forearms on the table like a card dealer, he turns his big, keen smile in my direction. (Oh, that smile. Evidently life in Hermann's universe is never less than *beaut*.)

'Morning,' he barks.

'Yes.' I offer a sultry pout. 'So it is.'

I have to hand it to my poor, dear mother: she knows how to pick them. This one is a male nurse. Apparently he was responsible for stitching Mum up after that unpleasant falling-out with her last male friend. And somewhere between the surgical swab and the sterilised dressing (mid-suture, I imagine) love blossomed. *Tres* romantic.

'Don't mind me,' I add graciously, taking my place at the table.

The comment is redundant since Georgia has paused only to glurp another spoonful. Then she's off again, oblivious to my glare at the Tupperware containing my low-fat organic muesli on the other side of her.

This morning's sermon concerneth Western medicine's policies regarding underdeveloped nations. Though Hermann's smile never falters, I can't believe he is unaware of the motive behind this diatribe, or the one last night about male chauvinism. Georgia is making no effort to disguise her feelings about this latest domestic arrangement.

I wait politely, reflecting that it is lucky my sister is academically inclined. God knows I've tried to encourage her appreciation of the finer things in life – and I'm sure with a little effort she could be halfway presentable. Sometimes I even suspect her frumpiness is an attempt to embarrass me. Anyway, I'm afraid it's clear I got all the charm and the looks.

But we are family. Thus, I feel obliged to ensure she doesn't catch sight of the commiserating eyebrow I raise at Hermann, who hasn't touched his Vegemite toast.

As Georgia buries her snout in her bowl again, I seize the moment to retrieve my muesli without getting showered by soggy cereal and bodily fluids. (Time enough for that later.) However, before I can pop the airtight seal, Hermann is saying he understands where Georgia is coming from and couldn't agree more.

Georgia sniffs. 'Yeah, right.'

In fact – Hermann continues mildly – he spends three weeks of his annual leave each year working as a volunteer medico in Rwanda.

Seconds pass. I realise I'm still holding my container of muesli and I lower it to the table unopened. Georgia's face is a splatter of dumbstruck awe, the likes of which I haven't seen there in years.

'How wonderful,' I observe, a moment later. 'We'll all have to be friends now, won't we?'

Finally Georgia acknowledges my presence. 'You don't have to be a fuckwit all the time,' she says, scowling. Then stares back down at her bowl as if she has suddenly noticed something Very Perplexing in its depths.

I am spared the bother of replying – which would certainly have involved some unpleasant home truths – by Mum's arrival.

'I'm so glad you didn't wait for me,' she says with a laugh as she flutters into the kitchen. 'I don't know why I'm such a slow coach in the morning these days. Old age, I suppose.'

She must have been slaving over the vanity bag since dawn. And the results, I must say, are quite effective. With her fringe brushed down it's almost impossible to see the pink weal that brought her and Hermann together. There's a slather of foundation around the eye, but the puffiness is nearly gone. As for the wrinkles and the pinched cheeks – well, there's only so much one can do.

Hermann is certainly impressed. 'Old age,' he repeats with a gallant chuckle. 'As if.'

Mum throws him a don't-think-you're-putting-anything-over-on-me look, which I doubt would convince anyone.

'Who's for coffee?' she chirps.

Hermann and I nod. I steel myself for Georgia's harangue on the exploited plantation workers of South America. Instead, she mumbles 'sure' so meekly that I glance at her in concern.

But she has again forgotten my existence. Her attention is now focused on Mum, her expression anxious. It appears she is waiting to see if Mum screws up, though it has never bothered her before.

Meanwhile, Hermann's gaze hasn't shifted, and I find myself following it back to Mum – bustling about the kitchen, apparently unimpeded by the weight of our combined observation. Her movements are purposeful, energetic. It is a bravura performance and I'm lost in admiration. I could believe, almost, that things really have changed and the recent past is history. No more tag-team attempts by Georgia and me to drag her out of bed; no more chronic TV dinners or long-forgotten laundry in the washing machine; no more of those gaping, vacant episodes. After all she's been through, there is not the slightest hint of how dreadful it must feel being a lonely, desperate middle-aged woman in a world that belongs to the young and gorgeous.

Hermann rises to help bring the mugs to the table. When we're all seated, I raise my mug and propose a toast: *Here's to happy ever afters.* From the pause that follows you would think I'd said something controversial. Mum's teaspoon has somehow become stuck solid in her coffee.

Then Georgia, once more her old self, helpfully suggests, 'Ignore him. He's been fucked up since dad left.'

I pity her. She has no idea. In hindsight I'm amazed our parents were so inconsiderate, waiting as long as they did for their divorce. Let's face it, these days it's a rite of passage. Seriously, it's incredible how the words 'You're the man of the family now' can throw everything into a whole new perspective.

I turn to Hermann to offer him a shrug of apology for Georgia's faux pas.

For the first time, though, he is not smiling. 'I reckon you've got guts,' he says. 'You must cop shit at school for that make-up.'

What is it with Hermann? As if he had any idea. And, frankly, why should he care? He's already won himself a season pass to Mum's bedroom. And accomplished the feat of getting Georgia on-side. Is that not enough for him?

Evidently not. It seems, happy as he is, Hermann won't be content till he has stitched us all up. What else could be behind this half-challenge, half-enticement to lower my guard and prove there's more to me than my glamorous exterior?

For a moment I consider grabbing the margarine knife and stabbing him in the heart. He is far more dangerous than I'd imagined. Because even while I'm marvelling at how he can deliver such a patronising comment with such sincerity; even while I'm asking myself how he could possibly believe I'd feel grateful for his charity; even while I'm telling myself that nothing in the known universe could induce me to give him the satisfaction – in the middle of all this I can feel a hot, sticky lump creeping into my throat.

Can it be possible I want to believe in the fairy tale? To imagine that just because things always turn out the way they do, it doesn't mean they always will? To wonder whether maybe if I made more of an effort... As if it's not enough of an effort just to get by.

'Since you mention it,' I say, exhaling slowly, 'it's a good day when I don't get the crap beaten out of me.' Calm. Self-possessed. I'm proud of myself.

Hermann shakes his head then raises his mug. 'To happy ever afters.' He is smiling again.

A moment later Mum follows suit, and then Georgia.

As soon as I've finished my coffee, I push back my chair and ask to be excused.

'Shouldn't you eat something?' Mum murmurs.

I assure her I'm not hungry.

I scurry through the laundry and lock myself in the bathroom. Slumped on the edge of the bath, I fumble the two tubes from my back pocket. As I try to unscrew the Warm Plum, I realise I'm trembling. But eventually the lid surrenders, and the sight is even more ghastly than it looked yesterday evening under the shop's fluorescent lighting. No right-thinking person could mistake this for one of *my* colours.

It requires a supreme exercise of will power to bring the stuff near my lips. But once I've started, instinct takes over and I do the job thoroughly. Then there's no time to lose. I tip-toe past the wash basin to the laundry basket. Hermann's shirt is still there, under yesterday's cellophane-stiff uniform.

I know I mustn't get carried away. The result has to be noticeable, but nothing that couldn't have escaped notice earlier. A few smudges on the inside of the collar towards the back should be more than enough.

It's worse than I imagined. My stomach heaves as I taste Hermann's sweat and smell the stale soup of his BO and aftershave. As soon as I've replaced the shirt in the basket, I have to swallow a mouthful of toothpaste and scrub my lips with toilet paper. Then I reapply the Electric Cherub. But the feeling of transcendence has gone. I just feel victorious and suicidal.

As for the Warm Plum, I'm sure one of the less discriminating girls at school will gladly relieve me of it. It's a pity – I'd put that money aside for something really glorious. But I know that none of us can afford Hermann's sympathy. Sometimes you have to make sacrifices.

His Painted Self
Rose Mulready

Even in this city, with its dim gold spires, its bundled women sweeping the streets with witches' brooms, its naked penitents, there is a billboard advertising the movie. He stands underneath it and looks at his own face. His painted self is screaming.

That night he sits on his bed – a stone platform with a bridal net – and unwraps his dinner from newspaper. A giblet handful of meat, fried beyond recognition, and a rough-hewn toffee. There is a chunk of unmelted sugar in the toffee, hard as flint. He removes it from his mouth and puts it in the cup of newspaper, where it sits like his own broken tooth.

He made a fortune from the movie, his first. There were parties, and hilarious carloads of people, and a white tide of flashbulbs. He stood on a glass terrace that spilled in wide stairs and an extravagance of garden to the sea, where a dark sun was sinking like a foundered ship. His drink numbed his fingers. He saw the twins long after they saw him. They had arranged themselves on the stairs with expressions so blank he felt safe to stare. They were not dressed identically – nothing so blatant – but there was a dandyish likeness in the loose knot of scarf around one's throat, the other's full sleeve. They were both wet from the sea, like pirates gone overboard, and their faces were flawless duplicates.

They waited until he was fairly hooked, then turned and went away down the glass stairs. Their bare feet made wet prints, and he followed.

In this city, the women paint their babies' faces to resemble monkeys, so that the hungry spirits will pass them by.

He had gained nineteen kilos to audition for the movie, all of it muscle. He had worked with a trainer who sectioned his body like a butcher and scourged each portion until he was mythical, his torso too wide for the narrow strip of mirror on his boarding house wardrobe.

The gun they gave him looked small in his arms, a toy, so they made him a bigger one.

The twins twined around a tree at the bottom of the garden, sinuous Adams, and suggested he drive them to the marina. They lived on a white blade of a yacht that looked simple but was full of cunning luxuries. False backs and spinning fronts concealed bathtubs, a ping-pong table, expensive liquors. The twins made him a drink, some kind of priceless white spirit with coriander crushed in it, and put on languid music.

And still they wouldn't tell him their names.

'You can call us Sailor,' said one, and the other laughed gently.

The guesthouse stands a few miles out of town in a dark fastness of trees. He can hear the birds, but he can't see them. He spends a lot of time here, lying in the small, blind world of the net. He can hear himself breathe, and feel it, one hand exploring his chest.

The twins didn't touch each other. He came back from a reeling search for somewhere to piss – opening doors to find polite ranks of jackets, walls he leaned on falling away from him, in the end he resorted to the sea – to find them curled naked on a green rug. There was something touching about the lack of tricks, no stripping or double-act.

'We bathed together as children,' said one.

'Since then, never.'

It was true there were two bathtubs on the yacht.

He searched their bodies for distinguishing features, but they were inscrutable. Matchless, smooth, flexible as heated toffee. One by one, their mouths. His cock spat like a Catherine Wheel, all through the spinning night.

Wandering through the city at dusk, he comes upon a street of prostitutes. They are as bulkily concealed as the rest of the city's women, but their clothes are bright as match heads. Ground powders are smeared on their lips and cheeks. He glimpses one in a doorway, engaged in a complicated gymnastics to free a passage through her clothes. Her client waits with his head down.

He walks and walks, turning at random, avoiding the lanes with their shadows and reek of fouled straw. On the main street, in a pool of smoking light, a woman kneels over the body of a prone infant – dead or asleep. Her hand is curled open on its chest, begging. He gives her a coin, and the hand closes.

He woke dry-mouthed on the yacht. His head lay in an unwelcome dazzle of light. The twins weren't in the room.

He found them breakfasting on the deck, one spreading marmalade, the other solemnly pouring tea. They both reached at the same time for the envelope.

He slipped it open, muzzy in the head, dread starting, and looked at the photographs. Saw his own blind eyes. His eager mouth open.

'We have a darkroom on board,' they chorused.

He crushed the photographs in his fist, and felt the slipping power of his bicep. He hadn't worked out since the movie wrapped.

'Who *are* you?'

The twins smirked.

'We are Siamese, if you please,' said one.

'We are Siamese – if you don't please,' said the other.

And then they pretended to purr.

He booked a flight and left that morning, choosing the city at random.

What he had never told anyone, a secret deeper than the twins' photographs: he had scared himself, making that movie. Stalking along the roof of the buckled train, oiled and hard, scoured by the sun, heavy with weapons, screaming. He had felt like an angel, the kind that brings fire. He threw one of the extras off the train in an unrehearsed move and broke the man's ankle. And they filmed even that.

He was sure they were going to show the movie on the plane – it felt inevitable – but they showed a romance. He watched as the film lovers held each other by a window. He couldn't stop looking at the gesture of the man's hand, the way it cupped the head of the woman.

The greatest secret he has is his tenderness. The soft parts of him that will never be filmed.

He sits in a booth at the phone shop, choking on a local cigarette. He hasn't spoken to Tomas since filming wrapped. They'd been together for three years, but the director considered him a risk.

Tomas wouldn't stand for being his skeleton. Tomas had boxed up his clothes and put the chain on the door.

He says hello and then quickly, 'please'.

There are dark whistles on the line, like hidden crows.

'You sound far away.'

'Not so much as I was.'

'I suppose you need help.'

He waits. A man in the doorway of the shop, hair braided close to his temples, leans to the street and releases a mouthful of red juice.

He says, 'I can't tell you...'

'Better *not* tell me.' The voice sharp. And then sharper, 'ah, don't start crying – not that cheap trick –'

He tries to stop and can't. He's there the way he has to be, making wet sounds into a dirty phone, and the sudden night has fallen down, and the man is moving back from the doorway, wiping the red from his mouth.

Orange
ANN BOLCH

The city is grey and cold and wet. Jude finds her favourite seat on the tram: in the middle, on the left, facing forwards. Outside people are coughing and sniffling, a rusty billboard reminds her to buy vitamin C tablets before winter.

There's an orange sitting on a seat across the aisle. With one flattish edge, it moves slightly with the tram's rocking, but mostly stays in the middle of the seat. Jude wonders whether to pick it up and take it home.

A grandmother pulls her way onto the tram with her grandson in tow. He sees the fresh unpeeled fruit. 'Don't touch that!' she says, 'you don't know where it's been'.

A woman with immaculate hair dressed in a black wool suit makes a beeline for the seat with the orange in it, thinking it empty. Astonished to find an orange, she looks down, pauses, looks around, and decides to sit in the seat beside the orange, glancing down at it every now and then.

On the street, orange is in vogue. Scarves, shirts – even the occasional jacket or beret. Burnt orange, mind. None of this bright fruity stuff.

As the tram continues to fill up, a man strides towards the orange-seat. He stops short when he sees the seat is occupied. 'Is this yours?' he asks the woman in the black wool suit. 'No,' she says, curtly. He decides to stand.

A woman with henna-streaked hair and armloads of shopping boards the tram. She is talking on her mobile phone, so she doesn't notice the orange as she sinks heavily into the seat. She quickly recoils as if poked with a carrot, and – because she is talking on her phone – doesn't bother to ask whose orange it is. Instead she stands at the front of the tram telling her phone-friend all about how an orange is taking up an entire seat. The aisle is congested, it's hard to keep tabs on all her shopping. She shifts her weight from foot to foot, stepping out of one new shoe, then the other. Jude had tried on a similar pair the day before. The shop assistant insisted on calling the shoes 'sunset', even though they were orange, as though conjuring the image of a romantic dinner for two would help flog off more shoes.

Then an old bloke wearing several holey layers gets on, carrying a faded, browny-red Ansett bag with the lettering peeling off. The 'n' has gone completely, so it reads like a dyslexic spelling of asset. Jude wonders if he does have all his assets in that bag.

He scans the tram for a spare seat and seems delighted to get one during peak hour, doubly surprised to find the orange.

He asks the nearby passengers if this is their orange. They assure him it isn't, so he breaks into the skin, squirting a fine spray of juice towards the lady in the black wool suit, but she's staring at a punk on the street with a bright sunset Mohawk.

The old man slurps and sucks and mentions to whoever is listening that it's the second orange he's found this week. 'A good thing,' he says, 'winter has started early this year'.

A Goitre-Shaped Protuberance
RYAN PAINE

At about quarter-past four, I offered my nipples to the wind and the wind said no thanks, but I'll have your pouch of tobacco. We were lumbering down the highway in Jetroe's jaffa-red Falcon, on our way to Corny Point to go fishing.

I was leaning out the window with my shirt unbuttoned, because I like to offer myself up like that now and then, when the world conspires to help me. In this case, when my best mate knocked off work with a 'headache' at the same time I did with 'stomach pains', I felt so blessed that I wanted to bare my nipples to the wind.

Now it's nearly five o'clock and we're at a service station in Ardrossan.

'Pouch o' Champion Ruby, thanks,' I say to "Serg", the guy behind the counter. That's what it says on his name badge: "Serg". Quotation marks and all.

'Got 'ny ID?' he asks.

A Goitre-Shaped Protruberance

'ID? I don't have any proper ID. I've got a student card, will ya take that?'

'Give us a look.'

I put my student card on the counter.

'Is this a joke? That's not you,' "Serg" says.

I knew that was coming; I get it all the time. You see, when I was younger, my brother seemed to like to see me vomit. He'd tickle me after dinner most nights until I coughed up on the carpet. One night after a particularly solid serving of Mum's 'goulash', my body wasn't able to regurgitate, the meal having set like Ice Magic in my stomach. My guts were straining and churning and my eyes were watering, but my body couldn't spew. My brother tried to poke me in the ribs but I arched away, vomiting only laughter, and something ruptured in my neck. I think it was my trachea. The doctor told me, but...anyway, one of my neck muscles ripped away from my right collar bone.

I was squealing and crying and trying to find his eye sockets so I could push my thumbs into them, but my brother kept tickling me. That's what caused the damage, the doctors said. My traumatised trachea, which had gathered in a goitre-shaped protuberance under my cheek and jaw, was permanently damaged in those crucial minutes. The doctors couldn't reattach the muscle to the bone, so they just left it hanging in there like a piece of sodden beef jerky hung in a meat safe.

Every time I laugh now, my coiled trachea forms the goitre-protuberance under my jaw. It's about the size of a cricket ball. The contraction distorts my whole face and pulls my chin into my right shoulder. Blood rushes to the area and my cheeks glow like sliced beetroot in the sun. My cheek and eyelid droop into a paroxysm of spasms, my ear stretches until it looks like a hot and sweaty sun-dried tomato and I can't speak or laugh or even breathe properly until my trachea relaxes and the face cramps let up.

So when I was getting my photo taken for my student card, some clown at the back of the room made a smart remark. My goitre was protruding in all its glory when the flash blared.

The nerve endings are rooted now, so laughing is relatively painless, and my student card is good for a wild party trick. I try it on "Serg":

'Eh? Yeah, that's me. Jetroe, make me laugh.' Jetroe walks straight over to the nearest fridge. "Serg" pushes the card across the counter, convinced that we're seventeen-year-old bullshit artists.

Jetroe turns his back to the fridge door and does a fart gesture (bending at the knees and lowering his haunches in a half-arsed curtsey) then makes a *parp* sound with his mouth. Then he turns around, squats, and pretends to write something in the imaginary fart-fog on the cold glass. It works a treat, and I break into a muffled and demented laugh that sounds more like I'm choking on someone else's vomit.

I turn my right shoulder towards "Serg" and throw my head back to reveal the goitre.

'Whoa,' he says, and laughs. He pulls my ID back to him, raises his eyebrows, then shakes his head and laughs again. My chin snaps back into my chest and my beer gut wobbles about. I can't swallow and a gob of drool slips out of my mouth. It lands on my shirt. I love it when that happens. A pang of sympathy invariably overwhelms any humour or disgust in onlookers. The drool is somehow worse than the goitre.

"Serg" grabs a pouch of Champion Ruby and throws it over the counter onto the floor.

I bend at the knees to pick it up, and remember that I forgot to ask for filters. I look at Jetroe and try not to think about the drool and the fart-fog. I hold my breath to stop laughing but the pressure builds up and I erupt with 'FILTERRG!' and then chuckle like I'm gargling pea and ham soup. I look over to Jetroe, but he's grinning and edging across the shop towards the door. I turn back to "Serg" and think about using my thumbs and forefingers to demonstrate filters, before realising the futility of trying to mime small, white cylinders. I look back at Jetroe.

I want him to explain that it was only a prank and that's me on the ID and I just want some filters. But my face is starting to hurt, so I just squat and then drop one knee to the floor, holding my guts. I try to concentrate on the dirty, non-funny grout between the floor-tiles. Then:

'Chris!'

I look up. I'm an idiot – I need to calm down so I can get some filters, but still I look up. Jetroe's walking in tight circles with his knees touching. He looks like a pigeon-toed duck with a twisted ankle.

It's all over. I roll onto my back and stick my legs in the air. My face is aching but I don't want to stop laughing. I laugh at the sound of my own uncontrollable laughter, and rejoice in the idea that I might never stop. I remember the old wives' tale: don't pull faces or the wind'll change and you'll stay like that forever. Shit I hope it's windy on Corny Point. Maybe then I'll be forced to come to terms with my bung face, to learn how to exist in perfect harmony with my self and the world. Maybe I'll find a place where it doesn't matter that I laughed at a fart joke. A place where they don't have bombs, or child pornographers, or *Australian Idol*. A place where it smells like mangoes all year round, where clouds are only white and the temperature is always twenty-four degrees. A place where my arse crack doesn't get scratched on the gravel when Jetroe drags me backwards across the car park.

Life After Death
Daniel Wynne

You're going to die. Nobody can really say when or how, but it's definitely gonna happen sooner or later. Not exactly uplifting, is it? But there's hope. If you believe in the concept of life after death, you can relax a little about your impending doom. It offers reassurance that although your body may be unhandsomely decomposing, your soul is partying on in the spirit realm.

So what exactly happens after you die? Well, there are a number of possibilities:

1) Heaven & Hell
Pros: If you get to Heaven, you're treated to eternal bliss.
Cons: To get to Heaven, you have to give up fun things like gluttony, sex and murder.
Pros: If you do go to Hell, everyone you know will be there.
Cons: If you do go to Hell, everyone you know will be there.

2) Reincarnation
Pros: If you've had a crappy life, the next one could be better.
Cons: Realistically speaking, it'll probably be even worse.
Pros: You get to witness what the world will be like in the future.
Cons: It's a pretty bleak future.

3) Becoming a Ghost
This one usually happens when you have unfinished business on Earth.
Pros: You can make spooky moaning noises, scrawl threatening messages on the wall and spy on people on the toilet…without them ever seeing you!
Cons: You can't have sex, which may be the reason so many poltergeists seem so angry and want to chuck stuff around. I know how they feel.

4) Limbo
This one is horrible. You have to do a stupid dance and lower your body under some terrible bar while managing to remain upright. And really annoying music plays. It's kinda like a Gold Coast nightclub.

Of course, there are a whole lot of spoilsports who are eager to suck the fun out of death. They will tell you that after you die… nothing happens. 'It's like being asleep forever,' they say. What these party-pooper atheist killjoys don't realize is that every full moon at the stroke of midnight the dead bodies in the cemetery come back to life, crawl out of their graves and perform a synchronised dance routine to C&C Music Factory's 'Everybody Dance Now'.

    It's the truth.
    Believe it.

Low Flying Planes
ADELE SMITH

I.

On my desk were the following things: a red stapler, made in Taiwan and prone to jamming. A wristwatch, the face removed from the band and stuck to the Formica with a piece of Blu-Tac. A plastic container of coloured paperclips with a magnet at the top. A white mug with a cracked handle. Sixty-four paper cranes. The school was a tiny thing, the kids sedate, and my job often involved making paper cranes to keep from falling asleep at my desk.

'Stress cranes,' I explained to my wife on the telephone one afternoon, when the kids were all behaving and the two absence slips had been properly followed up.

'Don't you mean anti-stress cranes?' she replied.

Our school play was a week away, and I had been given the job of rousing the choir. I had chosen two songs for them to sing, a slowed-up codeine version of Lionel Ritchie's Dancing on the Ceiling, and an old Irish folk song I had taped from a horror film that featured the words 'Corn Rigs and Bonnie' in almost every verse.

Although the school had seventeen choir kids, only one of them could really sing. Ian Ford was a boy who came from out of town and was not quite old or perceptive enough to realise the embarrassment he caused his thick-wristed father by being a falsetto supreme. It is my understanding that more than once, Harry Ford had had words to the boy about what an excellent game football was, and how a career in that sort of thing would be much better suited to a boy of his 'manly' character. It's true, I did have somewhat of a forceful tone when I explained to Ian that he would not be giving up his chair in the choir on my shift. After all, the rumours about my involvement in the missing kitty money were spreading like chicken pox, and making everybody sit through the off-key truth about public schooling was not going to add to my credibility.

A couple of days before the show, a garbage bag appeared in the space between my desk and the staff refrigerator. Stapled to the top of the bag was a sign that read: 'New and Used Waistcoats'. They were awful grey things that sat top-heavy and thick breasted on the most proportionate of children and looked like the remnants of some Soviet-style fashion experiment. I rang my wife to discuss the options.

'Do you think you can alter them?' I asked.
'Why?'
'Because they look…so…dumb.'
'Why bother? They're kids. Everyone is entitled to look ridiculous before they've gone through puberty. It's a privilege, nay, a rite of passage.'
'If Harry Ford sees his son in this thing, I can only imagine what kind of ball sports he'll inflict on him.'

My wife agreed to alter a few of the things provided I also helped with the sewing.

'Alright.' I agreed, and rounded up the children for their first fitting.

II.

I wanted my wife to know that I loved her, so I kissed her before asking her to un-jam the overlocker for me. She agreed politely and even said there was something erotic about watching me at the helm of a sewing machine, that I could have been a French tailor with a creamy satin cravat.

'Inside the cravat is a camera,' I said, 'and the camera is spying on a beautiful woman so that he can…can…'

'Can what?' she replied suggestively, emphasising the corner of her mouth when she smiled.

'Can…tell the police?' I offered.

'And when they get these women into custody what will they do with them?' She stuck her thumbnail between her two bottom teeth.

'I don't know. Hold them for a few hours and realise they have nothing to go on?'

She seemed disappointed, and turned back to where the fabric was running beneath the humming foot. The phone rang and the shrill call caused me to stub my finger on the needle. I threw the thumb in my mouth and ran towards the kitchen.

On the other end of the line, the voice was dry and sounded like it came from behind a wall of cotton wool. I listened for a moment before I slammed down the receiver and went back into the loungeroom to sit with my wife.

'Them again?' she asked.

I stared at the pile of waistcoats that were lumped on top of each other like excavated dirt from a hole.

'Unplug the thing. Fuckers. Small town gossips. Unplug the phone Ed.'

She got up and went to the kitchen and put the kettle on. As it boiled I heard the sound of the cord being ripped out of its socket.

III.

Because there was no allocated funding for a school play, we had to hold the event in the gymnasium at 2pm, which meant that roughly 40% of parents couldn't attend. This narrowed down the chances of seeing Harry Ford to roughly one in three. I had managed to get out of most of the days proceedings, citing on-going back problems, but I had to make a brief appearance to give a speech about the direction the music department was taking, its bright future etc. etc.

On the morning of the play, I sat in the loungeroom with a cigarette dangling out of my mouth while Lionel Ritchie provoked me from an old CD player in the corner. On the coffee table were some flyers I'd forgot to give out, advertising the annual Hilldown Primary Fiesta. I picked one up and began folding it with my shaking fingers, the cigarette jumping around in my mouth between folds and shedding a grey dust over the hand typed letters.

'Anti-stress cranes.' I mumbled to myself as I folded the corners together.

I'd tried to take my job seriously. I liked kids; I liked the odd things they said about their parents and the surreal couplets they drew during art classes. I liked it when a bunch of them pretended to be action figures in the playground or they asked questions about the colours of dinosaurs. I even enjoyed staying up until midnight with a row of pins in my mouth and a bunch of ugly grey waistcoats. But I knew my time at Hilldown was over as soon as the July surveys came back and someone found some concrete evidence about the kitty money I'd loosely tucked into my shirt one evening last month. It wasn't just the job that I was tired of. It was the small town and the parents committee. It was the principal's navy pants suit and the canteen food. I hoped my wife wouldn't be too angry.

IV.

When I pulled up in the school parking lot, I tapped my fingers on the dashboard for a few minutes before I got out. I was fifteen minutes late, and therefore, according to the running schedule, almost on time to give my speech.

I strode awkwardly through the car park and stopped at the big doors of the gymnasium, staring at the cut out pictures of body builders and basketballs glued to the windows. Inside, I could hear a few kids scrambling about on stage and some random applause rippling through the gym like small change being dropped onto a wooden floor. I rubbed my chin. To my right, an old fire escape ladder led up onto the roof. I decided that climbing up there would provide me with a better perspective—on the day, on my life, on everything. I took a deep breath, grasped the fourth rung and hoisted my foot, looking up to where the sky was as grey as tucked motel sheets.

When I reached the top I could see the whole school. It wasn't very high, but the metal pointed up in various elevations and made it difficult to get a foothold. I slipped a little, my fist crashing onto the iron and making a thundering boom. The roof creaked beneath each step like an old door banging in the wind.

I heard voices below. I struggled to find a foothold and sat down, craning my neck over the edge. In the concrete square, I could see the taut face of the principal, Eileen Downs, and a high-chinned P.E teacher who had come out to investigate the noise. They looked up. I smiled at them. Eileen's mouth dropped open and I could see her metallic tooth filling glisten in the sunlight.

'Edward?' She yelled, her voice quavering in her small throat. 'What are you…'

The last of her words were obscured by the sound of a low-flying plane overhead. A few more people had come out of the gymnasium, including Harry Ford, who stood beside Eileen like a bodyguard and shook his head from beneath his black cap. My wife had come out too, and stood awkwardly in the back with her teeth clenched and her fists like shot-puts on the end of her arms.

I reached into my pocket and pulled out one of the twenties I had taken from the kitty. I folded the edges together and ran my thumb along the creases one by one. It wasn't the best paper crane I'd made, but the salmon pink of the note was luminous against the grey sky. I raised my arm and dropped the bird over the edge of the gutter and watched as it floated down and landed with its back on the cement below. I smiled and waved to my wife.

Hemingway's Elephants
JOHN HOLTON

I suppose I should have been more shocked to meet Hemingway on the Broadmeadows train – not least because he blew his brains out in 1961, three years before I was even born, when Broadmeadows was just paddocks of Scotch thistles.

You could tell he was embarrassed to see someone reading *Men Without Women*. This was 1988 – 60 years after its publication. It was published the same year my father was born on a kitchen table in Coburg. It reads like it was written yesterday.

'I'm reading the elephant one,' I said to Hemingway. 'Do you remember the elephant one? We all read it at school. I bet you never dreamed they'd be reading it in schools after you were dead.'

Hemingway looked confused for a moment and then said, '"Hills Like White Elephants?"' His voice was much higher than I'd imagined, but that could be a symptom of death.

'Yes that's the one. I've always liked stories about elephants. I especially like Kipling – *The Jungle Book*. There were several elephants in that one.'

'I shot an elephant once,' Hemingway said with a certain pride. 'But it's not really about elephants.'

'But it says here about the colour of their skin through the trees.'

'Yes, but she's talking about the hills. It's about relationships. Not elephants.'

'But hills don't have skin,' I said dubiously. 'Why mention the skin if it's not about elephants?'

'Because it's suggestive of elephants,' Hemingway said. 'It's symbolic, don't you see?'

'Well, why mention elephants at all then? It seems a little strange – if they're not real. Aren't you just disappointing all the people who like to read about elephants?'

'Quite,' was all that Hemingway said.

'Quite, indeed!'

It was quiet for a moment, apart from the rhythmic clickety-clack of the train. Hemingway looked at his watch and scratched nervously at his beard.

'What about 'The Killers'?' I asked, not letting him off the hook. After all, this elephant fraud was a man who'd won a Nobel prize for literature.

'What about 'The Killers'?' Hemingway said, sounding agitated.

'Well, is it about real killers? It seems to be more about sandwiches. Are the sandwiches the killers? I mean are *they* symbolic?'

'What sandwiches? Hemingway was being downright aggressive now.

'He orders sandwiches. You wrote it – how can you forget the sandwiches? Are they like the elephants? Are they just symbolic sandwiches – is that what you're saying?'

Hemingway was wiping his brow with a handkerchief as the train pulled into North Melbourne station. He was out of the door in a flash – swept up by the rush-hour crowd – his camouflage hunting jacket fading into the jungle of commuters.

I didn't see Hemingway on the Broadmeadows train again. I looked for him every day, though. I had some serious questions about the opening page of *A Farewell To Arms*.

Floating Above the Village
LEE KOFMAN

My mother eats herring for breakfast. She uses her fingers to retrieve the bare bones out of her mouth and puts them back on her paper plate. She sucks in the moist flesh and stares blankly at me as I clean my brushes.

'Mama, would you like anything else to eat?'

'Don't worry, I'll manage.'

Feeding her is never simple. She only eats kosher food and refuses to use any of my kitchenware because it is 'impure'. Since her arrival in Australia, a week ago, we shop for her food around Elsternwick and East St Kilda. We enter the dark shabby shops stuffed untidily with imported goods bearing Hebrew labels. The floors are sticky and the shop assistants wear bouffant wigs like my mother. She feels at home there, perhaps more than in our flat of large windows and paintings. We come back loaded with canned gefilte fish, egg salad and frozen *cholent*.

My mother watches me experimenting, mixing cornflower blue with lemon chiffon, but as always, she doesn't ask me anything about my painting. She is bent over the food, her elbows solidly on the table. Her lips are oily with the fish.

'Are you okay?' I am as disgusted as I used to be in my childhood.

'Shhh...' says my mother, 'The kabbalah teaches that when we're eating, we feel God's presence.'

She finishes her meal, absentmindedly picks her teeth and whispers an aftermeal *brakha*.

'So what are you going to do today?' Daniel breaks the silence. It is Sunday, but he has to work. Here is the day I have been dreading since her visit began; the two of us alone. For the first time in five years, since I left Israel.

'Look! Look! Chagall!' My mother urges inside the National Gallery with its stony, industrial-looking floors and walls. What a setting for the luxury of past art – is it mere misunderstanding, or the deliberate contempt of pioneers? I always feel incurably foreign here, craving long marble stairways and flowers of chandeliers, soft silk and polished boots from my Russian childhood. My memory draws an invisible frontier between me and my new home.

In the Modern Art sections the minimalist exhibits, bleak like anorexic partygirls, match the building's spirit and make me wonder whether my own masquerade paintings, made with gold and silver splashes of color, have any future in this country. The critics write I am too European; as though it is a new measurement of failure; as though decadence is outdated in Australia, and more equivalent to *decay*.

I feel more comfortable in the Modernists section.

'Chagall was Jewish,' my mother pants behind me. We stand before a large canvas depicting a village of black fences and cherry-red roofs. Its houses, trees and hedges – painted in rough, thick brushstrokes – are pushing through, climbing on top of each other, invading. I move away from this density, and from my mother. From the distance, as I breathe deep, I notice two lovers, dressed head to toe in dark clothes like mourners, floating in the spacious, yellow-green sky, high above the village. The young man with curly hair gently cups the breast of his beloved. I stare into their sad, dark eyes, finding there a reflection of their village. Perhaps they are eloping, but will they ever break free from this memory? I feel like crying. I need to be alone.

My mother grabs my arm, tight: 'Chagall was just like us, born in Russia. *Nyet*, actually it was Byelorussia. What a rotten place, I tell you. Those Byelorussians, they hated Jews so much. There were always pogroms, always pogroms. After the revolution Chagall ran away to Paris, but all he ever painted was his village. How could he, after everything they've done to us?'

She lets go of my arm only to put up a wavering finger: 'Look at these people, flying. He always painted dreams. What a big dreamer he was...to paint Russia like some fairytale. Huh! What a joke. He should have got on with his life, just like I did.'

Her voice is that of a young and slender girl now. I can picture her back in Israel, lecturing to her students: '...so I said to those Russians: "Either you let us out of this country, or I'll burn myself right in Red Square." They let us go.'

I shut my eyes, pretending she is like her voice.

My mother is truly excited. I've never observed her before in such public situations. In Israel our paths would cross mainly over nervous Sabbath dinners: *Dochenka, your dress is too short. Wash your hands. Be quiet now, papa is praying...* Even now, in my home where she is my guest, it is the same on Friday nights: *Daniel, wear this yarmulke. Hurry, let's light the candles.* She cannot calm down until the conditions are just right, the *Kiddush* wine gulped down and the bread blessed, but even then she seems busy. I snap at her more often than I would like: 'You and your God... What would you do without him?' But she just ignores me. She sneaked a photo of the late Rabbi Lubavitch into my car ('for safe driving'). On long drives I stare crankily at the holy man's austere bearded face, but feel oddly secure.

We have never just spent time together and it has never occurred to me that we could both admire paintings. I try to draw out the moment. Now it is my turn to introduce her to one of my little passions:

'See this painting? Dorothea Tanning was one of the only women surrealists in Paris in the 1920s. These surrealists, they wrote a manifesto saying a woman's job is to inspire. Women weren't supposed to paint. She's been excluded from most art books, but here she's next to Magritte. He's probably turning in his grave.' I smile at my mother.

'Tanning...' she repeats. 'Didn't she have a Jewish husband?'

I also have a Jewish husband, but we didn't have a traditional Jewish wedding. I didn't circle Daniel seven times and he didn't break a glass under the *huppa*, but instead took me to Kakadu for a honeymoon. Perhaps this is why my mother is here now, to remind us of our Jewish duties. Purposes make her happy. Chagall makes her happy, not Dorothea Tanning.

We decide to go see the Early Renaissance.

'You should have babies,' says my mother before the *Madonna and Child*. 'I told Daniel, all this painting-shmainting... My silly girl.' She pats me with her oily-fishy fingers. I shake her off:

'Mama, stop it! Let's have fun. C'mon, I'll show you Melbourne.'

It is her first overseas trip, but she is more interested in ironing our clothes and vacuuming the carpets. It is not housework she performs, but an elaborate dance. She tiptoes skillfully on her sore toes, as though if she stopped, she might cease to exist.

She says, 'I came to see *you*, you silly girl. One day you'll have your own daughter… All right, all right. Anyway, when you have your own, you'll understand.'

Melbourne grants us a beautiful day. The sun peeps green through the abundant suburban foliage and the scant wind cools our sweating bodies. I navigate between cars: 'Mama, look at the Yarra.'

Small boats glide across its glossy surface like swans.

'Very nice,' my mother nods. Her gaze is fixed on my profile. Intermittently she watches the road and reads the signs out loud: *Left to City Rd*; *Slow down, children crossing*; *Seventeen parking spots available*. Occasionally she informs me, 'The truck behind is going too fast. Careful!'

I have no idea how others manage to go for a coffee or movies with their parents. My mother was always too busy for leisurely things, preferring productive activities, like studying kabbalah, marking her students' homework, arguing with my father or cooking large Sabbath dinners.

As I keep driving, rather than enjoying the view she grooms her new pet project, Daniel's family tree: 'So his paternal grandfather was from Poland? And what did he do for a living?'

Since her arrival, I've started breaking things. The frame of my newly mounted painting. Daniel's glasses. I trod on my palette. I can't work anymore. I just want her to go. Since her arrival I've counted the hours, not the days. This is the secret I'm keeping from Daniel. My secrets are mounting, not my paintings.

Last night I pushed Daniel away. 'Have I done something wrong?' he asked.

My tears flooded his chest.

'My mother's in the other room. She's alone...'

'So what? What's the big drama? She seems pretty happy to me. Anyway, soon she'll be back with your father, babe.'

I hid my face in his body. How could I explain? How could I explain my drifting father, daydreaming with the Russian radio as his lullaby? How could I explain my mother's erratic movement, as though escaping some memory? Or her bare legs, which she'd shown only to me? Their dark-purple veins trap her like fishing net.

The night was metallic blue. Daniel's breathing had grown steady. I stood on the balcony, peering into the giant orange windows of the city's skyscrapers, bright like stars. I wished my paintings were as bold as them, dazzling the onlookers, filling them with emotion. How do you paint feelings if you're not Chagall?

I could paint the thick veins on my mother's legs and the reviewers could again praise the intricacy of their patterns, the virtuosity of my brushstrokes. But this would be just another failure.

I couldn't sell you so cheaply, Mama. I want them to see my pain. That choking pain about your aging legs. But how?

Perhaps I'll paint you as you used to be, when we rented a wooden hut in a Siberian village and in the frosty mornings my father used to drown mice in the outside toilet. You wore that red dress there, the one with puffy princess-sleeves that you'd got on the black market. You'd saved for five months and then stood before my father, your hourglass body tight-wrapped in red. *A new haircut?* he asked, then went back to his books.

I want to show my mother my iridescent, sparkling Melbourne – but instead we drive in circles.

'What else would you like to see?' I ask, casually turning the wrong direction down a one-way street. I know the answer. Something like: *All I want to see is you and Daniel. That's my greatest pleasure. Besides, of course, having grandchildren…*

'I have to see a kangaroo.'

I almost collide with a car heading towards us. Rabbi Lubavitch, with his white Santa Claus beard, promptly rescues us while giving my cleavage a nasty look.

'Your father told me before I left not to come back until I'd seen a kangaroo!'

We leave the city behind. The houses recede, the horizon yawns its grand, pink mouth, and the energy of the city lets us go. Even Rabbi Lubavitch lets go of my cleavage. I open the window, breathing in warm grass. I hope one day to transplant this smell and the endless Australian space onto my canvas. This will be my private version of pioneering, of possessing this tough land.

But perhaps, like my mother says, I'm just vain and self-absorbed.

My mother ignores the changing landscape, the low hills and small makeshift graveyards. Instead, she looks at me; I can smell her breath: 'At your age I already had two children. I wasn't so silly. I knew what was really important.'

'I'm not you. You wanted to make babies, I'm making paintings.'

'Do you think that I wanted to have children so early?' My mother diverts her hazel, perpetually intense gaze from me. 'Those were different times then. In Russia you had to bribe the Abortion Commission. We were students and didn't have the money. When we got married, they kicked us out of the university hostel.'

I stop the car. My hands are shaking: 'You never told me these things.'

She stares blankly ahead, her wig is askew.

'Why did they kick you out?'

'Because we were Ph.D. candidates, because we were too good. So they gave us the privilege of sacrificing our youth for the mother country. It was either career or marriage; no grey areas for us. We had to focus on our studies, not babies. You never understood.'

I look at my mother as though she is a stranger. For the first time I notice how smooth her skin is. Her voice is unusually smooth too, and slow. She sits very still.

'After they kicked us out, your papa sat on a bench at the bus station, not moving…it was winter, minus forty. I wandered around in a neighbouring village, knocking on doors, begging people to let us in, to rent us a room. I didn't have time to even think about an abortion.'

She sobs quietly, her fleshy cheeks shiny crimson. She wipes her eyes with one determined gesture and adjusts her wig. I want to hold her, but I can't; that's not how things are between us. When I was younger, I craved to make her happy, but she would say happiness was God's business. And perhaps this memory is just another excuse.

'Russia was no good to its people,' says my mother. 'It ate them like that Australian spider that eats its children. What's its name?'

'I don't know.'

'You know, I'm really happy for you, *dochenka*. It's different today. Your papa and I didn't have our own place in our first years together. I'm so happy…' she sobs.

I'm weighed down with her sorrow, the sorrow that has always – since I was very young – driven me away to the strangest places: kinky nightclubs, artistic communes, and eventually Australia. She has infected me with incurable restlessness. Yet now, rather than running away, I have this odd urgency to get to our original destination:

'*Mamochka*, please don't cry. Another ten minutes and we'll see the kangaroos…'

I repeat these words like mantra, then turn on some music.

'Would you mind turning it down?' asks my mother.

'Mama, remember in Russia when we listened to opera records together? You used to tell me the story of *Onegin*.'

'I can't believe you remember that.'

'I remember more: your red dress. I thought you were a princess.'

'Me? A princess? You mean your papa was a prince, always the prince – not from this world. He was so spoiled…'

'Mama! Listen…'

'Sorry, sorry. Go on.'

'*You* were like a princess. Remember? You weren't religious then. Your hair was long. You were beautiful, mama. We played piano together. Remember how I could never get it right? But you didn't care. You never cared about those things.'

My mother stares straight ahead into the snaky road, 'Who would think children could remember so well…' This time she doesn't cry.

At the Healesville sanctuary my mother limps towards the jaded spaces, her heavy buttocks moving quickly under her skirt.

'Hey, mama, look what I've got for you – seeds to feed the animals.'

'Oy, oy,' says my mother.

'Here, have some.'

'Oy, oy,' my mother keeps saying, 'If only your father could see this… a real kangaroo…in Australia…' Her eyes are glued to the smooth-skinned kangaroos as they stroll around royally. She grabs both cones from me, gathers up her skirt and, panting heavily, but determined, pushes her way through a group of school children. Her limp is severe, but the cones are steady in her hands.

'Mama, will you give me one, please? I want to feed them too.'

There is no reply.

The sky is transparent, light blue. I can see two trembling naked figures floating high above, their movements awkward and mismatched. The man resembles my young father with a head full of curly hair. He shyly covers his groin with one hand, puts the other on my mother's abundant milky breast. I can just hear her voice: *Baruch Ata Adonai… Blessed are you, God. You who has saved us from our village…* She floats suddenly upwards, then back again, sinking beneath my father, and so on, till she disappears and only her voice remains.

Baruch Ata Adonai…

Here she is, back on earth – blackskirted, sprawled frivolously like an odalisque on the humid grass, fondling the muscular bodies of kangaroos.

'What the hell are you doing?! It's dangerous!'

But she is busy talking to a fat, pale wallaby, spilling words like seeds: 'You lazy boy! Look how they've spoiled you here in Australia. You can't even be bothered coming to get your food… Come on, lazy. Come on, beautiful!' Her voice rises and rises, its music strips her of her body, of our shared memories.

'Look how sweet he is.' She points at the wallaby that has eventually accepted her invitation and is swaying towards her. She stretches out an open palm laden with food for the *lazy boy*.

I sit down, close to her: 'Mama, you're spoiling him. In case you didn't know, he's not Jewish.'

My mother smiles at me and lifts her head, glaring intensely at the summer sky, as though she too can see the floating lovers.

365
Carolyn Court

Norman sits on a chair near the window, haloed by the neon sign across the road. He looks down and watches. He can tell which night it is by how late people stay at the bar below him.

The upstairs floor of the bar building is directly across from his window. There is another bar set up on this floor but he's never seen people drinking at it. Sometimes he sees women going up the stairs. When the blinds are up there is a big aquarium visible along the windows; he can even see the movement of the fish.

The lift squeaks up the lift well. It cranks past his floor and up to the penthouse apartment. The small dogs that live up there yip in joy to see their owners and their hysterical chorale floats down the lift well.

If he looks at the building next door to the bar, the number 365 stares back at him. The number is also in neon and is arched over the door. He doesn't know what the building 365 is, but he can't help thinking that it is either a magical number or God's daily joke.

The world of the bar at 367 is only a few steps away. If there was a flying fox he could fly across and drop in, Zorro-style. It's only a thought though; he doesn't really have any interest in meeting the bar people.

Norman opens a bottle of wine from his uncle's wine collection. It seems to be the only thing to do under the circumstances. It isn't a way forward but it is a way, if not the truth and the light.

The Friday night bar noise is building. In about an hour's time it will be boiling over and will erupt into a punch or two. The people in the bar might change from night to night but they are predictable in their rhythms. The men in their tousled suits become more obnoxious and the women become bolder as they get drunker. For his own part he wishes he was looking down at barflies like the ones in the Edward Hopper picture he saw in one of his uncle's books: phlegmatic, not messy. He's not sure why he needs to look at the people in the bar at all but he is drawn to do so. Finally the voices get sparse and someone pulls the blinds down. The aquarium vanishes.

Norman squints at his old watch with its fluorescent green numbers. The time is 3.30am and time for him to sink into sleep on the couch. Green enters his eyes and blocks out everything else. He finds himself completely bathed in the light. He has woken up inside the 365 sign. In a dreamlike way he believes that it is the green of kryptonite and green lights all rolled into one. He is Superman but the kryptonite isn't hurting him. Nothing can hurt him.

Outside his building the garbos arrive and roll the recycling bins to the trucks, shouting and cursing. The glass bottles shatter inside Norman's head. He escapes the sign and drifts into the bar across the road. He slides inside and finally gets to look at the fish up close. They are tropical exotics, impossibly beautiful and colourful.

The downstairs room simmers with silence and the residue of smoke. Someone has left their scarf on a chair. It is a woman's silky scarf. He sees the open cash register. Norman feels that he is staring down from the ceiling. The furniture is small. He likes being in the bar without the other people.

In the morning he feels refreshed. When he leans his elbows on the window ledge the 365 sign is harmless and mediaeval, dull without its electricity.

The dog noises go down the lift well and out for walkies, maybe he will go out too. If you never leave home nothing happens. He read that once although he's not quite sure he agrees.

Norman enters the lift and turns the key. He is committed to his mission now and descends to the lobby. He is jolted by bumping into other people so soon.

Office workers are smoking in the doorway, staring aimlessly across the empty rubbish bins. There is a woman with dark hair and rich brown eyes. If she were in a Latin American novel she would be someone with a name and a proud character. Norman himself would be Don Quixote and his awkwardness would be an attribute. He wonders that she is reduced to the title of office worker and he is reduced to the title of weirdo with an inheritance, but that is the way things are.

He passes through the smoke and walks bravely along the street. The light is harsh and he has no sunglasses. The sounds around him are loud and he can feel them in his whole body. He is already looking forward to returning and being able to congratulate himself on leaving his sanctuary.

When he looks up he can see many signs but they are all lifeless and he wishes that he had the courage to leave his home at night, so that he might see the fairyland that the signs would create. He goes to the safe coffee shop, the one where the woman is soft-voiced and kind. Here they make him perfect coffee with a design painted in the froth. There is a small chocolate muffin which he savours.

When he walks back some girls giggle and look down at his legs. He has left his serviette tucked in his pants. There are so many things to remember in the outside world.

A pigeon is moving like clockwork, darting here and there on the road as Norman waits to cross. A hotted-up car speeds past him and over the pigeon. Norman's heart skips a beat and his mouth opens. The pigeon is left there stunned but alive. Its feathers flutter around it. The bird is a Picasso dove paralysed amongst the hurrying world. Norman cannot walk over and lift it to the footpath. If only he had the courage to go and move the bird to safer ground but he can't touch it.

He has to get home now and his pace quickens. When he reaches his building he struggles with the key and his heart beats furiously until the lift doors open and he has metal behind him. Norman wonders how people outside seem so confident and unfazed. He curls up on the couch and puts his hands over his eyes and doesn't unfurl until the sun has gone down again.

The Line
PHIL GUY

The cicadas start up and two things happen: Kirk traces lines in the telly and Pop goes out to the shed.

I used to think Pop went out to the shed because of the cicadas; because of their everywhere chorus that not even the trains out back can shush up. But this summer I see that Pop goes out to the shed only *after* Kirk traces lines on the telly. So the cicadas start up, Kirk traces his lines, Pop goes out to the shed. But why wouldn't Pop just say 'Flamin' hell Kirk, give it a rest or there'll be a kick up the blot.'

Anyway Pop is up and gone, out of his sticky black chair that doesn't like to let go in the heat. The veranda door bangs and Mum's in the kitchen making the face Mum makes when the veranda door bangs.

I'm lying on the lounge room floor between Pop's chair and the lounge with the faded pattern that Uncle Pat gave us, looking at rocks in a book of rocks. Mum says that since I'm the smart one I should know what's good for me, and keeping my nose in books is what's good for me. Our teacher Mr Timmins, he says hot air rises. That's why I'm lying. It's hot today like it was yesterday and I don't see much changing tomorrow. The cicadas love the heat because the hotter it gets the louder they sing, and if you sing louder things must be good.

Kirk is kneeling right up close to the telly. He likes to trace around big faces, like on the news. If there're no faces as big as the news he'll change the channel and trace around the biggest face he can find.

Pop works on the roads. I've never seen him at work but I've seen other kids' Pops working on the roads. I wonder if my Pop's the one who has to do all the work while other kids' Pops watch or if he gets to watch too. I figure Pop mustn't do too much watching, because he's got arms big like rope I once saw hanging off a boat at Port Phillip Bay. On one arm he's got a tattoo of a flag. It's got a cross, sort of like the one they stuck Jesus on, except with a star in the middle and at every end. Pop said it was done by a regular flamin' Albert Namatjira and that's why it's crooked.

The cicadas are singing together now, a throbbing chant you can't keep out no matter how hard you try. But there's something else too. Something I feel before I hear. It's a train. I'm nearly eleven and I've lived in this house nearly eleven years so I think I know when a train goes by. I can tell when a train's coming before Mum and even Pop. And Kirk too, but he doesn't count. Once when Aunty Bid was over, Mum got me to yell *Train!* when I knew one was coming. Aunty Bid said 'That's some talent you've got there.' Pop said 'It's no talent when there's trains goin' past like ants to jam.'

Mum's at the kitchen table cutting out squares of cellophane for stretching over her jars of plum jam. She leans back in the chair so she can see into the lounge room. 'Where's your father?' Mum says. Mum knows where Pop is, but I still have to say 'Out in the shed'. If I don't, Mum won't be able to say 'out in the shed, eh? He's happy as a box of birds out there. I'll see the box of birds when I'm grown-up, and when I do I'll say 'See Mum? Those birds aren't happy, they're sore.'

Last summer Mum was at church and Pop was asleep in his sticky black chair, so me and Kirk got one of Mum's jars of plum jam, a full one, and ate it with teaspoons. Kirk said he felt crook and I said 'You'd better not spew or we'll get busted and I'll give you the biggest Chinese burn in the world.' Mum got back from church and we pinched our noses while we ate the pumpkin soup that we have for lunch every Sunday. Kirk was looking funny but he never spewed so I didn't give him the biggest Chinese burn in the world. Mum never said 'We're short a plum jam', so we got away with it. Best of all, Mum keeps her plum jam in the same cupboard every year, so there's plum jam for me and Kirk until we're grown-ups.

I'm wondering if lying down is as good as Mr Timmins says, because down here you can see all the cat hair on the carpet. There's a cat hair on my shorts and singlet, and now I'm choosing between standing up and the heat, and lying down and the cat hair. Even though there won't be Mum's plum jam to eat when I'm grown up, at least I'll have better things to choose from than heat and cat hair.

There's no news on the telly and nothing even close because Kirk's tracing around the heads of people bent over in rice paddies. His finger barely moves as he outlines their far-away heads. I get up off the lounge room floor and brush cat hair off my shorts and singlet. I'm hungry and I go to the kitchen. Mum doesn't look up, but she says, 'Look at you all covered in cat hair.'

I ask what she's doing even though anyone can see she's covering her plum jams.

Mum says, 'I'm making your favourite – pickled onions.'

I'm supposed to pull a face and say 'gross' and then laugh, because pickled onions are the worst food in the world and I almost spewed the one time I tried them.

I open the fridge and look inside. There's not much: four eggs, half a bottle of milk, some strange green –

'What are you after?' Mum says.

'I dunno.'

'Well don't stand there with the door open.' She says. 'You'll spoil the lot.'

I shut the fridge door and try to remember what I saw. Four eggs, half a bottle of milk, some strange green –

'Mum, why don't they make fridge doors like windows? So you can see what's inside.'

Mum lifts here eyebrows. 'Could be something your father might know.'

Our house has a front yard and a backyard but no side yard because people live of the other side of the walls, and it's like that the whole way down our street. There're two bedrooms upstairs, one for me and Kirk, and one for Mum and Pop. Downstairs is the kitchen and lounge room, and a laundry with a dunny or a dunny with a laundry.

To get to the shed from the kitchen you go through a hallway that's not really a hallway to the lounge room. Then you walk through the lounge room to the back door and out onto the veranda. There are two ratty chairs on the veranda, but hardly anyone sits in them because the veranda roof is tin and when it's hot you might as well run yourself a hot bath. Also they're right next to the dunny. It's hot in the lounge room but when you go from the lounge room to the veranda you think to yourself go back to the lounge room. You can't see much from the veranda except for the trains going by, and if you want to watch the trains going by you sit in the mulberry tree.

The veranda door is slappy and will nip your heel if you're not smart. It bangs shut and Mum says, 'don't bang the door!' but it bangs no matter what. Four steps go down to the yard from the veranda. They're slats of wood, and Pop's always saying the bottom one's about to go so don't put ya flamin' foot through it. Our cat Millie lies under them on some dirt. For all her lying around in the dirt she doesn't look dirty. Mum says it's because she licks herself clean. I reckon if you're licking yourself dirty isn't half your worries.

The yard is small but there's room for two plum trees, a lemon tree and a mulberry tree. Pop used to spray the lawn for bindis, but he doesn't anymore so there's a million of them. The shed is in the back corner next to the veggie garden. You used to have to walk down the middle of the veggie garden on bricks that Pop set out like stepping stones between the seedlings. But that was ages ago. Now there's a path worn straight across from corner to corner, so you don't have to worry about stepping on the bricks anymore. I remember when pop put those bricks in, because he laughed and said 'Bugger 'em, we'll grow what we need. ' He still says bugger 'em but he doesn't laugh and say stuff about growing.

The back fence is high, higher than me. But the train line is up on a pile of rocks just as high. I don't know what kind of rocks they are, but I will soon because of my book of rocks. When trains go by it looks like they're running along the top of the fence. We can see all the people everyday, but I never see anyone that I saw the day before or the day before that. Sometimes you watch a train go by and there's no-one on it except for a face at the last window. They probably don't know that they're the only person on the train, and I reckon that's good because if you told them they'd only get lonely.

I call *Pop!* and knock and push the shed door open. He's leaning against the bench with both arms, looking down at the floor. I can't see the cigarette in his hand but I know it's there because a line of smoke goes straight up. And because of the smell. I went with Pop to the races once and I smelt like that for days.

'Don't come in,' he says. 'Sit on the step.'

Pop says, 'Them cicadas are getting awful bad.'

'Why don't you like cicadas, Pop?'

'Never said I didn't like 'em, just said they're getting awful bad.'

I reckon if someone at school said I was getting awful bad, I'd have to figure they were looking to job me. There're two shovels hanging on the wall.

'Why've you got two shovels, Pop?'

Pop says, 'You're the bright one. Can't ya figure it out?'

'For digging two holes,' I say.

'One shovel's enough for two holes.'

'But if there's two of you –'

'If there's two of you!' says Pop. 'There's hardly flaming one of you!'

He sucks long on the cigarette. Then he sighs and the shed fills with smoke. I wonder how it is that me and Pop can talk about shovels but I still don't know why he's got two of them.

Mum's sweeping her arm across the table, collecting up bits of cellophane. The jars of jam are gone from the table, and I think of them sitting in the cupboard like treasure on an island that I know all about.

'Well?' Mum says.

'Well what?' I say.

'What did your father say? About the fridge door.'

After all that I forgot to ask him. But I'm the smart one so I say something quick because that's what smart people do.

'Pop had a gob full of smoke and couldn't talk.'

'Oh he did, did he?' Mum is up quick and off through the loungeroom.

There's the fridge and I'm still hungry. Four eggs half a bottle of milk, some strange green and that's all I remember. There's also a cupboard full with Mum's plum jam. If I don't eat a whole jar, Kirk will have what's left. The veranda door's not banging so I go to the cupboard and open it. There's no plum jam only a jar of pickled onions, and now I'm not so hungry.

Brackets (the story of)
Andrew McDonald

Life is like a box of chocolates because chocolates are like a pair of brackets – you never know what you're going to get inside. We judge the meaning of sentences by what is contained within brackets and we judge ourselves by what is contained within our lives.

The information contained within a pair of parenthetical brackets can be likened to the guest at dinner parties who never shuts up – for the sake of the example, let's call him Laurence. If someone at a party is telling an amusing anecdote about, say, polygamy, will Laurence either clarify parts of the story for those not overly *au fait* with polygamous customs:

> I believe in polygamy (the practice of having more than one wife at a time). In fact I have fourteen wives (they all call him their 'husband'). I rotate them over a fortnightly period (he has a lot of sex).

Or will Laurence annoy everyone with his own irrelevant opinions and prejudices?

I believe in polygamy (you dirty bastard). In fact I have fourteen wives (someone should stop scum like you from brainwashing these women). I rotate them over a fortnightly period (things would be different if the fascists were still in power).

Bracketed information can have its benefits too. If you had a twenty-year-old son whom you had kept locked in a cupboard all his life (possibly because you were afraid he'd grow up to be a polygamist) he may have some trouble – once freed – reading, and indeed, adjusting to the real world. But brackets could help this poor chap along. For example a sentence like the one below may confound him:

'A bird flew into a tall tree where it was subsequently shot dead by a dingo with a rifle.'

But the inclusion of brackets and bracketed information may help the socially unfamiliar youngster to understand the meaning of the words:

A bird (feathery flying thing) *flew* (flied) *into a tall tree* (phallic structure made of wood and leaves) *where* ('erehw' spelt backwards) *it was subsequently* (then) *shot dead* (made to die) *by a dingo* (they're cheap this time of year) *with a rifle* (another phallic symbol).

And so the twenty-year-old retard would not get into a fix when confronted with a similar, real-life situation – thanks to the bracketing system.

But possibly the most important lesson we can learn about brackets (and there is a lot to learn [much as with polygamy {which is like a cult but with more sex<and less suicide>}]) is not to overuse them.

As we move further into the twenty-first century our adoption of the bracketing system grows stronger and stronger, but not without change. As we have evolved so has our usage of the bracket. More recently brackets have been used to express significantly profound emotions such as:

    (: and):

Whether communicating happiness at being married to numerous beautiful women or dismay at a total loss of monogamy, brackets are an undeniable part of our modern day languages and consequently, our lives. Life and death are but a pair of parenthetical brackets and what we find in between can be likened to a maxim about a box of chocolates. But maxims are a different story.

So Many Things to Think About
MARIKA WEBB-PULLMAN

(the story – setting the scene)
I am there to watch the girl with the violin.

The girl with the violin is there to play music.

I am fascinated by her. I can sit for hours before her intent stare; watching her fingers moving effortlessly over the strings, elbow see-sawing, bow sliding seamlessly. Watching the notes pour out and write themselves on the surrounding air.

(digression – one)
The human body isn't really designed to hold a violin. Have you tried?

I picked one up once.

It made me very aware of my arms, of the triangles my elbows were creating with my arms, of my chin hard against the violin, of the violin hard against my shoulder. All angles and jerky movement, arms jolting like they were being moved by something else. I felt puppet-like, maneuvered by something outside me, and was relieved to put it down again.

So Many Things to Think About

(the story – girl with the violin – part one)
I am there to watch the girl with the violin.

Her playing speaks to me in a voice louder than a thousand instruments, it calls me so that in her I can sense salvation. Of a kind.

She doesn't jolt or jerk, each movement bleeds into the next with the consistency of sugar syrup. Sweet and slow, even when she's playing fast.

I am drawn to her in a way I can't fathom. I know we are meant to connect, I know we have so many things to talk about, but often when I see her I am squirming and speechless. It makes conversation difficult.

I comfort myself with the thought that if I feel so much then of course she has to feel something; that kind of electricity can't be generated by just one person – if there is a magnetic pull to or away from something, the laws of attraction and repulsion say there is a force being exerted by that something, and that the force is equal and identical.

I know I probably can't talk about magnetic pulls without sounding naïve at best, clichéd at worst.

Yet there it is.

In a way I cannot explain we are being written together, our stories are intersecting. We are seeking each other equally and not knowing why.

(interlude – incidental character # 1)
I am there to watch the girl with the violin and I am with a friend. A close friend, so close that many assume from our ease with each other, the casual way in which we touch, that we are lovers.

She's being chatted up behind me by some guy. He's young and agreeable, by which I mean he is agreeing with everything she says.

His earnestness is touching.

My friend and I exchange frequent glances; it is a soundless touching base, a reassurance. I will save her if her eyes ask me to. He notices and, unable to decipher the true language of our gazes, he assumes we are together.

'I think your girlfriend is jealous,' he says and I turn away to hide my smile. There are many things wrong with that sentence.

I have never wanted to own anyone. I always end up shedding my possessions.

(story – little old man – part one)
I am there to watch the girl with the violin.

The old man with the ball of wool is a bonus I'm not expecting. He's tiny and bearded, neat in his navy tracksuit. I notice him first while he's dancing. Small feet shuffle across the floor, while he waves his arms in spasmodic twitches, up and down, side to side, up and down again. He moves through the space timidly, yet it is as if he belongs there and it belongs to him.

When he sits down again he sits opposite me. I don't notice the ball of wool at first, but when I do I'm surprised I missed it. It's at least six times the size of his head.

He is finger-knitting single ply wool into a thick, colourful cord that is wound into a ball. It is almost ludicrously oversized, like a prop from a movie about a giant world; a giant world where the hero is of course smaller, but proves himself to have more courage, more strength, and more heart.

(in this story the old man is the hero)
I ask him what he's doing.

'Knitting,' he replies with a sideways glance in my direction.

I ask him why.

'Breaking the world record,' he replies.

He scratches around inside his shirt for a few seconds, somewhere near his shoulder, and draws out a dirty orange piece of paper.

There are pictures of Elvis on the wall behind him.

He pushes the paper across the table to me. Written on it is a name, a date and figure …15.03 km.

'World record,' he says, motioning to the paper.

I ask him how long his ball of wool is so far.

He leans across and turns over the piece of paper, where there are a series of figures that have been crossed out. He points to the only one that hasn't been.

The little old man has 13,700 metres to go.

(digression – two)
Suddenly I find myself wanting to take the little old man home and install him in a corner of my living room. I want him to tell me his story, I don't want to make him up. I am sure his truth will have more richness and depth than anything I might be able to create for him.

I used to think it didn't matter, the distinction between real and not real. I thought a story was just a story.

I was wrong though.

(the story – girl with the violin – part two)
I am there to watch the girl with the violin. In between sets she comes and talks to me. My heart threatens to pound its way out of my chest, I am visibly pulsing. I point out the ball of wool to her. She has a hard time understanding what I am talking about – it is loud and I talk softly. Eventually I get it across, and she is suitably impressed.

She puts one booted foot on the table as we talk. Her hair is slightly tousled, she curls a strand around her finger constantly;

her fringe is cut short and uneven across her forehead. Her cheeks are the softest flesh I have ever seen, they curve from her face like the rounded bodies of question marks.

For all that she appears like a bird – a regal bird, intense gaze; an eagle, a hawk. There is also something catlike about her; a self-possession, a certain alertness. She seems equally ready to curl up or flee; she has claws.

She is strong, this girl with the violin.

The little old man senses it too. He draws closer to her, yet turns his back at the same time, as one does on a fire, wanting its warmth, but not in our eyes, upon our faces.

Not wanting to have to squint against the smoke, the melted air.

(digression – three)
I once wrote a story about my ex-girlfriend.

It is my way, you see, to write stories about the people in my life.

She doesn't see herself in the spaces the way I do, though. The place where blue eyes become blue-green, where I becomes she, where love becomes a fiction and we both walk away in the end.

She hates my story, I think.

(interlude – incidental character # 2)
I am there to watch the girl with the violin and I am also watching the door. I am waiting for another friend, who I suspect isn't coming.

If she does though, I want to show her I am looking out for her.

We have been house-sitting together, and sleeping in the same bed for the past four weeks. I have become accustomed to her form next to mine, to the way our limbs tangle together as we sleep.

I have become accustomed to the smell of her hair when my head presses against hers in the night.

She never comes.

(digression – four)
My friend is still being chatted up by the guy behind me as the band takes the stage for their second set. I don't think she really wants him, but I think she's enjoying the attention.

I have forgotten that this is what people do when they're out.

(the story – the girl with the violin –part three)
I am there to watch the girl with the violin because I have started to see her everywhere. At intersections where our bikes almost collide, on the street. Every time my body leaps a little, imperceptible to anyone watching, but it is physically jolting for me. My breath snags on my throat, possibly my heart, and I am dizzy and shaking for minutes afterwards.

When she closes her eyes as she plays, the sides of my vision blur and darken until it is only her I can see. The space around her closes in, it contracts, she pulls it all to her in one huge inhalation.

She is central, she is featured, she is swaying as she plays.

She claims that emptied space as her own in a moment if stillness then expands it with each following note and movement, her entire body attuned to the sound, from melody to demonic screeching, twitches and scratches, gentle picking and plucking at the strings.

She breathes in, breathes out and the room moves with her.

The tempo increases, her eyes opened now, intense and focused. She plays more and more frantically, there are sparks flying off her bow and becoming spiraling ribbons of light that fly across the stage, illuminating everything they touch, but nothing more brightly then her.

The girl with the violin is radiant light, she is incandescent, the air around her is dissolving and I am leaning forward on my chair, knees drawn up to my chin, arms wrapped around my legs.

I have quite forgotten where I am.

(the story – little old man – part two and the end)
Outside the air is icy.

I blow rings with my breath, and wish for a cigarette for the first time in months. My friend goes home with the boy, both of them smiling. He is triumphant, she is embarrassed.

The door opens behind me and I turn. I am hoping for the girl with the violin, but it's the little old man with the ball of wool.

He stands there shivering, holding it out to me.

'Take it,' he says, and I do.

He begins to walk away. I stand still, watching him go, feeding out the wool slowly, keeping it slack, but off the ground.

Maroon wool becomes pale blue, and then orange. Green follows the deepest red. I keep my eyes on the little old man until he turns the corner and then I stare at the ground.

I feel dazed, timeless.

Finally there is no wool left to unravel, and instantly the gentle tugging stops.

I stand outside the bar rolling the end between my thumb and forefinger, wanting to go back inside, knowing that I will not.

My hands are numb.

I start to walk, looping the wool loosely around my palm as I do. I have no idea where I'm going, but I really don't mind.

A Frangipani Friendship
Leigh Coyle

The indigo-purple sky ferments over his head as Reginald Cartwright III throws best grade mince to the birds. At the same time every day he perches himself here, on the back steps, watching feathered families come and go – fighting and procreating – stealing lives and dreams in their swirling wings as they float up and over the tin roof. Cheeky noisy mynahs, dinner-suited magpies, twisting pee-wees, and of course, butcher birds, singing songs of beauty for a few clumps of prime meat. New birds join the afternoon ritual slyly, without invitation. There may be a slight hesitation as Reggie eyes the newcomer with the challenge of acceptance. And this, in turn, could be met with a gentle head cocking side-to-side as the bird calmly stands before him examining the contents of his age-etched hand. But then, the knowledge is passed between them and they understand each other.

The step is worn and shiny where Reggie's generous bum has sat, day after day.

When the brazen bird-stranger swishes its way down next to Reggie, he is so taken aback with this detour from conformity that he slides down two steps to the concrete at the bottom, drops his mincy Tupperware container and sits stunned, watching the bird peck belligerently at the fallen food. 'What are you looking at?' the bird says rudely, flicking its tongue. With this, Reggie is compelled, more quickly than ever before, to leap up and run to the greenhouse, where soft verdant things bend and unfurl all day and stand still all night. From there, he can see the bird picking and stabbing at the reddy-brown morsels as other would-be diners stand by politely, wishfully.

Fat drops plop sporadically as the sky-vat overflows and it is only a matter of time before Reggie will become a sodden weed. So he makes the decision to rebuff this ornithological anomaly and return to the sanctity of his house, where Faye is no doubt mashing potatoes with her usual ferocity.

Through the mesh of the greenhouse walls, Reggie examines the back of the bird's glossy head as it bobs and bobs. What sort of creature is this? Am I finally as crazy as Faye reckons I am? This is *ridiculous*. Bugger it. It's just a bird, after all. Not going to be trapped here all night. I'm getting back into my house whether it likes it or not.

Breathing heavily, prepping. Reggie moves and his legs quickly become gleaming in the downpour. Thighs rub together in lightning moments, but the stairs are successfully reached and mounted. 'What's your hurry buddy?' the bird shouts out to Reggie's back as the door is slammed shut like an exclamation mark. Inside, Reggie peers out through the ten centimetre square, but the glass is dimpled like a scotch bottle and the bird appears distorted and demonic.

'Oh my god, Faye,' Reggie clutches at his chest, showering sparkles of water around the kitchen and over the clean floor. 'You won't believe what's out there – it's the devil in a brown suit!'

'What on earth are you talking about, Reggie?' Faye continues to mash the last fragments of life out of the potatoes as she rolls her eyes upward.

'It's a...tal...a...talk...a...talking bird and a real bully if the truth be said!' Reggie sputters out the words as sweat spurts from greasy pores. 'Come and see, come on!' He pulls Faye and the masher over to the door and opens it three centimetres. Out there the bird has finished its feast and sits on Reggie's shiny spot looking out at the sodden garden.

'It's just a bird, Reggie. What's all the fuss about?' Faye says in her not impressed voice. She pushes past Reggie and stands at the top of the stairs looking down. 'Shoo. Shoo. Off the step, you'll make it all dirty. Don't want nasty bird droppings on my stairs. Shoo. Shoo.' She steps down two stairs, waving the masher about. The bird turns purposefully around and calmly preens under its wings, lifting them one at a time like the royal salute. 'What a cheek – scoot! scoot!' The masher is now being brandished like a knight's sword. And with that, the bird winks at Reggie and takes off into the pepper tree at the back of the yard, disappearing into the melting leaves.

Next door on the right, shrivelled Ernie Falcon (with an extra toe on his left foot) has pruned his box hedge down to the bare branches to reveal Reggie's backyard. He maintains a network of intricately clipped peep holes in the twisted mass and with his gummy eye adhered to the spiky hedge he spies the bird taunting Reggie as it plays with a spider web like a magical harp. Ernie's back never straightens, but this is normal for him, so he stands there like an allen key, viewing the world next door through gnarled grey twigs.

On normal days, Reggie's laughter and joy mingle with outdoor sounds which drift through the box hedge leaving Ernie breathless and overwhelmed by their strange perfume – heady with memories of past times when the two men would chat for hours under the poinciana tree; dual time pieces shiny with good home cooking and a shared love of green things. This was before the sickness came and took dear Cynthia away and Ernie could not be dissuaded from believing that the birds had caused all the trouble, scattering lice like chemical weapons, making Cynthia's air impure, tarnished; collectively creating heavy weights at the bottom of her lungs which pulled her down so at the end she lay limply on the bed pinched by the burden.

With narrow eyes, Ernie watches the bird fly into the trees.

The next morning, Reggie is woken earlier than usual by a tap-tapping at the window. Under the raised venetians, he blinks with crusty eyes at the sparkling beady bird eyes on the other side of the glass. 'Good morning sailor,' it sings in a shrill but friendly tone. 'How're they hanging?' Reggie shuts his heavy lids, closes shop. Then opens up again. And the bird is still there. Staring right at him. Reggie drops the blind down, then moves backwards, fast. He strides out of the bedroom in slippered feet and marches to the back door. Then he stops, eye to the dimpled glass and spies the bird sitting in *his* spot, waiting.

Deep breaths again, for courage this time, not speed. Reggie opens the door and faces his nemesis.

'What took you?' The bird examines Reggie's puckered yellow dressing gown with distaste. With that, Reggie's fleshy legs buckle under his ample bum and he crumples inside his dressing gown, fallen like an enormous frangipani, wrinkled hands held to his throat.

But that is not the end of him. When his eyes twitch open some time later, Reggie notices his body is covered with small sticks and pieces of soft moss and a red and yellow butterfly is poised like a ballerina where the dressing gown cord is tightly knotted over his tummy. He looks around for the bird, but it is not there. A feeling of soft tranquillity washes over him as the butterfly kisses his cheek and floats away on the breeze.

From then, Reggie and the bird come to their own understanding. In the afternoons, the other birds stand back discreetly, while Reggie and the bird gossip about the neighbourhood and laugh at politicians. In the mornings, their special time, they walk together down the street to the park and watch babies take their first steps, as exultant parents croon and squeal. They become luminaries – man and bird – the pudgy man in wrinkled trousers and singlet, accompanied by the swirling, diving, graceful bird, wings gleaming in the sunlight and an air of proprietary. People gather in clusters to watch the two take the air and the local paper sends out a reporter to scoop this latest nature-loving story. The bird preens its feathers especially for the front page photograph and they both smile discreet smug smiles of togetherness. The bird takes Reggie to secret damp places where bright things grow greenly. They marvel at the flat black creatures hiding under rocks, scurrying in the same direction when sunlight strikes their backs.

When not at his hedge-side post, Ernie creeps up to the back of his own yard where the malting white oak sends small yellow parcels on the air. The effort is worth it. From here he has an unrestricted view of Reggie and the bird; looking down-yard to his neighbour's back steps. Ernie packs a small esky for this journey and sits on the tufty hill munching egg sandwiches as he massages blood into his arthritic knees. Once when he sits there, the bird flaps over Ernie's head in a holding pattern, around and around on the same plane, in an ever diminishing circle. Filmy white feathers drop like soap flakes onto his head and he feels his back snap straight for the first time in forty years. His anger peels away in layers, until only the soft pink parts are left and he finds himself searching for the bird with unusual feelings of respect.

Straight-backed Ernie spends idle hours standing at the side fence, examining the pointy tops which he has been unable to see for so long. And to watch Reggie and the bird. Today, Reggie purposefully strides over to the fence, with a beatitude only a bird-friend can have and offers Ernie a staghorn and air-fern, fresh from his green-house.

'Here you go mate (the plants are thrust into Ernie's surprised hands). Good to see you up and about again. It's been a while since I've seen you in the garden.' Reggie reveals frighteningly pristine teeth. The words seem fresh despite a use-by date long surpassed. With a quiver and leaning backwards some distance, Ernie nods in acceptance of the situation.

'Yeah...feeling pretty well these days...' Ernie glances in the direction of Reggie's jasmine, where the bird plucks nonchalantly at a caterpillar, which is making its tortuous way to greener pastures. 'I seen you two out here together. Buddies hey?' Ernie fidgets with the fronds and disappears for a moment in his thoughts. 'Remember that old cat of mine? Polystyrene? Buggered if I know why Cynth called her that. She drove me crazy with all her scratching and sniffing. Used to tear dirty big patches right off her elbows. And wouldn't leave me alone. Not for a second. Ended up having her sleep in the bed with me, though it would've made old Cynth turn in her grave... Yeah, miss her sometimes.' Ernie's voice grinds to a halt and he stands breathless watching the bird fly above the pomegranate.

Two sets of eyes watch the ants' endless trail along the fence as they wait for the moment to pass.

'Anyway, how're the knees Ernie? Still using that infrared light you rigged up?' Reggie rearranges his cap, until he's sure Ernie has recovered sufficiently from his previous soliloquy.

'Oh, don't worry about me mate. It's the only thing that works. Can't complain.' Ernie gazes at his crazed watch and blinks twice. 'Look at that. Dinner time. Have a hot dinner these days and just a light supper. Better get that chicken out before she's all shrivelled. Thanks for the plants mate. I'll put 'em near the door so as I'll be sure to water 'em.'

Ernie creeps off into his bruised house, a shuffling frond-laden shadow merging to black. The bird drops frangipani flowers in each of Ernie's boggy backyard footsteps, fluttering to and from the tree like a process line until the last one is gently placed at the bottom of his peeling back stairs. Then Reggie and the bird go home to let the afternoon wash over them.

But then, the next sharp black day, the bird doesn't come. No tap-tapping on the window. No walk to the park to watch the babies teeter. No afternoon best-grade mince. Instead, Reggie stands quietly at the back door and stares out while inside Faye mashes her way through the day. The clock marks time in short spasms. Ernie stands at the side fence sky-gazing, studying each branch for a sign and the other birds congregate beside the hills-hoist clearing a flight-path for the waited-one. No bird.

That night, no bird. The next day, no bird. And for days and nights and days and nights, no bird.

Until.

2:40am on a cold Thursday night in August and the street dozes in the moonlight. Black-teeth houses in a black smile, separated by a tongue of bitumen. Trapped snores and dreams bouncing about inside. And a flicker of red light at Ernie's window.

At first, Reggie doesn't recognise the tap-tapping as anything more than a frantic heartbeat in a dream chase, but then he slides into reality and (after carefully slotting feet into slippers) dashes to the venetian blind and reveals Ernie's house fringed with red against the blackest of all skies, clouds puffing up into the fig tree.

'Oh...my god!' Reggie darts across the cimmerian lawn and springs up and over the fence into Ernie's yard. He grabs something flaccid off the clothes-line and with unusual strength breaks open the back-door. Assuming a commando-style crawl position he slides along the floor over which the smoke hovers like dwarf storm clouds, taking a shocked split-second to find he has Ernie's faded underpants pressed to his face. He slithers along the hall like a just-fed anaconda, but with arms grabbing at the floor boards ahead, wishing the house to move to him. At the front room, an ominous silence. A warped closed door hiding truths and memories and a jerry-built infrared bulb gone berserk.

Later, the firemen find Ernie, the oldest foetus in the world, clutching his knees behind the sofa; on the window ledge, two charred plant pots search for the sun.

Accidental death. But he was old afterall.

And on the butchered box hedge in Ernie's backyard, blackened Reggie finds the bird, limp and damp. Unnecessarily cold in the bright winter light. Wings calm, all songs sung. Grasping the bird to his dressing-gowned chest, he closes his eyes so he can fly and finds himself soaring over the street, a chenille-winged bird of unknown species viewing the world below in ever widening circles.

George Robertson Was
HELEN ADDISON SMITH

On the day George Robertson was born, rain hit the hosptal windows like gnats, and George Robertson's mother was in the lift, screaming. The lift was going down and she was going down too, her knees collapsing under her scream. Her blood washed the floor. That scream froze the heart of the nurse who was holding her hand, and froze the mechanism of the lift too. So George Robertson was born on the floor of a lift going down that wasn't going down anymore.

The nurse's name was Elaine, and her part in George Robertson's life was as short as she was, five foot one in white spongy-soled shoes. She took George Robertson out of his mother, and as she did so, she took in a gasp of air. For he was a little black baby. Not black skinned, but covered in a thick fur of black hair. Nurse Elaine grasped the tiny baby by his tiny heels, and when he cried, she put him on George Robertson's mother's breast and whispered, 'Don't forget he's your son'.

George Robertson's mother's second scream unfroze the mechanism of the lift, and soon she was being trollied to Recovery for light sedation.

George Robertson's mother got used to her hairy little baby. She even learned to pat the little monkey while he was breast-feeding. She would look down on him and smile and stroke his shiny fur. But George Robertson's father didn't like the hairy baby, a monkey at his wife's breast. He didn't like it, but he couldn't forget it. And it was because he couldn't forget that sight that he never touched his wife's breasts again. Instead, when George Robertson's father was on top of her, he would grab one of George Robertson's mother's plump biceps in each hand and pinch them, hard.

On the advice of doctors, George Robertson's parents gave him medicine from a bottle and all his hair fell out. George Robertson's mother gathered it together and put in a plastic snap-lock bag. She put this bag in her top drawer, under her best black underwear.

George Robertson's first word was 'Fuck'. He said it to his mother's mother, ninety-three years old, an old paper bag of a woman, scrunched together in a polyester dress belted tightly at the waist.

'What a beautiful baby!' she'd said, sticking her witchy finger in the cot.

'Fuck,' replied George Robertson. 'Fuck you.'

That was George Robertson's first kill, although grandmother didn't die straight away. When George Robertson said 'Fuck', grandmother had just a small seizure, a tick of her eye and a flap of her arms, but a tiny hole had opened up in her brain, and blood flowed in and in a couple of days, she died. She had had a good innings, though she had been bored like fuck most of the time.

The second person George Robertson killed was his older brother. Nathaniel Robertson was a blond boy with a quiff of hair as tight as a fist. He was a bully. He would tell George that they were going to play hide-and-seek and George should go and hide and he would find him. And then he never would. George Robertson's mother would eventually have to go and find George once the sun had gone down. He'd be under the house, not crying, not until his Mum pulled him out and gave him a hug. They would hug in the backyard under the banksia tree and his mother would cry too for the bully that her first son had become.

One day, it was a fine day, George and Nathaniel Robertson were playing Cowboys and Indians. George was the cowboy because Nathaniel wanted to wear the feather head-dress his father had bought him. Nathaniel told George, 'I am the Indian and you have captured me and now you have to hang me by the neck until I'm dead.' So George went into the shed and got some rope. Nathaniel went into the house and got a chair. Nathaniel stood on the chair. George made the noose. Nathaniel tied the noose to the tree branch with a double-handed half-hitch he'd learnt at Scouts. Nathaniel told George, 'Take the chair away.' George did, and when Nathaniel went blue in the face and kicked his legs about, perhaps George thought he was still only playing.

Then George Robertson went inside and did his piano practice. He played *Für Elise* all the way through three times with no mistakes and his mother said that it sounded very nice. His mother asked him to call Nathaniel for dinner. And it was then that George Robertson told her that he thought Nathaniel might be dead.

The coroner came back with a finding of suicide.

'I didn't think he was *that* unhappy,' George Robertson's mother cried into her white handkerchief. Nathaniel's teachers and doctors had offered evidence of behaviour, bad behaviour, setting animals alight, torturing other children, putting razor blades on chairs, and so on. 'Psychopathic tendencies,' the family doctor said, a face on him like a day in court. By the end of the inquest, everyone was a little bit glad that Nathaniel was dead. They all left the building with smiles inside them somewhere secret.

Everyone, that is, except George Robertson's father. He cried for his bully of a son and went down the pub and drank beer and strong spirits that scratched his throat on the way down and on the way back up again too. Then he stormed home with the footpath rolling under his feet. And as he walked his mind felt a great weight growing in it, squeezing his thoughts together into a hard little ball, and that ball was his fist, and when he walked through the door that fist fell into George Robertson's mother's face. Again and again while George Robertson pressed his face into his mother's waist and they cried together again. Then George Robertson's father told them, 'Wait here' and rolled out towards the shed. George Robertson grabbed his mother's hand and pulled her smeared face into the bedroom. He ran over to the big lattice-work trunk at the end of his mum and dad's bed. He threw out all the sheets in big white puffs and he and his mother climbed inside the trunk and shut the lid. Bang.

The slivers of light in the trunk lit up George Robertson and his mother, and they stared at each other as they breathed each other's breath. It was quiet, so quiet that George Robertson could hear a ringing in his ears like a far-away cicada, and he turned over and cuddled his back into his mother's front and felt her stomach panting up and down.

George Robertson's father's footsteps on the floor were as heavy as hobnailed boots. The breath whistled out through George Robertson's father's nose, and there was the sound of something metal being dragged across the floor. And George Robertson's father shouted, 'Where are you? I'm not going to hurt you.' And then George Robertson's father's bum sat down loudly on the lid of the trunk. 'Where are you?' he said again, but softer and more blurry this time, and his breathing was more blurry too. George Robertson and his mother heard the clatters and the thumps and the snores that told them that George Robertson's father had fallen over, asleep, on top of the trunk. And soon George Robertson and his mother fell asleep too. Inside the dark bedroom, the whole family slept together.

The next morning, George Robertson's father got up off the trunk and went off to work. After his car had shuddered its goodbye, George Robertson and his mother got out of the trunk and went their separate ways.

That night George Robertson's mother cooked chops and mashed potatoes and peas for dinner.

And George Robertson's father asked for tomato sauce.

And George Robertson's father asked for mustard.

And George Robertson's father said the chops were burnt.

And George Robertson's father didn't eat any of his peas.

And George Robertson's father drank a glass of stout.

And George Robertson's father took the spade back out to the shed.

And George Robertson's father sat down in front of telly and watched current affairs.

And apart from George Robertson's mother's fractured cheekbone, two cracked ribs and broken arm, everything was normal again.

George Robertson looked at his father differently after that night in the trunk, or rather, he didn't look at him at all, not at his face anyway, never anything above the breast pocket on his shirt. George Robertson bided his time. He breathed in and he breathed out, like he had in the trunk. He practiced the piano, though not *Für Elise*. He went to school and he came home.

One day, George Robertson got a new friend. Robert George was a very white boy, with freckles that chased each other down his arms. His gold hair trickled and curled down his back. His mouth was red and wet, like a just-sucked lolly. He laughed easily and he laughed a lot, when the bullies took his bag, and when the sports master kicked him in his stomach. He kissed George Robertson in George Robertson's shed, where they were making a model aeroplane together, and they ate each other up. George Robertson let Robert George put his lolly mouth all over him, even though he knew his father would be coming home any minute.

It was five-thirty in the afternoon when Robert George put a hard part of George Robertson in his mouth.

It was five-thirty-two when George Robertson started groaning.

It was five-thirty-six when George Robertson's father entered the shed.

It was five-thirty-seven when George Robertson's father felt something bursting in his chest.

It was five-thirty-eight when Robert George spat something milky on the ground.

It was five-thirty-nine when George Robertson's father finally stopped staggering around and fell on the floor.

It was six-twenty-five when George Robertson's father was pronounced dead. The ambulance had been delayed.

George Robertson knew better than to smile at his dead daddy looking at the ceiling like it was all a big surprise. He knew better than to hold Robert George's hand in front of other people, too. And he knew that he should hug his mum as his dad was being zipped up, so he did just that. He knew that if he buried his face in his mother's neck, his laughing shoulders would look like he was crying. So he did that too.

Soon George Robertson's dead daddy was a long-dead daddy, and George Robertson and his mother had lots of hugs and kisses. Sometimes George Robertson's mother would call out in the night and he would come into her room and sleep in her bed, not under the covers, she wasn't having that. George Robertson would curl up on the end of the bed, like a cat. He'd put his nose on his knees and sleep to the sound of his mother's breath, and when he'd wake up in the morning he'd be alone.

She'd be in the kitchen making him a high-fibre breakfast. He'd eat it all up before going off to art school where he'd paint pictures of Nathaniel, his granny and his daddy, in heaven and in hell.

On the day George Robertson turned nineteen, the sun was shining as bright as a lightbulb. George Robertson and his mother sat at the kitchen table in the sunshine and spooned bran and prunes into their mouths. George Robertson's mother put her spoon down and took him by the hand and stared into him, eye to eye.

'I'm leaving you, George,' she said. 'I've lost my mother, my husband and my son. I'm going to India. I want to find God and I hear he is there. You can have the house. Don't try to contact me.'

George Robertson started to laugh and only stopped properly three days later when he dropped her off at the airport, when he started to cry instead.

George Robertson came home and fell down on the couch and cried for poor him, all alone. And then he got on the phone and invited all his friends around for a party. 'My mother's left me,' he said. 'I need cheering up.'

The party went for two nights and two days. George Robertson's friends dressed up in their tight and glimmering best and descended into every corner of the house. They brought George Robertson presents of clear liquors and white powders and brightly coloured pills. And George Robertson put them all in his body until he felt radiant. Music pumped like from a heart. His mother's furniture, the brown velvet couch, the walnut veneer side tables, the doily-covered television, were pushed out into the street and everyone danced shoeless and swaying. George Robertson danced in the middle of the crowd, waving his hands like a revivalist. As each new person arrived, they'd kiss George Robertson. Sometimes those kisses would grow long and George Robertson could feel himself melting into the kisser. And then they would have to go into the bathroom and fuck like they were drilling for oil. Tits, cocks, tongues, all the bits and pieces. By the end of the party, as the last survivors wandered away into the blue day, there was no part of him that hadn't been wet.

*

It was the most aggressive case of Crohn's disease that he'd ever seen, the specialist told George Robertson. His chronic diarrhoea was just one symptom. Then there were the fistulas, small tunnels that were opening up from George Robertson's colon to the skin, allowing seepage of faecal matter. And there was already some infection. And there would be more fistulas coming, as inexorably as birthdays. The next thing was internal bleeding. And then there would be surgery. They'd remove part of his colon. His lifestyle would be, the doctor said as he stared at the desk, seriously compromised. But he shouldn't blame himself. He'd done nothing wrong.

'An act of God, if you believe in such things,' the doctor smiled.

George Robertson came home and lay on his couch and stared out the window at the roses his mother had planted. He rang his friends, one by one, and told them the news. Gasps were gasped, tears were cried, and promises to see him soon were made. 'I'm going to throw a fistula party,' George Robertson said, and his friend laughed, but not for very long.

But George Robertson didn't throw a party and he didn't see his friends soon. Sometimes they would ring, but he couldn't go out to the bar, or the club, or the cafe. Soon he couldn't even get off the couch. His house started to smell and if he did manage to keep one of his friends on the phone, all he could talk about was his guts.

The last person George Robertson killed was himself. The phone hadn't rung for seventeen days when George Robertson took the prescription bottle out of the bathroom cabinet. He took a cut-crystal glass that his grandmother had given his mother, and took the gin bottle out of the freezer. George Robertson swallowed and swallowed again.

On the day George Robertson was buried, rain hit George Robertson's tombstone like gnats. The bruised sky rumbled and shouted at his friends as they hurried away. They drove in their old cars to a smart pub, and they got drinks with ice, and they talked about George, and said they were sorry for his disease, and admitted to each other they hadn't seen him for a while, and they wondered why his family weren't at the funeral and they asked why such a terrible thing would happen to someone. The ashtrays filled up and the barmaids took them away.

And then night fell, and at George Robertson's grave his mother stood, in cheesecloth. She looked at the inscription on her son's tombstone. It read in letters like a newspaper headline 'George Robertson Was'.

Her eyes were dry. And she whispered to herself, 'George Robertson Is. George Robertson Is Dead.'

Blood Drunk
ADAM BROWNE

The day I ask Josephine out is the same day the media first mentions the virus – just a curiosity piece in a couple of the papers. It gives us something to chat about during our early awkward dates. I think the story is an urban myth, but she's not so sure. I press the point – even on a biochemical level it seems unlikely, I say: a disease that renders serum fats into glycerine, then generates nitrates from urea, then blends the two compounds in the correct ratio… If it's real, I say, it must be a *very* smart virus. She nods reluctantly, deferring to my training, but I can tell she's not convinced.

Things progress. The development of our romance coincides with reports of further deaths. The accounts are more credible now, the nature of the disease becoming clearer. The news pieces, though brief, have a more serious tone. The commentators who continue to doubt the reality of the virus start to sound a little shrill. Some claim the victims are suicide bombers, although they certainly don't fit the profile: a Scottish minister of parliament; a househusband in Canada; a girls school ice-hockey team in Laugaradlur, Iceland.

Then one morning I wake and realise, just like that, that I believe.

Josephine was right. I'd simply been afraid to face it before. This thing is real.

I begin reading virology journals. Those researchers who give the virus credence are still in the minority, but the number is growing. There are debates about whether it's a bioweapon or not — it seems impossible that such a thing could evolve on its own. I read papers suggesting it's a rhinovirus, transmitted in coughs and sneezes. Then others speculating it's like an explosive variant of Ebola, transmitting itself in the aerosolised spray of blood and bone produced in the victim's final moment. Later, it turns out both models are correct.

A new phrase comes into use: 'blood drunk', referring to the disease in its early stages. I see a television documentary about the brave epidemiologist who wore the body armour of a bomb disposal engineer to isolate nitrous oxide from the blood of patients. The theory is that it's a byproduct of the nitrogen reactions generated by the virus, producing dizziness, euphoria etc.

But we've always been blood drunk, Josephine says over dinner one night. All this is nothing new, she says, a little drunk herself. She feels no different now to how she's felt all her life, she says. I remember she spent part of her childhood in Belfast. Her father died there, she'd told me that early on. She's always felt the need to keep her head down, she says, to keep out of the crosshairs of history — the difference now is we no longer need bombs to blow ourselves up. The arms manufacturers must be furious, she says, laughing, but then the laughter turns to sobs, and I take her home. That night we sleep together for the first time.

The next morning we see a news article that indicates the virus is non-species specific. The term is *zoonosis* – transmission between humans and animals. There are reports from South America, some obscure seabird. Olrog's Gulls, dying in sad little blood-and-feather bursts over the South Atlantic.

Then, later that week, it's the gastric-brooding frogs. Shots on TV of entire colonies going up like Chinese New Year in the depths of the Queensland rainforest. Next day, it's the cattle. Herds of them hamburgered in nasty chain-reaction cluster-blasts, meadows turned to cratered moonscapes smelling of blood and barbecue.

And suddenly things are going downhill fast. We're at the steep end of the curve. More and more species, a global epidemic. Attempts to create a vaccine are unsuccessful or disastrous. The economy falters, not just here, but world-wide. Those countries not in a state of denial are in a state of emergency. Looting, rationing of food and water. It feels like the end of the world.

Josephine moves in with me. My house is bigger, better security, should that become an issue. I'm sick with dread – but Josephine is oddly cheerful. She has a kind of happy fatalism. She's more relaxed than I've ever seen her, despite suffering a miserable head-cold.

And after a while I begin to find her mood infectious. I relax into a feeling of luxurious resignation. When, soon after, I see my first actual example of the disease (it's in the garden, a flock of cabbagemoth butterflies disappearing in a brief wet-crackle cascade) it seems almost festive. Childhood memories of cracker-night.

A few days later, we go upstairs to watch the sunset from my balcony. I've got Josephine's cold by now, and should be feeling wretched. The sky is beautiful, reminiscent of that time back in the '90s when Mount Pinatubo made the dusks so spectacular. Birds wheel clamorously overhead, sparrows, swallows and mynahs returning to their nests. I turn to look at Josephine. She's swaying a little in her seat – as, I realise, am I. Have we been drinking? – I can't seem to recall.

I take her hand, tell her I love her, but the words are lost under a series of explosions from above. Charred feathers over the balcony. Another flock detonates in an elm nearby, wet thunder, pyrotechnics backlighting the foliage. In the yard next door, a labrador barks, frightened – dogs are always afraid of fireworks – until, with a big boomy bloodburst, he's gone too. Things are speeding up, I say, and Josephine nods abstractedly. I see all the trees are burning, on my property and up and down the street, autumn colours bright among the branches. But Josephine's more interested in the lawn, which is alive with flashes of blue light; cicadas, I guess, popping merrily, their little deaths lighting the dark. Now the air itself is sparkling – mosquitoes flaring in pretty little glitter-twinkles – is it *our* blood that has infected them? A fruit-bat is spinning by, spewing Catherine Wheel flames, when we hear a big roar from down the street. A house has gone up – then another – the smoke smelling of Sunday roasts, and the street is awash with blood, calligraphic rivulets bright-burning blue, and suddenly Josephine and I are naked to the bonfire night and laughing as we make sick-giddy love, the virus taking us closer and closer.

The Honey Machine
Rose Mulready

Synge is the pediment, and Lotta is the ornament. He is loaded down with all kinds of instruments: drums and glockenspiels, bells and cymbals. He blows into flutes, saws his mouth over a harmonica. His feet are shaggy, like a monster. On his shoulders he carries the frame of the trapeze. And she is up there, singing. She teeters and swoops, toes pointed; she swallows fire.

The act is called the Honey Machine. His name for it. She is his third girl. The first girl got pregnant. He won't say by who. The second girl fell and broke her leg. He found Lotta at the border, trying to cover her breasts, the guards laughing. He offered her room in his caravan and taught her the high wire. She has papers now. She can leave any time.

Synge has a face like a stone idol. His lids are smooth and heavy and he's always smiling just a little. He wears a heavy jade dragon around his neck. Girls are always asking about the dragon, its cultural significance. It's an excuse for touching him.

They pick it up with light fingers, testing the warmth of his chest. And Lotta stands there in her comet-white costume, starving to death.

Synge is very strict about her diet. He says he has to carry the whole show and if she puts on even one pound she'll cause him an injury. He says she's too heavy as it is. She balances on her bunk, trying to see in the high-up mirror. Nubbed bone and string; but he pinches her hip as she comes down from the trapeze and says no supper tonight. You're breaking my back.

Every festival they play, miles of food. Sugar air, meat sizzle whisper, voices calling ice cream. From the trapeze she sees food colours, floss-pink and red-hot, yellow-squirt, ahhh. Her mouth raw with kerosene.

He is leaning against the caravan, still in his shaggy boots, his overalls pulled to his hips. Three girls from that night's town. Milk-and-honey tits. Heart-shaped charms on their musical wrists. Lotta the wolf in the shadows. Or not even. Some ridden-out dog.

She practises her arabesque.

Blue stifling nights, the height of the season. She puts her powdered foot in his hand and hoop-la! up to her perch. He is stamping, bells on his ankles. Bellowing drum on his back. His teeth clench the mouth organ, haw! The flute whimpers. She gets a good swing up. Singing in bursts. Giddy pirouettes. The stars reel around her head. He is the pediment, so she must be the goddess. She blows fire, pffff! Tonight she isn't coming down.

And so she sings all the songs about honey in a mean gravel voice, all the ones she can think of, on and on. And Synge has stopped playing, he is calling for her to stop, stop Lotta! Stop you stupid and she triple flips, turning like a drill above him, singing (you better put some sugar in my bowl) until he moans and falls on his knees, the drum punctured.

Lotta jumps off lightly, preens. The crowd applauds uncertainly. She walks over to the crepe stall, adjusting her ruffled plumes, and orders herself a dozen Suzette, with cream.

Fith
Mischa Merz

Rory could hit like a cunt. And I mean that in a positive way, don't get me wrong. He really had it. He showed no fear and no mercy, which is exactly how it should be, believe me. You need that ruthlessness in the fight game. That's why he was the champ. Things have changed of course. You can't be a cunt in life as well. People tire of it. Even those who love you.

But at one time it was the cunt in him that everyone wanted to see. And I'm not being gratuitously vulgar using that word either. It's a legitimate word in boxing. Everyone knows what it means. It's more succinct than 'killer instinct', which, to my ear, is a little too euphemistic. The word 'cunt' has that guillotine snap, like the crack your neck makes when someone hits you with a good left hook.

Everyone who ever laced on a pair of gloves will have been told at some stage that aside from being quick, fit, smart, brave, strong, cunning and resilient, you also need a bit of cunt in you. In fact, you can never have too much of it. Except in life.

Those who know how to tuck that side of themselves out of sight, when they don't need it, are the ones who survive. I mean in life. Not the fight game. But people do like it when you're a cunt inside the ropes.

And when Rory was inside the ropes they felt the vicarious glory of his destructive powers, they were in love with his grace and his rage in equal measure because he was a craftsman too, don't forget. But once retired, they eventually realized that what made him great was also something pretty loathsome. I don't know why anyone was surprised when he hit the bottle.

There's a truckload of goodwill if you come home with a big gold-encrusted championship belt, as Rory did. But it didn't take him too long to use most of that up. There are just so many blokes' wives you can feel up, just so many people you can insult, just so many times you can turn up drunk and in a shambles to occasions held in your honour. And the cold shoulder from a crowd of admirers can be pretty icy. Personally, I was never one to go looking for heroes to worship. I knew what he was. I mean as a man. In boxing and in life. I'd seen the bloke up close.

Rory used to come spar us amateur boys in his heyday. We had to wear big pillowy 16oz gloves that made us look like clowns, while he had his sleek, compact fighting mitts on that made him faster and made his fists feel like hammers, as if he even needed the advantage. But that was him. He was a cunt through and through. He wasn't interested in even pretending that we were equal to the task of sparring him or that he might need to adjust to our lesser skills. Some fighters are like that. They won't turn up the volume unless it's for real and there is something at stake. But Rory beat all our heads in one after the other just for the hell of it until we were like a shrunken, demoralised army that had marched too long on no food and in boots that gave us blisters.

There were plenty of tears. Oh yeah. But private, choked up changing-room tears that no one ever acknowledged although we all heard them. Personally, I preferred to save mine for the car. I'd drive home with an aching jaw and a lacerated mouth and floaters in my vision and caked blood in my nostrils, which I would loosen with tears. Globs of blood and snot would be smeared on my track top as I wiped with one arm and steered with the other. They were not, however, tears of pain, at least not the kind of pain most people are familiar with. We all could take physical pain, you get accustomed to that, to the thuds and the sharp stings and snaps. It was the humiliation that got to us. It was the realisation that our daily, arduous grind, our early morning roadwork, the repetition of practicing our combinations, the sit-ups, the push-ups, the high-jumps, the burpees, the padwork, the bagwork, the dieting, the unending disparaging criticisms from the trainer; none of all that had got us even close to feeling capable when Rory shaped up to spar. We felt like plodders. And he didn't even have to try. He had what they called 'natural talent'. And great lung capacity. Funny to think that the fuel for such terror is the benign air that everyone breathes.

At first, when they brought him in, I didn't recognise him. The lean, greyhound, junior lightweight frame had blown out to light heavy. He'd gone soft and puffed and pitiful, his skin like crepe paper, white and fragile.

When I felt his body, because he needed my help to walk to his room, it was fat and hard, as if it was full of fluid. He smelled of aftershave and beer and had dried blood caked in an ugly lump on his forehead. He didn't recognize me either, of course, but then I had been able to read the name on his admission form before I looked a little more closely. The part of him that still looked familiar was that horrible little Hitler moustache that he grew in the 1970s, probably to make himself look older because he was just nineteen when he won the title. But it was still there and made him look like some bloated white supremacist. And he had the same eyes too. Those killer eyes, arctic blue and dead like a shark's. When he spoke his thoughts were too fast for his thick tongue and it seemed to trip over his teeth.

'Hey, mate, whazzup?' he said, trying to focus on my face.

'Rory 'the destroyer' Cooper,' I said, 'IBF junior lightweight champion.'

'Not no more mate,' he said, 'now I'm a fucking champion of stupidity.'

'Let's get you cleaned up,' I said and helped him to the bathroom.

As I watched him stagger in that special way that alcoholics have, as if they are trying to walk on a vibrating floor, I recalled the speed with which his feet carried him around the ring, the superb balance that allowed him to change direction suddenly and punch from such a range of angles it felt like you were fighting three men, not one.

'He could hit you on the soles of your feet while you're skipping,' I remember my old trainer joking as he watched another of his rising stars hit the deck.

And there he was at the bathroom sink looking a little unsure where the soles of his own feet actually were. He splashed his face with water and took off his black shirt which he let fall to the floor. I picked it up and put it on the back of a chair.

'You know my problem mate,' he said, 'Everywhere I go, people want to buy me a drink. I never have to pay for a drink myself, ever. It's all free, mate. Can't knock back a free beer can ya?' he said.

'Guess not,' I said, remembering the reaction when he won the title and all the people who had come to the airport to greet him and pat him on the back, all the kids who had run beside him along gravelly roads on barren suburban estates where he trained. New suburbs full of brown brick veneer houses and cul-de-sacs waiting for more to be built. Flat paddocks of drying grass. I remember seeing his lean, gaunt face on TV before the fight, saying he couldn't wait to get in that ring.

I left him to have a shower and went and had a chat to Doig, the director of nursing.

'What's with Cooper?'

'The old pug?'

'Careful. He's the same age as me.'

'Gawd. Is he?'

'I mean I can see that he's been drinking, but.'

'Official diagnosis, darl, is FITH.'

'FITH?''

'Fucked In The Head. Sorry, I know this job's full of acronyms.'

'He seems ok now.'

'Darl, he's very much not ok. He's very fucking FITH. Call it depression and a bit of OCD and personality disorder if you want to get technical, and I know you like all that stuff. But to me, he's FITH.'

Doig delivered everything in the same deadpan way. She knew I was interested in improving myself and she'd leant me some books. She called everyone 'darl', a byproduct of looking after so many FITH people over the years, I suppose.

'Just get him cleaned up, into bed, ok darl?'

'Ok, darl,' I said and she did a double take.

I went back to Rory's room. The bathroom door was closed and the water was still running.

'You OK in there, champ?'

There was no response so I went in. He was sitting down on the tiles under the running water, hugging his knees like a frightened kid. I turned off the tap.

'What's up mate, you get tired did ya?'

He looked at me for a second or two as if he was trying to recall me from all those sparring sessions. But I don't think he'd have any clue. We were all just bodies to him, guys trussed up in protective gear that made no difference. Those big helmets just made our heads a bigger target for him.

'I'm the champion of stup-fucking-pidity,' he said.

'Well, good for you. Better than not being the champion of anything at all, like me.'

'You can teach a bloke most things.' He began what sounded like a familiar speech. 'You can teach someone how to run and punch and skip. But you can't teach a young bloke how to handle success. I couldn't handle it, mate, couldn't handle the success.'

'Well, then. You don't have to worry about that any more.'

Rory had dished out the punishment when he came to our gym, but I had my whipping boys too and my small successes as well. You'll find eventually that there is always someone you can physically dominate and in the end it might not be so much about strength as it is about character. And when you realise that, the fun goes out of it, in a way. For me, the challenge was always to overcome, to merely survive, not to overwhelm. I didn't follow through enough, my trainer always used to say. I'd get them on the ropes and step away, let them out.

'What are you doing? Dancing with the bloke?' he'd shout as I sat on my stool, sucking in the air. 'Finish what you started, son.'

But I wasn't a finisher. Once I saw that I was on top, that was enough for me, it took the wind out of my sails. I didn't want to see anyone humiliated.

Now from the tiled floor Rory looked up at me, those killer eyes gone all milky and hurt: 'Whaddayamean by that?'

'Well,' I said, 'success isn't your problem anymore, is it champ. Look at yourself.'

He rested his head on his knees and his rolls of fat started to suck and contract and his shoulders began to heave and shake.

'Never mind. You were great once.'

He looked up again with eyes as red and raw as my own had been after a session in the gym with him.

'I was great, wazzen I?' he said, with all the questioning vanity of an aging movie star.

'You were,' I said. 'But not any more.'

As I watched his lower lip tremble and the ugly moustache moisten, part of me felt sorry for him. But I have to say that I also tasted the cold dish of revenge I had yearned for from the time when his black leather glove caused me to stumble like a drunk and for a few seconds forget who I was. We've all got a bit of cunt in us I suppose. It's just some people know when to show it and when to hide it.

'C'mon mate, let's get you into bed. You'll feel better after a good night's sleep.'

'Champion of stupidity,' he said.

'You can say that again, mate. You can say that again.'

Since She Hasn't Gone
NATHAN CURNOW

Since she hasn't gone, my brother Lucien's been talking to her. He tells me what Mama knows about the monster. I don't hear the monster. I smell the monster. I smell it since she hasn't gone.

Lucien's been talking to her over and over. He says, *sorry, Mama, sorry*, non-stop. She lets him drink some from the cabinet. She never used to let him drink some. He drinks more and more like Papa did. Then Lucien stops talking. Nothing wakes him up. If the monster's gonna come, it'll come then.

We don't want Papa coming neither. She says he's the worser monster. Since she hasn't gone, we do better without him. Mama stabbed him one time for being so wicked but he did wicked a long time on us.

Lucien's enough Papa now. I have to listen to him. If the town comes snooping we be mouses. Someone came up here like he said they would; walked the porch, called for Mama, tried the lock. Lucien lay on his belly in the hallway with the gun, was gonna shoot them if they broke in.

Papa will come and get us if they know she hasn't gone. Take him five days this time of year. If we have to go outside we be foxy about it. I'm scared of that monster but I'm staying.

Snow's been coming down. Can't go out now. I been stuck in the house for long. The monster knows it too. The monster's been smelling. Can't be smelling any worser soon.

Lucien's done it. He boarded up the attic to stop me saying *Jesus* so much. He don't like it when I say *Jesus. Lord Jesus*, non stop. He says Mama don't want to hear it. But Mama liked prayer words, I remember she did. She would say them in the sickness she would.

Since she hasn't gone, we've been melting snow for the drinking. It tastes clean but don't work on fever. We tried that on her when she got real hot. Lucien hears her, he swears it. I don't.

Lucien's enough Papa now. I have to listen to him. He's Papa more and more with the gun. He boarded up that attic but it's still been smelling. I miss her since she hasn't gone.

Now Lucien's gone too. He don't come back none. I'm scared at night, want my Mama. Lucien's being foxy. I think that sometimes. Think he's testing if I believe him. He must be hunting in that blizzard, might bring me some food. I heard the rifle go off one time. I heard the rifle go off but he must have missed. If he got something he'd bring it home.

It's been snowing I tell you. Monster's smelling so close. Must be getting so hungry itself. I say *Lord Jesus*. I'm getting so cold. I'm tired of being the mouse.

I'm cold like she got. Want to be with Mama. Think I'll take off them boards if I can. Pray the Lord Jesus on that monster and climb on up. Try and cuddle her the warm back in.

Molluscan Princess
RACHEL LEARY

I always liked snails. As a child I collected them, housed them in shoe boxes and fed them lettuce. They were my pets. My brother used to find them, my slow moist little friends, take the whole box of them down to the bottom of the backyard and pelt them one by one at the fence, my cries and protestations only adding to his wicked boyish delight. As I held them between my fingers and they frothed green through their broken shells I found in myself a deep sympathy for them and their slimy fragility. And it was a sympathy that only deepened when I began to observe that my friends' fate in life (or should I say in death) so often seemed to involve being squished into a wet footpath, their guts spewing out under their shells in a most undignified fashion.

However it was years later, when I was twenty-eight and working as the Parksbridge Rivulet Catchment Officer, that I came to realise I didn't like snails much at all; not compared to how much it was *possible* to like them. Not compared to how much the Snail Man did.

I met him at a conference on water quality in urban and semi-urban rivers. I first saw him when I rushed into the room early in the morning on day one, my hair slightly damp, my demeanour frazzled. He stuck out in the crowd because he was the only person who looked like Doctor Who. He had buoyant curly brown hair and wore a brown skivvy, denim jeans rolled once at the cuff, white socks and white Dunlop Volleys.

At morning tea on the second day of the conference I was loitering in the foyer with my friend Josephine, who worked for a local organisation responsible for frog conservation. She nudged me with her elbow and gestured in his direction.

'There's the Snail Man,' she whispered.

'The *what* man?'

'The Snail Man. Everyone calls him the Snail Man. I don't think anyone even knows his real name.'

'He's into snails?'

'You could say that. Obsessed, I hear. Like weirdly so.'

'I think he looks kinda sweet.'

'If you like Doctor Who.'

'What's wrong with Doctor Who?'

'Nothing, he's just not exactly pin up material, is he? You know, move over Brad Pitt here comes Doctor Who.'

I was introduced later that day to Dr Marcus Shackelton.

'Marcus, I'd like you to meet Alex Taylor. Alex's the new Parksbridge Rivulet Catchment Officer at Springvale Council.'

Brian Russell, the man responsible for the introduction, was then called elsewhere and I was left standing with a Doctor Who look-alike, apparently known as the Snail Man.

It turned out he was Associate Professor of the Department of Environment and Ecology at Guilford University. We stood by the steaming urn, sporting nametags and hot cups of coffee. We spoke for a while about work. About rivers, toxins, new policy, the future of urban waterways and snails. Snails, of course, were his speciality. He gave a talk about them on the afternoon of the third day, 'Managing Urban Waterways and the Life-Cycle of *Austropeplea lessoni.*'

A week later I was sitting at my desk at work looking out the window and chewing my right thumbnail. I was thinking that on the weekend I might paint my toenails red because I didn't do enough nice things for myself and when you're single you have to do nice things for yourself. I was thinking that it might be nice but that I wasn't sure, because I don't like the smell of nail polish much at all, and I was thinking that perhaps I could paint them with a peg on my nose, but I didn't think that would be nice either because it would hurt and I've never been masochistic enough to enjoy pain, especially not on the weekends. I was thinking all of those things when the phone rang and I expected it to be Sally Mason from Environment and Planning.

'Hello, Springvale Council. Alex Taylor speaking.'
'Hello Alex, it's Marcus Shackelton here.'
'Marcus Shackelton?'
'We met at the conference last week.' *Oh my God, the Snail Man!*
'Oh yes, of course. Hello Marcus, how are you?'
'Well, thank you. I hope it's ok to call you at work.'
'Fine.'
'It's a personal call.'

I tried to think what to say. It is difficult to panic and think at the same time, so after a longer than comfortable pause, Marcus spoke again.

'I'm going on a field trip on Sunday. I just thought if you weren't doing anything you might like to come.'

We walked through wet bush. My legs were scratched by low-lying scrub. He talked about snails.

'There are one hundred and seventeen species of snails in this state alone. There is one particular species that can live for days in sub-zero temperatures. Last year I discovered…'

I began to wonder what I was doing there. No wonder they call him the Snail Man I thought, it's true, he's obsessed. He knew everything there was to know about snails. He knew about terrestrial snails, freshwater snails, marine snails and probably intergalactic snails as well. Not my type at all. But still, as I walked behind him I noticed the light wind was laced with his smell. It was an unusual smell, almost musty but sweet, and its olfactory peculiarity pricked my curiosity. As I traipsed up the hill, I watched his calves flex and felt hungry.

We rested for lunch. He had prepared a picnic and brought a blanket. He laid it out and as we ate he found a snail and placed it on my bare arm. He watched it move along my arm leaving a wet trail behind it. He looked from my arm up into my eyes. 'You are a very beautiful woman.'

When his hand went down under the elastic of my underpants and he found my wetness he groaned and called me his Molluscan Princess. I laughed and he smiled back at me, even more urgent then in his enjoyment of what he later referred to as my 'molluscan delights'. He called me Little Snail as he entered me and groaned some more. I was amused, but I would be lying if I said I wasn't enjoying myself. He was quite gifted. I decided there were worse things in life to be than a snail substitute.

The next Sunday was a beautiful day, sunny and clear. He arrived at my house at 10am with a box full of regular garden snails. I asked him what they were for.

'I want to show you something,' he told me. We drank coffee and then he led me into my bedroom. I had just made the bed.

'Will you take your clothes off?' he asked me. I thought it was a little unromantic, but he obviously had something in mind. I undressed in front of him and he stood watching, holding the box of snails.

'Now lie on the bed,' he directed me.

He placed the snails on my body carefully, one by one. The positioning of them seemed to be important. One went just under my belly button; one on each breast, over the nipple; one on each of my upper thighs and so on until I was covered in them. Their feet were moist and cool and they tickled slightly as they moved. He undressed as they moved about on me. He was already hard. I was hoping he wasn't planning on lying on me and squashing them into me – I would have to draw the line at that. But he stood watching them for a while and then removed them again, one by one, collecting some of their moisture from my skin with his index finger. He tasted it and looked at me as he licked the thick mucus from his finger, then he rubbed the snail trails into my skin, massaged them into my thighs, into my breasts and then felt down into my own moisture, calling me his Molluscan Princess, over and over.

I didn't tell anyone about our sex life, about the kind of sex we had, but I was enjoying it. He was a wonderful lover. Yes, a little strange it's true, but wonderful. My days and nights began to be about waiting for the next encounter, waiting for the snails.

It went on that way for three months. I had never felt so satiated. There was a cushion of air under my feet. Everywhere I went people told me how well I was looking. They said I was glowing. I think it must have been all the snail goop that had been rubbed into my skin. I was saving money on moisturiser.

He called me one night, later than usual.

'Princess, I just heard. I am going to South America,' he said. 'They have discovered a new species of snail. It lives in the mountains there. Isn't that great? They say its shell is like pearls. Opalescent.'

He said he'd come around tomorrow evening.

Two months. He said he'd be two months. It's important, he said. I thought about quitting my job and going with him. I imagined my skin dotted with pearly opalescent snails somewhere on an exotic South American mountain. But he didn't invite me. He didn't ask me to go with him.

He called when he first arrived sounding so excited to be there that I thought the phone might explode. In the first month he was away I received a couple of postcards. I sat in my house alone and after the rain I watched the snails crawl around on the paving outside the back door. I thought about taking them into my bedroom, applying them to my skin and delighting myself. But who would be there to call me their Molluscan Princess? No-one. The postcards became less frequent until they dried up like a snail trail under hot sun.

I slid into a state of despair. My friends began to worry and visited more often to check that I was okay. My family worried too. It'd been two-and-a-half months since Marcus left. I hadn't heard anything for a month and I knew he wasn't back because I'd called the uni dozens of times.

Then one day my brother came to visit. We sat and chatted over coffee. It had been raining. The paving outside was crawling with snails.

I excused myself and told my brother I wouldn't be long. He watched me as I went through one of my junk cupboards looking for an old shoe box. I retrieved one and went outside.

Their trails glistened silver with streaks of rainbow on the grey stone. I picked one up and put it in the shoebox, then another, and another. When the paving was clear of them, I called my brother out. He leant forward and peered into the box.

'You still collecting snails, Sis?'

'Here.' I handed them to him.

'What are you giving them to me for?'

'Pelt them at the fence.'

'Pardon?'

'Pelt them at the fence for me. One by one, like you used to.'

'Why on earth do you want me to do that? You used to cry.'

'Yes, I know. I might still cry, but go on, please. I want you to.'

He looked down into the box and then at me. He's grown up. He's not a horrible little boy anymore. No longer made of puppy dogs' tails.

'I don't know if I can.'

'Try.'

'Ok.' He picked the first one up and studied it, turned it upside down to look at the soft nakedness at the bottom of its one big foot. As his fingers squeezed either side of the brown shell it stretched its thick neck out to probe the air with its feelers. Then my brother yanked his arm back and lobbed the snail at the grey paling fence. It hit and dropped, and I squealed with delight. I jumped up and down clapping my hands.

'Again. Again! Another one!'

My brother looked at me questioningly and hesitated, but I urged him on. After three or four he had found his old fervour. Soon we were hunting around the garden for more.

With the great snail massacre over, we went inside, both of us worn out. We sat together at the table in silence.

'Alex, are you alright?' My brother looked at me tenderly, his face full of concern.

'Yes Leroy,' I said. 'Yes, I'll be alright now.'

On My Goat
Jamie Buchannan

You know what gets on my goat? Hopefully nothing because it would be one bumpy ride.

I remember a time in the not too distant ages when riding a goat was a civilised affair enjoyed by gentlemen and ladies alike. Persons of gentry would mount a hand-made saddle, which had been made entirely out of hands (it made their pants fit like a glove), and ride to their heart's content – or at least until the chafing became unbearable.

The goat races at Royal Ascot were a sight to behold and the day that the 150-to-1 rough outsider Sassafrass Surprise won by a short half-head was a day like no other, evidenced by the fact that the nag had never won before and never raced again (I am told by those reliably informed folk who know such things that the said stallion decided to go out on a high, so he won, smoked a large reefer and disappeared like a thief in the night). The fact that he had a short half-head stapled to the tip of his nose helped in his success, but it also compounded the issue for the race caller.

The announcer on the day was the legendary Sir Cecil Supine, who called all races lying down in a cot that was then propped up against the window. He also had a terrible lisp that drenched anyone who got within earshot of the man in saliva within two minutes of his oration commencing. A shortsighted man (he believed that electricity was just a passing fad and that penicillin was nothing more than herbalistic nonsense), he was longsighted in his ocular capacity, which made him something of a paradox.

So too did his gait, which befitted a man of much taller stature. That is, his legs were far too tall for his body. They towered above him in an ungainly way that put most people off their tea and scones. Rarely invited to afternoon soirees, he died a lonely man in someone else's trousers. But in his own bed, which was a nice touch.

All of this meant nothing to my goat however when the local larrikins decided to, and I shall paraphrase here for fear of misquoting the lovely little urchins, 'take it for a spin'.

Now in my opinion spinning a goat is unsound behaviour not fit for any member of a golf club, let alone the children of the local postmaster. I would have thought (and in fact, did think) that the offspring of a man with a profession in which the word 'master' was contained would have had respect for my domesticated *capra aegagrus* but evidently I was wrong to have thunk it. These delightfully demonic descendants of my demurely decorated dispatcher decided that spinning the goat was only the start of their festivities.

Allow me to elucidate.

At first, I hadn't even known this occurred at all – although my suspicions were aroused when I espied Cedric, my goat, behaving in a manner entirely non-Cedric like. He was stumbling around the backyard as if drunk and staggering his way home after a heavy night on the sauce with his mates followed by a quick cheeky one at Madame Bovine's Stable of Ill-Repute. The fact that he was singing a naughty version of 'Three German Officers Crossed the Line' in a bleating fashion only stiffened my resolve in believing that Cedric was indeed inebriated.

However, I received in the mail that very same day (and now I know why it came in the mail – you see how this all knits together so well?) a videotape of Cedric's previous night's dalliance. Yes he had been spun in no uncertain fashion and yes he had partaken in beverages of an entirely unwholesome influence. But he had also engaged in acts so carnal in their depravity that I have no desire to explicate. However, to say that there was cottage cheese involved will give you some idea I am sure. And I was pretty sure that it was my cottage cheese too!

I couldn't look Cedric in the eye after this, I felt cheated upon. To his credit Cedric did look a bit sheepish himself which is not easy for a goat, especially when you consider the disdain in which they hold their woolly cousins. After he had sobered up and whipped himself with leathers for an hour I decided that we had better part ways. It was probably best for both of us.

He agreed saying that he had only stayed because of the children anyway which was a supremely idiotic thing to say considering we neither had children nor the capacity to produce any. But I let it go, choosing to end our association amicably rather than in an argument about the propagation of both our respective species.

I am now over him, it's been three years and I have decided to move on. I have another goat now who is much more accommodating. Geoff is much more of a homebody than Cedric was and we get along like a house on fire. I must admit that I have never really understood that analogy, as a house on fire wouldn't really get along with anyone. I would like to think most sane and rational people would want to get as far away as possible from a house on fire but then again I'm not most people.

I now sleep a contented sleep. I can hear the little bleating of our children (turns out I was wrong about the whole propagation thing) in the yard with their father, gnawing at the roses and smearing cottage cheese on one another. Ahhh, the joys of simple folk.

Cicada
LEANNE HALL

1.1.1

I forgot my body when I left the house today. I ran through my mental checklist (wallet, keys, phone) but it never occurred to me to check for the obvious. I don't know how it happened, even though cicadas do it all the time.

1.1.2

There's no way of knowing why you notice some people and not others. Sometimes your eye passes over a scene and stumbles on someone as if they were a pot-hole. Those kinds of people don't hold your attention for long. Other times it seems as if one person in a crowded room is flooded in light and you have no choice. The lights on the tram were harsh fluorescents but she sat in a warm glow, next to the window. The tram was full, not that I could tell you anything about anyone else. Once I'd seen her I couldn't look away.

The first thing I noticed was that she wore her temper extremely short, shorter than most people I knew. I would have been tempted to say she was just having a bad day but the temper was ragged around the edges as if she was in the habit of chewing on it. I looked for a fuse or even a button or two, but she was turned sideways to look out the window, leaving at least half of her person unseen.

When she shifted in her seat I saw that she had a large confidence, peppered at regular intervals with fear. It was a strange combination. On paper it wouldn't work but on her it made perfect sense. I would even go so far as to say that it was what made her so intriguing. She'd clothed herself in indecision, which I'm sure made her attractive to a certain type of man but proved fatal at job interviews.

I want to know you, I thought. *I want to know you but how will I recognise you tomorrow when everything might have changed?*

Without warning she grew tired of looking out of the window and her gaze slid quickly in my direction. When she noticed I was staring at her, she froze and the warm light around her died abruptly. I looked away immediately, pretending that I was interested in the floor. I counted slowly inside my head. How long before it was safe for me to look in her direction again? I felt like an idiot. When you take seashells out of the water they lose all the colours that made them interesting to you in the first place; I'd ruined her by looking.

1.1.3

Outside David Jones I saw someone who had gone the opposite way. Flesh vacuum-packed into skinny jeans; boots that made a soundtrack when she walked. If you stripped away her highlights her hair would crumble; if you removed her sunglasses you would see two golf-ball sized holes where her eyes should be. She looked fantastic.

It's easy to imagine how this could happen. You could be looking in the mirror one day. Maybe you went there for a purpose; say to see if your hairline was receding or if any new freckles had sprung up. But once you got there you were caught by the sight of your other two eyes and couldn't look away. You kept staring until you weren't sure which were the real set and which were the fake. You knew your eyes were the window to your soul but which ones? Without even meaning to, you stared in the mirror too long and your self poured out (like a snake, like honey) into your image.

I saw what was left. It was like injection-moulded plastic. It was like the dolls you eagerly examined when you were a kid only to find they had no genitals and no body hair. It was what's-wrong-with-this-picture. It was perfect, so I followed it down the street. Could I buy apples as fresh and crispy as her? I don't think so.

1.1.4

The couple stood close to the shop window, pretending they were looking at shoes but really they were waiting for the tram. When I moved closer I realised that they weren't looking at shoes or waiting for the tram, they were having a conversation.

She was covered almost head-to-toe in crackly white static; he stood under a rain cloud of boredom.

'Over the years' she said 'I've tried everything to prise those two apart. Acid, speed, Johnny Walker…but nothing's worked. My mind has its fingers deep in my brain and heart and guts and it won't let go. It's growing there, like a tumour. I'd give anything to lose it, even for five minutes.'

1.1.5

I said:
>Do you have any newspapers left?

It was a long-shot; they always sell out on the weekend.

He said:
>This is going to sound strange but the way you bite your lower lip really reminds me of my ex-girlfriend. She always used to do that when she was concentrating. See you're doing it right now and you don't even realise it. I guess you're not the only two people in the world who do it, but you'd be surprised how many different ways there are of biting your lip. Your way — oh, you've stopped now — your way is the same as hers. You bite a little bit to the left, not in the middle, and you bite in a sustained fashion, rather than gnawing away. It's amazing isn't it, how that could make you look so much like her. When I looked up just now my breath caught in my throat and for a split second I *really* saw her. Now that I look at you properly I can see that you don't look like her at all. Well there are some similarities of course, like you have eyes and a nose and a mouth and she also has straight hair, but that could be said of most people. It's like chimpanzee and human DNA you know, they're almost exactly the same. I don't know the exact figure, ninety percent or ninety-nine percent, something like that. The point is, we've all got nearly the same components but the magic is in those tiny variations.

I said:
>I'm biting my lip because I'm worried there are no newspapers left.

He said:
>I can't help you there. Sorry.

Counting Buttons
MEG VERTIGAN

Tuesday

The end always comes suddenly. It doesn't matter how long you've been expecting it. Today I finally made the call that I knew would end it all. It was just before lunchtime. It only took them eight and a half minutes to get to the house. Sitting on the porch, I waited while they went to get him from inside.

They asked me questions. So many questions. Repeated again and again as if I was giving the wrong answers. I felt confused.

Then they carried him off right in front of me, not even stopping so I could say goodbye. Just shoved him in the back of the van and left him there all alone, knowing the neighbours were staring from their front porches.

They took me inside to ask me more questions.

'Why didn't you call sooner?'

'Why?'

Why? Because I knew you would come and take him away. Because I am afraid of being alone. Because then everyone would know and stare at me up the street. Because I still love him. Because I haven't finished counting the buttons yet.

Monday

I keep thinking that he will be back. His things are here. His sock balls are still sitting in the middle of the floor. I walk around them carefully. He can't go far without his socks. Not in this weather, anyway. He's never liked the cold.

We will be together unless I make the call. I know they will take him away forever then. How can I make the phone call that will separate us forever, except for stony visits, one-sided conversations, and too much silence. If I call now how long will we have left together? Twenty minutes? Twenty minutes at the most to say goodbye. Maybe even ten. Ten minutes. It's just not long enough. I'll have a cup of tea first, finish counting the buttons, and then I'll call.

His apple-core is still sitting there on the kitchen table. I can almost see his tooth marks on the skin, the angle where they cross at the front. The apple keeps me company as I sit down and start sorting the buttons into groups of ten. Its flesh, as dull as dust, has shrunken in on itself so that the skin around the top of the core now hangs, loose and wrinkled. A marching army of ants forms a line across the wall from the window. They are stealing his apple.

I arm myself with the Mortein from the cupboard under the sink and spray their trail across the wall. Reaching up I bump into the table and some of the buttons fall onto the floor. I'm so clumsy. I'll have to start counting again now. I hold my finger down on the trigger until the ants smear across the wall.

Reaching as high as can I let a few poison droplets fall onto his apple to protect it. Then, following their trail to a small crack in the windowpane, I squirt into it until ants come to the surface, hundreds of black dots trying to swim in the toxic froth. Outside I continue my assault all around the window as high as I can reach. Sue Stuart is on her balcony next door and she calls down to me.

'How are you today, Mrs Cloak?'

I pretend I can't hear her.

Go away, I can't hear you. Don't speak to me. I can't speak to you. You'll only ask me questions. Don't look at me. How am I today? You don't care anyway. That's why you built that big wall between our houses. I heard you talking on your balcony, saying I always catch you on the way to the clothes line. Talk for hours. You think I can't hear you up there? All right then, I am deaf. I can't hear you shouting down at me from up there.

She takes a step closer and leans over her balcony towards me. A lone spider has spun a web connecting her balcony to my overgrown garden. It watches to see if Sue will fall into its trap, but I know she won't come any further. The wild thorns on my rose bushes will protect me.

She calls again. 'Mrs Cloak, are you ok?'

Am I ok?

I have arthritis. The vacuum cleaner is too heavy for me to lift out of the cupboard. Sometimes I don't speak to anyone else for ten days in a row. Nobody visits us. He hasn't woken up yet and it's nearly lunchtime.

As if you care, on the other side of your new wall.

I go inside and turn the heater off, hoping the cold air will preserve his apple. When I go to bed I can't smell him in the shirt anymore. It smells like me. I go to the laundry to find another, but I washed them all yesterday. They smell of soap and nothing. I cry for hours, knowing that I will never smell his smell again.

Sunday

I wake up in that time between night and day. At first I'm not sure whether it is the sun or the moon that is starting its shift.

'Are you awake?' I ask, and his stomach gurgles in response.

I can't get back to sleep so I get up and get ready for church early. The first hymn is 'How Great Thou Art'. Then all of a sudden too many hands are helping me back into my pew. Someone is trying to force me to drink a glass of water, saying, 'Are you alright to hold it yourself?' Like I am a child. The whole church is in disarray. It is such a big fuss about nothing. I just stood up too fast, that's all. They tell me I should go to the hospital to get checked out.

'There's nothing wrong with me,' I tell them. 'The church is stinking hot with all those heaters burning. It's no wonder I fainted.'

They want to take me to the hospital, but I tell them I have to go home to take care of my husband.

But when I get home I don't feel like visiting his end of the house just yet. I clean off the kitchen table, when I notice the apple. About half of its skin still remains. I fed it to him on Friday. I took a bite and then held it to his lips for him to suck the juice. We did this a few times, I took a bite and then he sucked the juice while I chewed.

We met over an apple, a whole lifetime ago when we were in our last year of school. We were both on crutches and so were given the job of scoring the hockey on a Friday afternoon.

I sat like an idiot on the grass next to him with nothing to say. Girls kept coming over to talk to him. They all had long legs and long hair in plaits that shone in the sun and bounced when they walked. I brushed my bangs out of my eyes and tried to smile. I felt short and dumpy and regretted the short bob style I'd cut my hair into. *No wonder I can't think of anything to say to him, with this stupid haircut,* I'd thought. The teacher was getting annoyed because none of the girls would play properly while he was watching. They kept hitting the ball out of the field in his direction, and then they'd come over and make witty remarks and roll their eyes behind the teachers back when she called them back to the game. He grinned at them, and I knew that if I looked like them I would be able to think of something funny to say too.

At half time he started rummaging around in his satchel. I stared straight ahead, pretending I wasn't trying to see what he was doing. Eventually he pulled an apple from his bag and took a bite. He must have caught me watching him because he winked and said, 'What's wrong? You want some?'

My heart jumped. I couldn't believe it. He was holding the apple near my mouth, his bite just inches from my lips. I could see the mark where his teeth crossed in the skin. I couldn't talk so I just shook my head.

'It's so sweet, try some.'

He held the apple closer to me and I could see a small bubble of his saliva on its skin. My cheeks burned. I shook my head but he held the apple closer until it touched my lip.

'You have to eat it now, you've touched it,' he grinned, displaying his dimples. I didn't know what else to do, so I tried to take a bite but I was so nervous that only a bit of skin came off. The whole world stopped and looked at us.

'Now will you talk to me?' he asked, and we ate the rest of the apple together, bite for bite.

That's where my mind was on Friday as I chewed the apple, and held it to his lips for him to suck the juice. I forgot that he was sick and that I was old and that biting an apple could break my false teeth. I was sitting back on the grass feeling the sun and the envy of my classmates burning on my face.

By the end of that summer we were married. So now I have our washing, our ironing. There are a million little things to do around the house. Bake a cake. Vacuum the floor. Make a phone call? Maybe after seven o'clock. When it's cheaper. Keep busy until then. Hang out the clothes. Watch the news at noon. At five o'clock. At seven o'clock. At ten o'clock. With the heater on and all the lights burning to keep me company. And then finally it's bedtime. I wear his old gardening shirt to bed. It still has his smell.

We lie back to back. As if we'd been fighting. As if he is refusing to talk to me. I should be the one to refuse to talk to him. How dare he do this to me?

But he is cold, so cold. I get up to find another quilt out of the high cupboard in our bedroom. Something clinks in the cupboard when I'm taking out the quilt and when I look to see what it is I find my old button collection. Years ago now I'd put it up there where I wouldn't have to look at it.

Just before we got married my mother told me, 'If you put a button in a jar 'every time' until your first child, and then after that take a button out 'every time', the jar will never become empty.'

I told him that on our wedding night and the next morning he went straight out and bought me three bright pink buttons. I put them in an empty jam jar, and that was the start of my collection. We used to laugh about it and he often bought me a supply of buttons home of a Friday night as a joke. Soon we had filled up a couple of jars. The buttons came in many different colours and sizes. He used to put them on the mantelpiece so he could tease me for being embarrassed when visitors looked at them. I'd go so red.

After a couple of years it wasn't funny anymore. It began to seem as if I'd never begin taking buttons out of the jars.

Eventually I couldn't bear looking at them anymore so I put the buttons in the back of the cupboard to forget them, and he stopped buying them for me. Now looking at the buttons gives me happy memories. Suddenly I want to know how many are in there. I never wanted to count them before, just looking at them used to remind me. I am aware of him watching me as I pull the jars one by one out of the cupboard. 'There are five jars!' I tell him, blushing at the thought of it.

Putting the jars on the bedside table I fold the quilt double on top of him. I turn the heater on and get back into bed, rubbing his skinny arms and legs, no fat left to keep them warm. I turn and cuddle his back to fall asleep. Our smells mix together in his shirt.

Sleep conquers hours. Tomorrow I will count the buttons.

Saturday

I wake but my eyes stay closed. I hold him while he sleeps. His breath is so shallow I have to put my ear close to his mouth to hear it. There's a pause. Finally he breathes again, and then nothing, and it feels like forever. I lie awake waiting for the pause, and holding my own breath so I can hear his, so thin that it barely moves his ribcage. Sometimes he is silent for so long that I poke him with my bony old finger. I lie with my face right next to his and whisper, 'breathe,' and he obeys me in his sleep.

I touch the softness of his beard, the baldness of his head. My fingers feel the new thinness of his hips, his hollow belly. He reaches out and touches my finger. I hold his hand and feel him squeeze my fingers, like a child. I stay awake all night, waiting for the next breath. 'I'll stay awake forever,' I tell him. 'I'll look after you, don't worry.'

But I must have dozed off again because when I wake it is hot and sweaty under the bedspread. The sun shines through the crack between the curtains and straight into my eyes. Only he feels cold. I hug him and rub his body to warm him up. His eyes are open, but he isn't awake.

For information on the authors in this book
please visit
www.renewal.org.au/cardigan